With Be... Roy Grantham (handwritten)

Deeds and Misdeeds

Roy Grantham

Finding the body of a young girl in the woods whilst musing on the frailties of human relationships (particularly those with his mistress and his wife) fails to make Peter's life less complicated.

It tumbles him into a period of enforced maturity when he either has to start sorting out his life or give himself up to his sexual longings.

This adult-rated book explores the complex emotional and sexual relationships between: husbands, wives and lovers against a mounting police investigation that seems to be focussing on him.

First published in Great Britain in 2013 by
U P Publications Ltd Head Office: 25 Bedford Street,
Peterborough, UK. PE1 4DN

Cover design copyright © G M G Peers 2013
Photo © Egidijus Mika, Dreamstime Stock Photos
From an original design by Raoul Grantham 2013

A CIP Catalogue record of this book is available from the British Library

ISBN 978-1908135353
9 2 0 7 5 8 6 4 3 1

Also published for Kindle by U P Publications under

ISBN 978-1908135360

FIRST PAPERBACK EDITION
Published by U P Publications Ltd
Printed in England by The Lightning Source Group
www.roygrantham.com
www.uppublications.ltd.uk

Deeds and Misdeeds

Roy Grantham

ЧP

2013

For

Andy, Raoul and Justin

Chapter 1.

He still had sex with Naomi, occasionally, and then only after a complicated ballet of moves that made him wonder if it was all worthwhile.

If challenged, he would have claimed that it was her libido that had lost its vibrancy, while his urges in that direction were undiminished. He might even have gone on to say that it was the usual way male/female sexual relationships developed, but then, if pressed further, he would probably have admitted that he was far from certain in this case.

What really got up his nose, and made him reluctant to initiate sex often, was Naomi's attitude that, apparently, she was doing him a favour when she finally offered herself up and, even then, she usually had something to say about the way he went about it. Was that why...? ...of course that was why ...sex with Simone was so delicious. It was what they both wanted, no messing about, no games, just unadulterated glorious fucking. Perhaps affairs were always like that. Perhaps, in fact, that's what affairs were all about.

For Peter, post coital rumination often took the form of comparing the two women. It struck him that the really sexy women were those for whom sexuality is part of their personality, their everyday persona, their very being. In Simone's case her sexuality was demonstrated by her quite ordinary actions and movements. Of course such comparisons were unfair, particularly if he limited it to their sexual performances when, of course, Naomi was rather more than a sexual partner, being a working mother and, as she was always telling Peter, the rock on which their family was based. She certainly had the process of nagging off to a fine art, he thought.

He turned his head to look at the figure lying beside him. Eyes closed, mouth slightly open, a sheen of sweat on her face from their recent exertions, blonde hair scattered over the pillow. The sight immediately reignited prurient thoughts, pushing aside anything other than the need to re-establish contact with that beautiful body – his for the taking, or at least for the asking.

As he reached out a finger to touch her full lips, she opened her eyes to smile sleepily, but encouragingly at him, hunching up her shoulders sensuously, like a sun-drenched cat, and yawning voluptuously, the movement causing one ample breast to appear over the edge of the duvet.

Peter should have left half an hour ago but what the hell. How could he possibly turn down what was so blatantly on offer. Her touch, the ambient musk of sex had stimulated him to initiate another bout of sexual congress that left him trembling in culmination, wondering whether he would ever recover sufficiently to get out of bed and take a shower.

Even as the water began to jet away some of his post coital lethargy, Peter found the image of that wild display of golden hair coming back to him. Blondes definitely turned him on, so how on earth, he wondered, did he end up marrying Naomi, with her neatly controlled, dark curls.

When he arrived home, he hardly had time to get through the door, before he heard Naomi's voice from the kitchen.

"Will someone please take that bloody dog for a walk, it's not fair on the poor creature, shut up all day."

"Homework."

"Me too, got to give a presentation, first period tomorrow."

Peter was shattered. The last thing he felt like doing was taking the dog for a walk but then, he was supposed to have spent the afternoon on his writing course at college, so any excuse, in the circumstances, would sound feeble. His intended response was much too slow. His wife, who had come out into the sitting room, glared at him.

"Thank you all very much. In case any of you hadn't noticed, I would just like to point out that I've been working all day, and it's me who's cooking this fucking meal"

"Mum your language."

"Never mind my language, I'm getting pretty fed up with holding down a job, and running this house all on my bloody own."

"Alright, I'll take the dog for a walk, anything for a quiet life." Peter dragged himself reluctantly to his feet.

As soon as they reached the street, George immediately started his usual impatient straining at the lead. It was spotting with rain, but once under way Peter felt better.

Walking didn't impose too much extra stress on his fragile being. When man and beast reached the field, he was able to sit on the stile and watch George tearing madly round in circles, every so often changing course to chase an elusive rabbit, or at least what he thought was a rabbit.

What am I doing, he thought.

Here I am with the perfect nuclear family, and I'm risking it all because of sheer unadulterated lust.

He wondered if Simone saw it in those brute terms, which in turn led him to wonder further whether he really cared what she thought. After all she had gone into the thing with eyes wide open, no promises made, no expectations of onward development of the relationship offered. They both wanted to have sex, they were both mature adults, what the hell, it was just an interlude. Yet Christ did he want the woman, couldn't wait until the next time they met in that comfortable little flat of hers.

The child looked very peaceful lying there quite neatly on the ground. Peter had unthinkingly wandered into the edge of the woods following one of the dog's mad chases into the undergrowth, and there she was, quiet and unmoving. He didn't at once rush forward to see what was the matter with the child, playing a game perhaps; didn't do to go touching strange children in this day and age, and yet he knew, instinctively, that she was dead. It was no game she was playing. Cautiously he moved the few yards to where she was lying to kneel by her side, hoping against hope that she would spring up in front of him, and run away laughing.

There was no sign of injury on the pretty little body, but as he tried to lift her she flopped back like a rag doll. He laid her gently back on the ground, conscious that this was going to be a police matter. He had probably compromised himself already by touching her, DNA and all that. He tried to find a pulse despite it being patently obvious that she was dead. For a few seconds the great wave of sadness that came over him prevented Peter from thinking straight. He knew he had to ring the police but his mobile was at home. It seemed somehow uncaring to leave the little girl lying there, by herself, in the woods.

The arrival of George on the scene, back from his foraging, brought Peter to his senses. He pulled the dog away from joyously licking the child's cold face, although that seemed, to him, to be a kindness in itself. Then he ran, the dog jumping at his heels, ran until his lungs felt as though they were bursting. When he reached the road he turned into the drive of the first house he came to, knocked on the door pressed his finger hard on the bell, waiting with a mad sort of impatience for someone to answer his summons. Still breathless, his words quickly changed the annoyed expression on the face of the man opening the door into one of gaping shock when he explained the need to telephone the police and the ambulance, although the latter was more a matter of expediency, than hope. The man, eager now to do what he could, ushered Peter into the hallway and pointed to the telephone. For some reason George had lain down quietly just inside the front door, seemingly aware that something important was up, and that he should keep out of the way.

The person at the police station who answered his call told him to stay at the house from where he had telephoned. To hell with that, he just couldn't leave that poor child lying there alone any longer than necessary. He told the worried-looking householder he was going back to the woods and whereabouts he would be, so the police could locate him when they arrived; more trouble he supposed, but it seemed important to get back to keep a temporary vigil on the girl. To Peter, for that short span of time, nothing else mattered.

When the first policemen arrived Peter was sitting by the body stroking the girl's hair and crying. It was quite probable that he was making himself the absolute number one suspect, yet he couldn't help himself, feeling an overwhelming need to offer some form of retrospective solace. The dog was lying with his head on his paws, sad without knowing why, sensing of his master's distress.

"You shouldn't be touching the body, sir." It was the first of many admonitions that were to follow, different words perhaps, but all amounting to the same thing, interfering with a crime scene, will the bloody public never learn, they appearing to be saying.

When Inspector Goddard arrived, it was clear from his manner, that he thought this was an open and shut case. At first he ignored Peter, whispering with the sergeant before bending down, scrutinising the body and the area round about it.

"Well, Mr Shadbolt, this is all very unpleasant sir. You found the body I understand, walking the dog were you?" His tone was less than sympathetic, shocking Peter with what appeared to be his unfeeling attitude. He hesitated, frowned, wanting more respect.

"Yes, inspector, I found the child, where you see her now."

"Not exactly where she is now sir so I'm told, you moved the body I believe."

That was too much ."Of course I moved the body, she might not have been dead, what the hell did you expect me to do."

"Quite so sir. There's no need to get upset."

"For Christ's sake, no need to get upset, a child's dead, of course I'm bloody upset. This may all be routine to you inspector, but it's been rather a shock for me." The policemen ignored the outburst, asked Peter if he minded going down to the police station to make a statement, making it abundantly clear that he was really had no choice in the matter.

It was two hours before they finished their questions, an uncomfortable two hours at that. Of course they said it was none of their business how he spent his afternoons, and there would be no need to mention it to anyone else, except of course to Simone herself. Then they wanted to come home with him to have the later timing verified. Naomi was shocked when he walked into the house with two policemen. The kids too were, for once, gobsmacked.

When Goddard finally left, Naomi was unusually solicitous, pouring him a large Scotch, before bringing out his ruined dinner, then rather sheepishly offering to cook him something else. James and Charlie were very quiet, almost sitting at his feet as it were, waiting to hear the story from his own lips. It wasn't cold but he felt chilled somehow. He needed the whisky, appreciated the feeling of warmth as it made its journey down to his stomach.

Gradually he began to adjust, although the pall of sadness remained. The death of a young child was so much more terrible experienced at first hand like this than reading about it in the papers. At his request Naomi made him a sandwich, refilling his glass without being asked. As he told them the short, sad story of what had occurred, they listened in shocked silence, trying to say sympathetic things, which came over as banal clichés. Duty done, the children disappeared to their rooms to finish off their homework while Naomi kept asking if there was anything else she could do.

That night Peter slept on and off, dreamed about something terrible, but couldn't remember exactly what when he woke up for the final time. He did remember that when they had gone to bed, that night, Naomi had unusually offered herself for sex, which had caused him to think, with a trace of bitterness, that it took the death of a child to make her lower the barriers. That was unfair of course. The truth was that she was only being kind, twenty years of marriage had some substance in it, after all. He accepted the comfort of her warm embrace, but that was quite enough.

In the morning he was deciding whether to call in sick, when the decision was made for him by a telephone call from Inspector Goddard, asking him if he would mind coming down to the station again, preferably before lunch.

At breakfast the children were in less of a rush than usual and very quiet, even saying good morning, abstaining from their usual pre-school bickering. Naomi was being solicitous, telling him not to worry, even offering to accompany him to the police station, an offer he gently declined. An hour or so later, seated in front of the inspector's desk, Peter waited, with mild trepidation, to hear what he had to say.

Chapter 2.

"It's a very sad case Mr Shadbolt, a sad case indeed, the child's mother is very upset, as you can imagine. Little girl was called Sharon apparently, only six years old." He looked at Peter over the top of his spectacles. Peter wondered what was coming next.

"I suppose you think we were a bit hard on you yesterday, but we have to consider everyone a suspect in the early stages of an investigation. You've been eliminated from our enquiries now of course, the child had been dead for upwards of six hours, which leaves you well in the clear. I regret to say we have no positive leads at this stage. No motive, no sexual interference, we're at a loss. " He stopped as though waiting for a response. When it was not forthcoming he went on. "The real reason I asked you to come into the station was to make a request. The little girl's mother has asked if she could meet with you, a strange request I know, but she was quite insistent, name of Margaret Benson."

"I don't think that would be a good idea inspector, there's nothing I can tell her. I found the child by accident, got help, that's all there is to it." The very idea of meeting a grief stricken woman, in these circumstances, appalled him, he wouldn't know what to say, feeling obliged to offer a comfort he didn't know how to deliver. He was shaking his head, getting to his feet, escape uppermost on his mind.

The inspector, too, got to his feet, coming came round to the other side of the desk to shake Peter's hand. "I quite understand, sir, but I had to ask, as I said she was so insistent."

Peter left the police station, his mood restless, disturbed by the mother's request to see him, now feeling guilty that he hadn't agreed. After all it didn't matter if he felt awkward, if it helped that poor woman. He should have agreed, whatever his reservations.

Instead of driving straight home, he turned towards the coast, pulling into a parking place at the edge of Woodbury Common. Here there was plenty of space and fresh air, which is what he needed to clear his head. He walked for about an hour over the drab, almost treeless sandy soil, until he reached a tumble down building at the far side of the common. As he leant against one of the still standing walls, taking a breather, he was startled, nearly out of his skin, by the sudden appearance from inside the ruins of a gaunt looking, bearded, man in a raincoat that had obviously seen better days. For a moment they stood staring at each other, then the man turned, walked quickly away, shouting over his shoulder as he went "Fuck off, you bastard, fuck off out of it."

Peter had been shocked, momentarily angry, at the man's outburst, but the encounter had brought about a change in his mood. Now he felt the need to get back to civilization. With his confused mind full of regrets, he walked slowly back to the car, regrets that his love for Naomi had waned, regrets that he hadn't done lot of the things in life that he would have liked to have done, regrets that it was July and the nights already drawing in before he had got used to the idea that it was summer. He always felt like that at this time of the year. Spring so eagerly anticipated, then somehow time slipped through almost to Autumn, before he appreciated whereabouts in the year they were. The day wasn't much like Summer anyway, .thick scudding cloud, no sign of the sun, not particularly warm, it suited his mood.

Back home, he was easing himself, rather dejectedly, out of the driving seat, when he was startled to hear a voice. He hadn't noticed anyone around, when he drove in. The words, seemingly out of thin air, caused his heart to give a little hop of surprise. As he turned towards the sound, he saw a black clad figure emerging from the front porch, where she must obviously have been waiting. "Mr Shadbolt, I'm very sorry to trouble you, I'm Mrs Benson, you know, Sharon's mother."

It took a moment for the penny to drop, he hadn't really assimilated the little girl's name into his memory, although now he remembered having been told both her and her mother's name by the inspector, only that morning. Margaret Benson was a straight mouthed woman to whom humour was anathema, not through any malice towards anyone, but just because she found life too serious to smile about. As she came towards Peter, all he noticed was the strained appeal in her eyes. That was quite enough to make him feel desperately uncomfortable. He thrust out a hand awkwardly in her direction.

"Yes, Mrs Benson, I'm so very sorry for your tragic loss."

"Not sorry enough to agree to meet me, Mr Shadbolt."

"No, well, sorry. Look, why don't you come inside?" He gestured towards the front door.

"She was my life, Mr Shadbolt, and you couldn't find the time to talk to me about my little girl."

Peter felt this was unfair, although looking back, he realised his refusal to see her had been unthinking. Alright, he had little to tell, but if that little might have helped. He should have agreed to see the woman. "I may have been wrong not to agree to talk to you, Mrs Benson, but there is so little I can tell you. I thought talking about my small part would only upset you more." Fucking liar, he just hadn't wanted to get involved, that was the truth.

"Anyway, please come inside the house. I'll answer any questions you want to ask but, as I said, there isn't much I can tell you."

The woman didn't follow him as he moved nearer the door. Instead she stood, hands on hips, glaring at him with something like hatred in her eyes. Then, as if having come to a sudden difficult decision, she walked quickly towards him.

He opened the front door to usher the angry woman inside, then into the lounge, where he asked her to sit down, offering her a cup of tea.

"I don't want your damn tea, I want to know what happened to my little Sharon."

Peter didn't like the way things were going, but in these

circumstances he could only tolerate whatever the woman threw at him. "As I said, Mrs Benson, I don't know what happened to your daughter. I found her when I was taking the dog for a walk in the fields, just up the road from here. I called the police and the ambulance, I'm afraid that's all there was to it."

His body was rigid with emotional tension, the residual horror of what he had witnessed the previous day, but also from the perceived injustice of this poor woman's attitude. He had done what he could, had acted properly, had felt real grief. Then that was easy where a child was concerned, not quite so easy when confronted by, what appeared to be, an accusing grim-faced mother. He licked his lips, wanting this to be over quickly. "I really am very sorry, but there is no more I can tell you." He was conscious of repeating himself, but what else could he say.

The woman in black remained silent for what seemed like minutes, her eyes never leaving Peter's face, boring into him with what, he continued to perceive, as accusation. "You touched my little girl didn't you?" Again the accusing frown.

"I tried to see if I could help her, she might have been hurt." This was all very unfair. He tried hard to keep a note of exasperation out of his voice.

"The child was dead, had been dead for hours the police said, why did you have to disturb her?" The grim face had dissolved into tears now, shoulders wracked by sobs. All this time, in the fraught atmosphere that pervaded the lounge, the two of them had stayed standing. Now, emerging suddenly from her huddled misery, the woman crossed the space between them, flinging herself at Peter's chest in what, he first thought, was some kind of assault, but then realised was a plea for comfort. He stood still, rigid with embarrassment, his arms at his side as she clutched at him wildly. Then, as she made no move to break her hold, he slowly folded his arms round her to complete a circle of awkward sympathy, all the while wanting, with all his heart, for her to go away, yet knowing he owed it to this distressed fellow human being, to show he understood her inordinate grief, if nothing else.

They stood like that for, what seemed to Peter, like minutes, before she slid down his body, and slumped on the floor at his feet, to lie there motionless. She couldn't, by any means, be considered a bulky woman, yet it took all his strength to hoist her dead weight off the floor onto the sofa, where she flopped back like a rag doll, the folds of her black dress dragging high on her thighs, causing him to look guiltily away. Call a doctor, fetch a glass of water, undo some buttons, what the hell should he do? Before he could make up his mind what action to take, the woman showed signs of recovery, opening her eyes, staring at him in a fixed, yet puzzled way.

"Feeling better? You fainted, I'll get you a glass of water." He needed the respite, and anyway a glass of water was probably the right thing to offer. When he came back into the room she was sitting up, her dress back in place, her face was shiny damp, her breathing harsh as though she had just been on a hard run. "I'll get you a towel." He was off again, anything to escape the uncomfortable atmosphere..

Back with the towel, he found the woman on her feet, on the point of leaving the room. In fact as he started to enter through the door, she barged clumsily past him, appearing to be making for the front door. "Look," he hesitated before dragging her name up from his memory. "Mrs Benson, you're not well, sit down, have a cup of tea, wait a while." It was all in vain. Pulling open the front door, she hurried outside, then almost running, started making her way down the drive. Peter followed. "Let me drive you home," he shouted after her. At the gateway, she stopped, turned, directed her glaring eyes towards him.

"No way, don't know what might happen to me, just fuck off will you, leave me to grieve in peace."

He should have insisted, but then, once again, the unfairness of it all struck home, so he decided to let the woman go her own way.

Back inside the house, he found his thoughts ranging over that unfairness, guilt that he should have done more to make sure she was alright, and astonishment at how grief could affect a person's actions, which is how he sort of rationalised Mrs Benson's strange behaviour.

Time had got lost that day. It was only when he glanced at the kitchen clock, that he realised it was mid-afternoon, moreover that he was hungry, badly in need of a cup of soothing tea.

Chapter 3.

Later, as he sat there eating his beans on toast, sipping the hot, sweet tea, he thought again about that weird woman's visit, half wondering if he should mention it to Inspector Goddard, then deciding against. After he put the lunch things in the sink, he felt a wave of utter weariness flood over him. He went upstairs to lie on the bed for a few minutes. When he was woken by the sound of Naomi's voice asking if he was alright, it took him a few dazed seconds to understand that his few minutes on the bed had turned into a couple of hours.

Sleeping during the day always had a dulling effect on Peter; today was no exception. Watching the coloured kaleidoscope perform behind his eyes, as he pressed knuckles to eyeballs, he felt that dullness mutating into the beginnings of a headache. He wanted nothing better than to stay where he was until his mood changed into something lighter, but of course he didn't. For once Naomi's concern appeared real, rather than habitual. It seemed churlish not to reciprocate. "Sorry, dozed off, I'm alright, that woman came round, wore me out, seems to think I was somehow involved in her child's death, oh, I don't know, it wasn't very pleasant." The words came out in an uncoordinated rush.

Peter heaved himself off the bed, made for the bathroom, with Naomi following uncertainly behind. "What was she doing here? Why on earth should she think you had anything to do with the child's death?"

"I don't bloody know, do I." The truce was at an end. He just didn't want these stupid, unanswerable, questions being fired at him, yet, at the same time, he was quite aware, they were reasonable in the circumstances – would have asked them himself, had their roles been reversed. Then, where does fairness ever go hand in hand with petulance? Amazingly Naomi didn't take up the challenge, remaining, instead, frowningly concerned. "Are you hungry Peter? Shall I hurry dinner along? Can I get you anything? an aspirin?"

Guilt took charge. He dragged the tattered cloak of his emotions closer to him, tried to show his wife a more civilized aspect, a reasonable response to her apparently genuine worry on his behalf. "I'm alright, but I am hungry, beans on toast for lunch, that woman put me off my stride." He came out of the bathroom feeling better, after sluicing his face with cold water, and drinking a glassful. Naomi lightened, started to go downstairs with Peter following. Reaching the hallway, they were just in time to hear the end of a heightening argument between the children.

"Why should I want to go into your room anyway, it stinks to high heaven."

"No it doesn't you rotten bitch, just keep out."

"Yes it does, stinks of farts, feet, and wanking," Charlie sneered, sensing she had found a weak point in James's armour, ready to exploit her advantage.

At that point James came out of the kitchen, red-faced, nearly crying with anger, ran past his parents, and up the stairs, shouting back at his unseen sister. "Fucking bitch, fucking bitch, you smell of periods, bitch."

Peter, still somewhat dull of mind, nevertheless managed to shout at his son not to use language like that. The sound of a slamming door was all the reply he got. Naomi sighed, then moved into the kitchen to have a word with her recalcitrant daughter, and to get on with cooking their evening meal, leaving Peter to switch on the early evening news, before pouring himself an unusually large Scotch and Canada.

Sitting slumped in one of the deep armchairs, barely listening to the television, he found his mind going back to that last meeting with Simone. Sometimes he thought he might leave all this family stuff behind him, walk out on them, take the consequences. Then, he supposed, he still loved his children, even if they didn't often appear very loveable these days. On top of that, there was some sort of debt due to Naomi after twenty years of marriage. The whisky wasn't having much of a lifting effect on his state of mind, not that that stopped him pouring himself another large one, before Naomi put her head round the door to tell him that dinner was ready.

Three of them sat at the kitchen table. Despite considerable coaxing from his mother, James steadfastly refused to come downstairs to eat. Peter was still irritable. "Charlotte..." he only called her Charlotte when he had something unpleasant or very serious to say, "...it would help the atmosphere in this house, if you would stop tormenting your brother all the time."

"Me, you must be joking, dad, all I ever do is stick up for myself against the obnoxious little twit."

"Don't talk like that Charlie."

It appeared, for a moment, that there would only be two of them eating dinner, but after half-getting to her feet, Charlie sat down again with a point-making thump as her bottom hit the chair. "I shall be glad when I can get out of this house, away from grotty little boys altogether. Thank God for university that's all I can say."

Before there was time for either of her parents to express a view, the telephone in the hall rang. While Naomi went to answer it, Peter stayed toying unenthusiastically with his lamb chops, his earlier appetite having evaporated with his mood. He didn't feel as though he wanted his family this evening, his thoughts drifting once again to the ease of his relationship with Simone. Yet he was fiercely loyal when it came to his children, remembering his own continuing sense of loss when his parents divorced. In fact, despite some token efforts, he was virtually without a father from that time onwards. When his father died at the tender age of fifty, that was that. The hurt was still there, always would be, so he was absolutely determined that he wasn't going to leave his own kids with that terrible void in their lives. Then the saying came swiftly to mind – something about troubles coming in regiments, rather than single spies!

When Naomi came back into the kitchen, her face shouting that the telephone call had been rather more than casual, she sat down heavily and looked across the table at Peter, waiting for him to ask what was the matter. He duly did, with a resigned reluctance and was informed, "That was Rebecca on the phone." There was a pause, Peter raised his eyebrows. "She wants to come and stay for a while, bringing the baby."

Peter sensed that Naomi was talking about something more than a regular family visit. "Alright, what else? You wouldn't look like that if your sister was just coming to see us in the normal way."

Naomi put a hand to her hair, sighed looked down, then up, and straight across the table at Peter. "Of course you're right, some kind of row with Simon, says she can't stay with him any longer. What could I do Peter, she is my sister after all."

Charlie was interested now. "Has he attacked her mum, let's have all the lurid details."

"For God's sake, Charlie, this is serious, maybe a marriage at stake, no time to be flippant. As it happens though, it does appear that Simon slapped her, but then Rebecca was very upset, not entirely coherent. It seems that he stormed out of the house after their row. She's afraid of what will happen when he comes back, she's loading up the car now, coming over tonight." Her eyes appealed to Peter not to be angry by this sudden complication in their lives.

The truth was, Naomi wasn't too happy with this turn of events either. She knew her own sister too well, loved her, of course, but also knew what a pain in the arse she could be, temperamental in the extreme and manipulative on occasion. She remembered clearly, when they were kids, with only a year between their ages, how, whenever there was a quarrel, and there were plenty of those, Rebecca was always on the side of the angels, when it came to parental retribution. She could turn on a sweet smile at the drop of a hat, whatever she felt like underneath, and that smile won her many victories.

Naomi had always worried that her sister's marriage to Simon wouldn't last, they were much too similar in character, both needing to be the poor victim. That doesn't work when there were two of you.

Her mood darkened; she began to feel pretty sorry for herself. Would her kids ever grow up to be vaguely normal adults with just a hint of consideration for other people, would she and Peter ever cease being a constant irritant to each other. Now sister Rebecca was arriving with, no doubt, a bag full of hard-done-by complaints, to which she would have to listen.

It wasn't only family. At work, she was convinced that the senior partners were determined that she would remain in the second class, despite all the fine words and assurances, about it being only a matter of time. Christ, that Bill Clarkson was an oily bastard, charm oozing out of every pore, clients loved him, but always with his own hidden agenda.

There had been a time, she mused, after she and Peter were first married when, despite the lack of money, life had seemed bright, challenging and filled with a great deal of laughter. She didn't laugh much these days, despite their comparative affluence. Well, there was the spare room to get ready, life must go on, even if the zest had somehow gone out of it. Rising in silence from the kitchen table, she avoided any further eye contact with her frowning husband, before making her disconsolate way upstairs to get on with the job of preparing Rebecca's room. Peter watched her go, under cover of pretending to read the newspaper.

Charlotte, who had been expecting more fireworks, continued with her busy demolition of cheese and biscuits, but she too was thinking hard, thinking about her imminent escape to Durham, subject to her A level results, of course. Escape from, what she saw, as the stifling environment of home life, escape to a place where they would treat her as an adult individual, in her own right, not just part of someone's damn family. She might even have them call her Charlotte, at least at first, although she supposed she would revert to Charlie, when she got to know a few people.

Saying goodbye to Justin would be no hardship, something she should have done months ago. All very well this children of friendly families, nice boy and all that. He was alright, but she felt she had now outgrown him. She had to start her real life at university, meet some real people, live and experiment, get some experience behind her, grow up, at last.

Chapter 4.

"For Christ's sake, Michael, you know bloody well that I don't come in on Wednesday afternoons." Peter wasn't altogether surprised, it had happened before. Jackson had been against this flexi-hours idea from the start, particularly for managers. He always pretended it had slipped his memory, when something like this happened.

"Sorry old chap, but it really was the only time that both Smithson and Rake could get over at the same time, forgot about your bloody Wednesdays, didn't I." Like hell he forgot.

Peter felt like a child, suddenly deprived of a promised outing, and angry with it. After the events of the last few days, the invasion of his house by Naomi's sister, his regular assignation with the lovely Simone had seemed a light in the darkness, something to think about that set his pulses racing. If you can snarl inwardly, then that's what Peter did. Those meetings with Simone provided an interlude exciting enough to keep him going through the rest of the week. Now his bastard boss was taking away his toy.

There was no way he could turn down the meeting, it was his baby, no bloody need for Jackson to get involved, in fact, but then, he was always putting his oar in, seeking to take credit where there was any going. There had been times, quite a lot of them, when he had been tempted to look elsewhere for employment. It was only the fact that Michael Jackson was sixty-four, and decidedly creaky, that stopped him. He had a good chance, or at least thought he had, of being promoted to the board when his boss retired, and that carrot was sufficient for him to put up with the old man's irascible ways.

"Actually Michael, the contract is pretty well cut and dried, you don't really need to get involved if you're busy." Said with a forlorn hope of him agreeing, it received the expected response.

"No problem, cleared my desk, known old Jimmy Smithson since we were both at tech. Came up the hard way in those days, both of us, not like you university blokes today, all red carpets and expense accounts. Anyway Jimmy will buy us a decent lunch, save Marjorie cooking, alright son?"

Of course Peter nodded, smiled his acceptance of the fait accompli, while remaining seething inside. At once he started to consider whether he could risk some excuse to Naomi, allowing him to escape to Simone's place one evening. He didn't need justification, could put guilty feelings aside, he was owed an evening of relaxation was the way he looked at it, although relaxation was hardly the word for what he wanted. It had to be an evening because Simone had her own kids to stay most weekends.

Simone with kids, that was a laugh, he thought, remembering her more as a sexual athlete than a mother, or more likely wanting to remember her in that way. Anyway tomorrow was out, so he would just have to accept that the big boy had taken his lollipop away.

Peter was still in a deprived sulky mood, when he got home that evening. The fact that the baby was screaming, Naomi already looking frazzled, helped not one little bit. She appeared from the kitchen, tea towel in hand, as soon as he stepped through the front door, her expression one of supplication. "Peter, sorry love, would you mind, need a few things from the shops, Rebecca being here rather upset the old routine."

At that moment, the said Rebecca had been coming downstairs, holding the still-crying baby in her arms. ."Well thank you very much sister dear, so nice to know I'm welcome."

"You know very well I didn't mean that, Rebecca, but having you here does rather ring the changes, you know. As I said, in the first place, you're very welcome, but you must see that it makes a difference to our domestic routine."

Calm, she must keep calm, flesh and blood, yes, but a dangerous cow, when it came to arguments about who was right, and who was wrong. Naomi's smile may have been carved out of wood, but smile she did, while Rebecca strode out of the room, her buttocks moving in angry protest. She flounced, and sniffed as she took the noisy baby into the kitchen, muttering something about overflowing breasts, and nosey little boys.

Peter took the scribbled note from Naomi's hand and, without even a sigh, went back out again determined that, if he had to be errand boy, then he would take the opportunity of calling in to the Red Fox for a swift half or something of that kind, anything to delay returning to his invaded home. When he entered the pub, the usual culprits were there, sitting at the bar, grumbling about Tony Blair and the Muslim threat, the miserable recent performances of the England football team, and the price of beer.

"Got you doing the shopping then, mate? My God, Peter, didn't take you for a subordinate husband."

"Belt up Ronnie, I'm not in the mood, but if you're feeling sorry for me, I'll have a pint of Badger." Peter wasn't a regular in the same way these guys were, but he knew them. It was pleasant, in a way, going into a pub, being greeted, albeit often scornfully, by friendly faces. That first pint went down his gullet swiftly, and satisfyingly. He then felt it incumbent upon him to buy the next round, knowing full well, he should go back home to face the extended family music.

Conversation soon reverted to the old topics they had been worrying at, before Peter came in, nothing new, just a repositioning of views expressed many times previously. It didn't take him long to remember that his reluctance to become a regular in the Red Fox, was because he would die of boredom, had he done so. Their only interest appeared to be in running down whatever particular target they had before them that day, be it sporting, political, educational or female. The arguments went round and round, covering the same ground, in a way that had Peter dizzy, and he had only been there half an hour.

Half an hour: Christ he'd better be getting back, if he wanted to avoid a frosty reception at home. He left to a chorus of comments about who was boss in his house, and had he left his apron in the car. Back home he dumped the shopping bag on the kitchen table. The baby had stopped crying, but Naomi looked still stressed, her forehead damp, her mouth clamped determinedly shut, as she dealt with the dinner, her sulky son, unhelpful daughter and weeping sister.

Apparently Simon had been on the phone, and whatever words had been exchanged, it seemed that Rebecca was staying. At that moment, she was hovering in the kitchen, on the face of it trying to help with the cooking, but actually alternating between apologising for being a nuisance, and tearful declamations that her life was over, and what bastards men were.

"Would you ladies like a drink?" Uncontroversial you might have thought, but you would have been wrong. With a show of irritation, Naomi snatched the bag of shopping from him.

"For God's sake, Peter, can't you see I'm trying to cook the dinner. Judging from the time you took, you've already had a couple, so don't worry about us." She glared at her husband as though she hated the very air he breathed.

"Thanks Peter but can't, baby's milk and all that, don't want him to grow up a toper do we, like his fucking father." Politeness had turned to venom in the blink of an eye, as tears continued to trickle down her cheeks. "Please Naomi let me do something to help, I hate being such a nuisance to you."

"The best thing you can do to help, is to fuck off out, and leave me to it. Oh, God, I'm sorry love, I didn't mean that, but really everything's under control." She broke away from the stove, to put her arms round her sister. "That was very unkind of me. I know you're feeling rotten what with Simon, and all that, but there is nothing you can do, so why don't you go and talk to Charlie, she's only watching the box. I'm sure she would like a chat."

The telephone rang. Peter, being nearest, picked up the receiver. "It's for you Charlie, Justin wants a word."

"Fucking hell, what does he want?" Charlotte emerged from the lounge, looking peeved. Grabbing the phone out of her father's hand, she ignored his imprecations about her bad language. She had to do it soon. There was no way she wanted this thing to carry on, once she was off to Durham. It had become a habit, the boy next door, not this next door but the previous house. Thrown together by neighbourly get-togethers, they had slipped into a relationship, which as far as she was concerned had outgrown any raison d'être. Justin was a year younger than she was, and lately she had found him rather immature, particularly when it came to sex. No more clumsy fumbling with schoolboys she had decided, but how to tell the poor bugger. She was only too aware that he was still smitten.

"Hello Just, can't be long, dinner's about to go on the table. No, not tonight, few girly things to do, perhaps later in the week. Yes, alright Friday it is, see you at seven."

Her father was still in the hall. He knew how Charlie felt about Justin. He had masculine empathy with the boy, against the cruelty of the female sex. "Charlie, it's none of my business, but why on earth don't you put the lad out of his misery, letting him take you out to expensive dinners, when you're just marking time, it's not fair on the lad is it?"

She looked straight at her father, eyes unblinking. "You're right, it's none of your business dad, but you're also right, it isn't fair, and yes, I am going to tell him, probably on Friday as it happens, O.K. Dad?" She brushed past him to resume her place in front of the television.

Peter followed her into the sitting room, reached for the whisky decanter, needing something to soothe the tension, that was sloshing around the house that evening. He had no sooner poured out a liberal measure, when Naomi put her head round the door. "Dinner will be ready in five minutes, in the kitchen, alright, open a bottle of wine please Peter." She must has seen the glass in his hand, so discretion definitely being the better part of valour this evening, he put the tumbler on the sideboard, went into the kitchen to select a bottle from the wine rack.

So there they were, a grim-faced James persuaded down from his room, an angry wife and her unfortunate sister, his independent-minded daughter, and himself, still hating the fact that his Wednesday afternoon had been ruined by that old fool Jackson. Peter poured the wine, and for several minutes the only sounds that could be heard were those of eating and drinking: sounds which couldn't really be expected to do any tension-breaking. Eventually, when Rebecca asked James what A levels he was taking next term, a conversation of sorts got going. George, cadging under the table had to be expelled from the kitchen, another notch of relief, and then the wine began to take hold. Gradually civilisation was restored to the Shadbolt household.

After dinner Rebecca was eager to do the washing up, but the moment she put her hands in the kitchen sink, the baby started to howl again. Peter, rather than get an earful from his teenage monsters, stepped into the breach himself. "You go and sit down love," he offered Naomi, while at the same time attempting to put a consoling arm round her shoulders. She shrugged away with a curt, "Right it's all yours," before walking into the sitting room to slump down on the sofa and sit, head back, eyes closed, only to revive a moment later to shout, "and you can make us a cup of coffee while you're at it."

Chapter 5.

Peter got on with the chores, thinking all the time that, when he was with Simone, he was never asked to do the washing up, but then they never really had time for eating so that was hardly a fair comparison, he reflected. Thoughts of his lover, reminded him that he hadn't told her yet that tomorrow was off... Take the dog a walk, use the mobile, talk dirty for a few minutes, as soon as he'd done jobs in the kitchen. Thinking along those lines got him remembering how it had all started with Simone.

She was an independent financial adviser. He had seen her firm's advertisement in the local paper. Wanting some critical illness cover, he had gone to the hotel where she and her colleagues were seeing potential clients and, from the moment he first clapped eyes on her, he was hooked. When he seemed keen to do business, she invited him to one of the small private rooms at the company's disposal to discuss his requirements more fully.

There had been sexual lightening between them right from the start. Although nothing, other than a very long-held handshake, full of suggestion, took place that afternoon, it was obvious to both of them, that there was more to come. After a few days she rang him to say the policy was ready. She could either bring it round to his house, office, or if he felt like a drink one evening, he could come round to her flat to collect the documentation.

The invitation and expectation were blatant. It was all so unlike him, but probably for the first time in his life, Peter was certain of a woman, certain why she had invited him round to her flat, certain there was more to his visit than documentation. The feeling he had, ever since Simone's telephone call, had been one of adventure, new, daring and very exciting.

When he arrived at the flat the slow burn of anticipated pleasure burst into lustful flame when Simone opened the door wearing her dressing gown. They were down each other's throats, the moment he kicked the door shut. The bedroom remained undisturbed. Peter had a fleeting thought that this was no way to treat an almost new business suit, before they were writhing on the floor, seeking that primary culmination that would only later be replaced by love making.

It was all so easy, so natural, the first time he had gone astray since he married, and it was all so bloody easy. At first he worried that he might be found out, that there might be smells left over to betray his infidelity, but Simone was very practical about such things. On future occasions she made him change as soon as he arrived at the flat, and when they had finished, she made sure his shower left him smelling like a new man, as she put it, but had what they were doing anything to do with love?

However, had what they were doing anything to do with love? Peter thought back, as he mopped the last dinner plate, and if it hadn't, did that matter. Such considerations, at least at a distance, bothered him somewhat. As a youth, discussing such matters with his bawdy school friends, he had always held forth the view that sex was emotionally important, not to be taken too lightly, like most of his randy pals. He used to say that he wouldn't have sex unless he had some feeling for his partner over and above sheer lust. That was a long time ago, but faint guilt lingered in his consciousness over this thing with Simone. She was fine with it, or so she said, and he had made no promises, and yet that uneasiness remained. Betrayal of Naomi was part of it, but the other part was that there was something not quite right with unadulterated sex without accompanying affection, but then what was affection actually, anyway.

He took coffee into the two women, then said he would take George out for a brief stroll, to get some fresh air. As he walked out of the drive he saw, to his shocked surprise, Mrs Benson standing on the other side of the street looking straight at him. It was nearly dark, but he had absolutely no doubt it was her, same black dress as the last time he saw her, same rigid body posture, and that accusing stare. What should he do, cross the road and speak to her, perhaps, but then he remembered her less than friendly departure so settled for. "Hello, Mrs Benson," and walked on, jerking angrily at the lead as George strained to go faster.

The woman said nothing in reply, but Peter thought he could feel her eyes boring into his back. It took a mighty effort of willpower not to turn round, to confirm the fact. Yes, it bothered him, yes he was desperately sorry for her, but no, he didn't want to see her again, and no, despite the desperate circumstances, he couldn't feel any empathy with the woman, couldn't get inside her grief to see how she suffered. Rotten way of thinking maybe, but he couldn't bring himself to like Mrs Benson, and that's all there was to it.

Why she was hanging about, he had no idea. Whether she still felt he had something to do with her little girl's death, he, again, didn't know; he certainly hoped she would get whatever it was out of her system pretty quickly, and not come near him again, a hope which, as soon as it entered his mind, brought back that sense of guilt that was troubling him so much lately. As far as the Benson woman was concerned, he understood only too well, that he wasn't able to comprehend the grief a mother must feel at the loss of a child.

Peter reached the style before allowing George his ecstatic release. Sitting on the top step the unpleasant image of Mrs Benson, was pushed to a distant part of his brain, by his phone call to Simone. After the initial few minutes of apology and regret, came the prurient bit which left him with a craving for sex, almost adolescent in its intensity, accompanied by a frustrating degree of tumescence that, under instruction from his lover, left him no alternative but to seek relief.

With his mobile still clamped to his ear, he moved into the trees, and while Simone described what she was doing to herself, he quickly dealt with the problem, leaving himself drained and trembling, immediately bothered by the image he would present, when he got back home. When he finally rang off, his voice still husky with excitement, Simone was still laughing. Female triumphalism was how he would have described it, but whatever it was, he shouted for George and, still weak from spent sex, made his way slowly back to the house.

Take the dog for a walk. That bloody dog provided endless get-outs for Peter, but it was that sister of hers that was the more immediate problem She was her flesh and blood, she was in trouble, and yet Naomi had more than once wondered to what extent Rebecca was actually enjoying the attention, being the injured party, and all that.

Shades of their childhood, never knowing what was real feeling, and what wasn't. Anyway, unless she wanted a row to develop, she had no alternative but to take things at their face value, or at least until her exasperation overflowed into comment. Truth was, she didn't really know her sister when it came to personal interchanges, was never sure of her ground, always conscious that she was almost certainly being manipulated then, if she responded on that assumption, it usually turned out that she was the bitch, and poor old Rebecca was the one being maligned.

She hadn't been watching the television with much attention. Now, she got up from the sofa and, followed by Rebecca's quizzical gaze, left the room, restlessly moving through the kitchen out into the back garden. The stars were beginning to appear in the velvety darkness, the night smells were pleasant. There in the mellow air, she slowly sighed her way into a better frame of mind.

All her worries were pretty normal, frustration at work, difficult relations, and a marriage that had lost its gloss. On the other side of the coin no one she loved was dying, there were no financial worries and, although the children frequently drove her mad, they were actually doing alright. What came next she wondered. Once those two were launched into university education, what about Peter and her, what were they going to do with their lives, apart from getting up each other's noses, that was.

Her melancholic introspection was interrupted by a loud shout heard through an open upstairs window. The only word she could make out was "bitch" but the voice was James's, she suspected the fault was Charlie's. Why that girl took such a delight in tormenting her young brother, she really didn't know, and of course the boy always rose to the bait, absolutely no match against her feminine wiles. Thank God in another couple of months her daughter would be on her way to Durham, then perhaps there'd be some peace in the house and maybe, just maybe, Rebecca could sort herself out, leaving Peter and her with some space to negotiate a pattern for the next phase of their life together, or maybe not. Naomi walked back inside to quell the row, but by the time she reached the bottom of the stairs, all was quiet again, usual storm in a teacup stuff.

Then, as she walked back towards the living room, the front doorbell rang. She thought at first Peter had forgotten his key, but there on the doorstep was the figure of Simon, smartly dressed, and carrying flowers. She let him in without much enthusiasm and told him where Rebecca was before disappearing upstairs, out of the way. Naomi had only been in the bathroom a few minutes, washing her face, when she heard raised voices, then the front door crashed shut. Rebecca was here to stay a while longer was her immediate conclusion, as she made her reluctant way downstairs to offer half-hearted succour to her sister.

When Naomi, sighs tucked away at the ready, entered the living room, Rebecca raised a crumpled tear-stained face from her hands, looking for succour and comfort against cruel husbands. The flowers, that Simon had been clutching, were scattered in dismal disarray, on the floor at the side of the fireplace. Neither they nor whatever her husband had said had worked, and despite her sister's look of unhappy desperation, Naomi couldn't help but wonder whose fault that was. Disloyal, she knew, but then she knew her sister, knew, to her remembered cost, the penalties she extracted when it came to re-establishing relations after a quarrel. "Alright let's have it love, what's happened now? I thought from the visit, and the flowers, that the two of you might just be able to make peace."

The tears fell with renewed volume, her nose ran in sympathy, making it necessary to snatch at the box of paper tissues, Naomi had pushed in her direction. "The bastard hit me, it's finished, flowers don't make up for violence, saying sorry and expect everything to be back to normal, typical man."

"Well what do you want him to do? I'm sure he is sorry, but if you won't talk to him, what hope is there of resolving the issues between you." She knew, she should put her arms round the woman, comfort her, yet her feelings were ambivalent. If truth were known she could do without the complications of a long-term stay by her sister. Moreover, she wondered again quite where all the fault lay in that situation. Simon probably had hit her, then what provocation had been offered? Curbing her doubts, she sat close to Rebecca, making a half-hearted effort to put an arm round her shoulders, only to be rebuffed with a shrug and an angry look. Her sister's miserable desolation of a couple of minutes ago, had been replaced a wild anger that left her spitting venom in Naomi's direction, the nearest person available.

"It's all over, I tell you, not that I expect you to understand. You've always taken other people's side where I'm involved, always have done. Alright I know you want me out of the house so I'll pack and go, then perhaps you'll be happy." She rose and made to flounce out of the room, while Naomi raised a restraining hand.

"For God's sake Rebecca, you know damn well, you're welcome to stay here as long as you want. It's not a matter of sides, anyway. Surely you're not going to throw away a marriage, because your husband lost his temper once, it was only once wasn't it?"

None of that was what she wanted to say, but in the circumstances words had to be tempered to meet feelings. There was absolutely nothing to be gained by adding a secondary row to go with the one her sister was already having with Simon. Charlie came back in the room at that point. Rebecca brushed past her, could be heard running upstairs, then the sound of a door slamming, a noise heard quite frequently in the Shadbolt household lately.

Charlie looked at her mother, raised her eyebrows, shrugged, intending sympathy but coming over to Naomi as uncaring youth. Not that she said anything, and when Charlie asked quietly what had happened, she told her without hint of remonstration. "Looks as though we'll be having Rebecca to stay a while longer."

Chapter 6.

Peter got back to a silent house, not having sighted the terrible Mrs Benson again on the way, and, despite knowing he had already drunk quite enough for one evening, he helped himself to another Scotch. He picked up the Telegraph, but couldn't concentrate on the usual dire litany of news items; Iraq, Afghanistan, North Korea. Sri Lanka all vying for the largest share of misery, while at home, stories of violence with murder, drugs, guns and brutality featuring strongly. My God what a world we live in today, he thought, but at the same time he knew only too well he and his circle were among the lucky ones.

When Naomi came into the room, she sensed at once, his despondency. Years of marriage and feminine intuition, had equipped her well to recognise the moods of the individual members of her family. A fed-up husband was not something she wanted to deal with right now. Their eyes met, and held for some moments in unvoiced but mutual animosity. The connection broke when she said, in even tones, "I'll have one of those."

The ice temporarily broken, Naomi took the proffered glass, slumping down on the sofa, with a sound somewhere between a sigh and a groan. "Simon was round, didn't stay long though. I'm afraid Rebecca looks like being with us for a while longer."

Truce now firmly established, Peter offered his genuine attention. "You reckon this spat between them is really serious then?"

"Difficult to say really. He did hit her. As far as I can tell it was just the once, not that even once is on, of course. Anyway Rebecca is going to require an awful lot of retribution, if they're to get together again. I have to say, knowing my dear sister, I have some sympathy with Simon, though. There have been many times when I've felt like belting her one, and if truth be told I did, when we were kids."

Peter was rather surprised, when she made the peace secure by continuing. "You've been good about this, Peter. I'll work on her tomorrow, see if we can sort something out." She actually kissed him. He realised, with trepidation, that she was moving in the direction of sex. That was the very last thing he wanted, after his telephone conversation with Simone, but there was the dilemma. To turn down his wife's very infrequent initiative was to risk several days of frost, to go ahead risked an unenthusiastic showing in bed, which could be equally disastrous.

In the end her hand on his thigh, a suggestion that they take their drinks up to bed left absolutely no alternative. A short time later, when he came out of the bathroom to see Naomi sitting naked, on the side of the bed, he was relieved to feel a stirring in his loins. They made love, and as far as Peter could tell, she was reasonably satisfied with his performance.

The next morning feeling rather shattered, Peter came out of the bedroom, to find Rebecca on the landing, making her way to the bathroom. She had on a nightdress which left absolutely nothing to the imagination. When she saw Peter, she stopped at the bathroom door to smile charmingly in his direction and to say, "Good morning". He replied of course, but couldn't help wondering, as he made his way downstairs, how a woman supposedly distraught over her marital problems, could still manage to flaunt herself about the place in such an apparently carefree way.

"Doesn't that sister of yours possess a dressing gown?" was probably not the best way to start a conversation, but somehow the thought of Rebecca being their guest for some time to come, irritated him to an unreasonable degree.

Naomi looked up, surprised. "My sister embarrassing you, Peter? I'll have a word, although I'm surprised at you complaining about any display of female flesh." She showed her teeth in what might have been a passing smile, quickly substituted by a frown indicating that last night's truce had been just that, normal relations were to be resumed today.

James came into the kitchen, sulked a reluctant reply in answer to his father's insistent, "Good morning". It was only the fact that Naomi had booked him a dental appointment for that morning, and had accordingly shouted at his bedroom door until he acknowledged her cries, that he was downstairs at this time on a non-school day. As James lay in bed that morning, slowly gathering his wits, he decided he was depressed. Another day of boredom once he had seen the tooth torturer, was all he had to look forward to. School holidays were a bore. Two weeks in the Loire Valley, looking at fucking chateaux was not his idea of a good time, since then nothing. He had made a couple of attempts to join in football games in the park, with some of the guys he knew from school, but he wasn't much good at it, no one seemed all that keen to have him on their side.

Next term was going to be a bundle of laughs; A levels and the assumption by his mother and father that he was going to university. He had no idea what degree he wanted to take, and the subjects he was going to study were really just the easy way out, acceptance of his form master's suggestions. He liked literature, and that had seemed an option until both the school and his dad, had talked about the shortage of science students, and the fact that because of that, there would be good opportunities for someone with a science degree by the time he had finished at university. He had sense enough to understand though, that his resentment about people deciding his future education for him was unreasonable, given that he had no strong views himself.

James helped himself to some crunchy nut cornflakes, ate them, eyes down, trying to avoid any contact that might lead to the necessity of communication. His body felt heavily lethargic. He was vaguely worried that he might be showing some outward signs of last night's masturbatory session. That was another thing. His damn penis was for ever springing up at the slightest sexual thought that came into his mind, and there were lots of those. He had read it was nothing to worry about, common in fact amongst boys of his age, yet every time he did it, he was left feeling drained physically, with an unease of mind, telling him that he was weak to give into his desires.

Some of the guys at school boasted about having had sex with girls, "girls gagging for it," as they said, but girls frightened him to death. The idea of actually putting into practice his sexual fantasies, seemed a world away.

"You'll be late James," his mother sighed, looking with some dismay at her frowning scruffy-looking son, moping slowly through his breakfast.

"Yes alright, I'm going." He slammed his half-empty dish onto the draining board, leaving the room without further words. The sound of the front door closing with a crash, told his parents, that he had indeed gone.

Peter looked up from his newspaper, his eyes meeting his wife's in agreed exasperation at the demeanour of their son. "I'll be glad when it's term time again. At least school will get him out of that damned room, and away from that computer for a few hours."

"That's great coming from you. What do you do to encourage him? Fathers are supposed to bond with their sons, play sport with them, even talk to them occasionally"

Chapter 7.

As he drove out of the driveway on his way to meet Robbie Bankworth, his regular squash partner, Peter was slightly disturbed to see a black clad figure standing on the opposite side of the road. Of course he recognised her instantly, their eyes meeting briefly, as he swung out into the road.

He braked momentarily, half-thinking about having a word with the woman, then changing his mind, accelerating away instead. Nevertheless it bothered him. What did she want? It was a mild case of stalking, when all said and done, not that he would ever do anything about it, but he wished she would disappear. He understood full well that there was no way he fathom the grief of someone losing a child, particularly a young one, but what could he do about it? Having said that, for some inexplicable reason, he was assailed with a vague sense of guilt. Peter didn't like loose ends. As he drove, he mused over how he could tie this particular one up.

Despite the usual output of sweat and energy, he wasn't sharp on the court that evening. As the two men sat slumped against the back wall in between sets, Robbie poked him gently in the chest with his racket. "Getting past it are we mate, or is there something on your mind tonight?"

Robbie knew all about him finding the dead girl, but not about the unwelcome attention he had been getting from Mrs Benson. So far, Peter had managed to block out the image of the dead child for most of the time, but the sight of that black clad figure this evening, brought it all rushing back. The shock, the disbelief that something like that could happen to him, but most of the huge sense of regret at a little girl losing her life, came over him as strongly as it had at the time. He wanted so badly to turn the clock back, for the tragedy not to have taken place, useless thoughts he knew, but powerful nevertheless. "Sorry, Robbie, just not in the mood tonight. Do you mind if we call it a day."

Robbie still had no idea what was troubling his friend, although he was sure that there was something on his mind. He decided it was better to leave it until Peter confided in him, rather than push him for an on the spot explanation. "Suits me old son, but we were playing for the beer, so don't you forget it."

In the showers the two men were silent, some slight sense of unease hanging between them. As Robbie liberally soaped his genital area, Peter couldn't help a surreptitious glance down in that direction. Robbie had an unusually large penis, which the lads said explained why he had six kids, although Peter knew that that was more down to his earth-mother wife, Wendy, than anything else. Nevertheless it was difficult to avoid a prurient thought about what that great thing would look like when erect. The two men had been friends ever since the two families had been neighbours several years ago, keeping the contact going when Robbie moved to the other side of town when he joined in with other doctors to form the Wayside Medical Clinic At almost the same time, Peter and Naomi had moved up market, to a larger house.

By the time the men had towelled off, and were sitting in the club bar, taking the first sips at their beer, Peter had managed to shake off his troubled feelings for the time being, putting to one side his worries about him and Naomi, his job and his deep sadness over the little girl he had found lying in the woods. On the other side of the table Robbie gave a little sigh and shake of the head. "Shame about Charlie and Justin, I really thought they would make a go of it. Then I suppose being at different universities would have made things rather difficult anyway.

Peter shrugged, smiled a sad, but not very interested, agreement, which Robbie took to be a sign of his earlier distracted state of mind. Despite his earlier resolution to leave to Peter to speak out in his own good time, Robbie decided to ask the question. "Alright Peter, let's have it, got the sack or something, wife having it off with the milkman, spill the bloody beans, for Christ's sake, you're turning my beer sour." He reached across the table, to grip his friend's arm.

Selecting the most obvious of his worries, Peter explained about the woman in black, which is how he now thought of Mrs Benson. He explained how he felt helpless in the face of her persistence, deeply sorry, yet unable to help her.

"Why don't you have a word with that inspector chap. After all he knows the circumstances. I'm sure he would tread very carefully, given what the poor woman's been through. Whichever way you look at it, it's not your responsibility, no matter how sorry you feel for her."

"No, I don't want to do that, seems pathetic asking for police help in a situation like this. Might just have another word with her, try and get to the bottom of what she wants from me. It's quite ridiculous, I know, but I still feel vaguely guilty, as if I should have done more to help the child even though she was stone cold by the time I found her." He reached into his pocket for his handkerchief to mop up some of the sweat still pouring down his face.

Robbie shook his head, but felt it wise to leave the subject alone for this evening. They chatted amicably enough for another half hour or so, before Peter said he had to go. As he got near to his home he looked with slight trepidation towards the pavement opposite his house. Some sense of relief came over him, when there was no figure in black waiting to add to his unsettled state of mind.

Earlier in the evening, Naomi had heard small sounds of sobbing coming from Rebecca's room as she passed along the landing, and they certainly weren't coming from the baby. With a preliminary sigh, she tapped on her sister's door, ready to hide her feelings in the name of caring, while at the same time being only too aware of her own frustration with what she saw as a resolvable stand-off between Rebecca and Simon. She was sure that Simon was not by nature a violent man. Thinking back, she remembered the many occasions, when driven to distraction by the wiles of her little sister, she had clobbered her one. Of course there was no excuse for violence in any circumstances, yet she felt some of her sympathy moving towards her brother-in-law. Anyway she wanted her home back; babies crying in the night had, she thought, become a thing of the past. She was becoming mildly frazzled due to the broken sleep patterns.

A weak sounding invitation to enter the room, made it inevitable that she would have to listen to another round of recriminations against Simon, and his evil deeds. Her sister was standing over the carry cot, where the baby lay sleeping peacefully, stroking the child's head in what Naomi thought uncharitably, was a rather contrived way, almost as though she had set the tableau for when someone entered the room. "I thought I heard you crying Rebecca."

"Yes, well, I've been speaking at length to this poor little thing's father on the mobile."

"That's good isn't it? What did he have to say?"

"Oh, he just went over and over the same ground, he's desperately sorry, won't ever happen again and so on, but the thing is it did happen, there's no way I'm going to let him off the hook, the bastard." Naomi felt her heart sink, she had hoped for reconciliation, now this latest news did not augur well for any such thing.

"Look sweetheart what do you want him to do? Are you really prepared to throw away a marriage over one incident, violent or otherwise. It sounds to me as though he's genuinely sorry, and you know if you went back to him it would put you in a very strong position in the future." She was tempted to add that such a situation would be one her sister was well suited to exploit, but of course she didn't.

Rebecca came towards her, taking both her hands in hers. She smiled in a way that gave a lie to her sobbing minutes earlier. She had always been good at turning on that smile, her lips sliding open to reveal her teeth at the slightest provocation, almost as though she found it difficult to keep her teeth covered for long. "You've been marvellous Naomi, you and Peter, and the children of course, but my marriage is over. I can't stand physical violence, no amount of saying sorry can put it right." As though a switch had been pressed, the smile switched off, the tears were there again.

Naomi felt her earlier frustration surging back. Her sister was playing out a part, and not yet ready to move onto the next scene, was how she saw it. If the truth were known she wanted to shake Rebecca hard until some sense percolated into that stubborn brain of hers, but she knew that would only cement her satisfaction with her part, lead her to take it forward. Instead she shrugged her shoulders. "You know best of course. Have you been in touch with a solicitor yet?"

Rebecca frowned. She had expected further persuasion, not this bland acceptance of what she said. In actual fact the thought of legal proceedings frightened her. Moreover the thought of a possibly less comfortable life if she divorced Simon also worried her a good deal. Nevertheless, she wasn't yet ready to negotiate her husband's surrender. For the time being she rather enjoyed being a burden on her sister.

Chapter 8.

The solicitors where Naomi worked, was a long established firm. Bradford, Lang and Oldfield sounded good, but in reality there was only Roger left of the original partners, and he was a mere figurehead, putting in an appearance now and then, but dealing only with a few ancient ladies, who continued to value his gentlemanly presence. In fact the old boy farmed out the work to some junior as soon as the old dears left the office.

To all intents and purposes, Bill Clarkson ruled the roost of Naomi's particular firm of solicitors. He, together with a favoured few cohorts, made all the decisions of any importance, despite the weekly strategy meetings, which were supposed to do exactly that. Even the system of payment to partners and associates was shrouded in mystery, though it was supposedly based on a weighted system of clients billed.

Naomi was chatting to Rosalind Makepiece, one of the legal secretaries, when Bill put his head round her door, glanced from one to the other of the two women, then pausing for a moment, he switched on a smile. "Naomi, my love, could you possibly spare me a moment in my office." Without waiting for a reply, he removed his head, closing the door firmly behind him.

Naomi was well aware that Bill didn't expect partners or associates to be too friendly with the more junior members of staff. She knew that, in particular, he disapproved of the rapport that she and Rosalind had built up, although he never came out and said so in any direct way. By the time she had trailed him to his lair, the senior partner was firmly established behind that great desk of his, pretending to be concentrating on some papers in front of him.

"Ah, Naomi my sweet," he started, as though forgetting that only two or three minutes had elapsed since he had summoned her to the presence, "how are we these days, getting on, alright?" Before she could respond, he continued. "You remember Mr Longstaff, divorce case a few weeks back, well he's been to see me, complaining about being overcharged, says you could have settled the wording of the agreement roughed out in court, without the lengthy exchange of correspondence with the other side."

She looked across the desk at her boss's large fleshy face. It struck her in that moment that it represented a gross image of bullying masculinity at its worst. "Well I like that, it was due to your Mr Longstaff's very particular insistence on the actual wording, that caused most of the delays, and the additional correspondence that that entailed."

"Well now, my dear, he's not my Mr Longstaff. Anyway I've had a look at the file and I do feel that if you and that Smithson woman had spoken about some of the points over the telephone, some time could have been saved."

"We did and…"

"Yes well, I felt all things considered I had to make an adjustment to his account, can't get a reputation for overbilling can we?"

"Look, Bill, I am sure the original billing was O.K. You would be the first to complain, if one of us was less than thorough." She was furious, furious that the Longstaff guy hadn't come to her with his complaint, furious that Bill had accepted what he said without talking to her first, and furious with this pompous man who thought he could do exactly what he wanted in the firm.

"Your work is exemplary, my dear, but there are times when corners can be cut, time is money after all. Anyway Naomi, thank you for popping in." His eyes moved dismissively away from her to the papers in front of him. Feeling like an intimidated school girl in the headmistress's office, she took the only option available to her, which was to get up and leave the room. As she moved away, she glared at the bent head on the other side of the desk, felt an outburst coming on, before common sense kicked in. This was not the time to make a stand.

Nevertheless, she was seething as she walked down the corridor. Not for the first her thoughts dwelt on the possibility of looking elsewhere for a job. Back in her own office, she considered ringing Peter to complain about the obnoxious Bill Clarkson, before remembering that he wasn't at work on Wednesday afternoons. She rather resented those afternoons now she came to think about it and, when she thought about it some more, she remembered how little output she had ever seen from his so called writer's club. Partly because she knew it would annoy Bill, partly because she wanted someone to talk to, she decided to ask Rosalind to have lunch with her.

When the two women were safely ensconced in a corner of the Centurion, Naomi gave vent to a few of her frustrations, explaining all about her sister first of all, before running through her worries about her son's complete lack of social graces, Bill Clarkson's overbearing pomposity and finally her disappointment with the way her relationship with Peter was going.

Rosalind giggled quietly. "Apart from that, Mrs Lincoln, how did you enjoy the play?" It was one of their long established responses, when one or the other went on a bit. "But seriously, love, what you've just described is pretty much the sort of goings-on that happen in most normal families, isn't it?" She sipped her beer, raised her eyebrows, smiling across the table at her companion. Rosalind might have smiled, but there was a touch of irony in the smile. She was single herself, hadn't been lucky in her relationships with men, so the idea of her friend complaining, when she had all that lovely family structure to worry about, struck her as slightly ungrateful.

"Of course, you're right, Rosalind. I expect too much, the happily ever after romantic love is a very rare happening, I suppose. Here let me get you another beer, before we return to the lion's den." She went up to the bar, fighting her way through the lunchtime crowd. While she was getting the drinks in, it came to her that Rosalind was right about everything except perhaps that bastard Clarkson, there she felt her moans were justified. Returning to the table she smiled at her friend. "Anyway enough about me, what about your love life these days?"

Rosalind shrugged. "Still see Jeremy from time to time, but you couldn't call what we have a relationship. Trouble is when you're the age I am, and carry the weight I do, you're not much of a catch. Jeremy will never leave his wife. In fact I'm not at all sure I'd want him to anyway. He sees me as a very obliging, and non-complaining bit on the side, which adds a touch of spice to life in his world of accounts ledgers. Don't get me wrong, he's very kind, despite expecting me to be available at any time convenient to him. I should tell him to fuck off really. Then I say to myself, why do that when I enjoy what little we have, including I have to say the sex, which isn't bad with the old bugger."

Naomi was glad she had asked Rosalind to have lunch with her, she could always rely on her to cheer her up. She laughed at the description of her friend Jeremy, and their strange association, while recognising the sadness that lay behind the joking reference to her love life. It was pretty clear to Naomi that the woman sitting across the table from her would like nothing better than to have a family and kids. Then came one of those guilty thought surges, when she realised that despite the perceived problems, she had a stable family which she should be thankful for.

Chapter 9.

Peter arrived at Simone's flat, almost panting with frustrated lust, after the previous Wednesday's debacle. As she let him in it was obvious something was wrong. She didn't fling herself into his arms, which was the usual way she greeted her lover. As she stood back to let him through the door, he could see she had been crying. His initial disappointment was quickly pushed to one side by genuine concern. If Simone was upset, then there must be something to be upset about. She was usually so upbeat about everything. "What on earth is the matter darling?"

She didn't immediately reply, but as the tears came again, she threw her arms round him and nestled her head into his chest. Naturally he held her tight, waiting patiently for an explanation, all thoughts of a prurient nature shelved in the face of this emotion. After a while Simone raised her head to plant a weak kiss to Peter's lips. "I'm sorry honey, but it's Phillip, he's ill in hospital."

Peter, in the short time he had known Simone, had never discovered why it was that her ex-husband had got custody of their two boys, but now he remembered that Phillip was the name of one of her sons. "That's your boy isn't it, love, what's the problem, why aren't you with him if he's in hospital?"

She broke away from his embrace, slumping down in an armchair. "Make us a cup of tea would you sweetie, and I'll explain."

He went into the kitchen, happy to do what he could. Then, when he returned with two mugs of tea, Simone told him that her son had developed severe stomach pains while at school. His teachers had been worried enough to call for an ambulance, which was just as well, because apparently shortly after arrival at hospital they diagnosed appendicitis; then the appendix had burst entailing an emergency operation.

"That was three days ago, he's alright now, but Roger didn't let me know until after the operation, and even then he was his usual awkward fucking self, telling me as little as possible. I went in to the hospital straight away, of course, but each time I came back to this bloody flat, I worried there might be complications; there was no one here to talk to."

Peter left the mugs of tea on the table to offer comfort to a very upset woman, who was now sobbing loudly. Along with his sympathy there was an element of surprise in his reaction. He had only known Simone as an ardent lover, and this upset mother was a side of her he hadn't seen. She had mentioned her children, of course, but only in passing. Now here she was crying her eyes out because one of them had had a routine operation. "But he's alright now, you say."

"Yes he's fine, his father is picking him up tomorrow. What gets up my nose is that during the whole episode that bastard ex-husband of mine tried to exclude me. Now he says that Phillip won't be well enough to come over this weekend. I'm sorry love, but I needed a shoulder to cry on, you're the rather delayed shoulder, I'm afraid."

Peter looked at the drawn, tear-stained face, that was appealing to him for understanding, wondering where that vibrantly sexy woman, who had captured his libido, had gone. He was surprised that he could hold her in his arms without the urge to ravish her there and then. His selfish side was telling him about another lost Wednesday, although his sympathy was real enough, ready for the sacrifice.

He was very surprised when, given what had gone before, Simone still clinging tightly to him said quietly. "Fuck the tea Peter, take me to bed."

"For Christ's sake, Simone, you're obviously very upset. How on earth can you talk of going to bed in the state you're in."

"I want you to comfort me, you great fool. I'm not asking for anything sexual, I want you to hold me in bed, sooth the pain away. Can you do that?" She seemed to be angry with him, for some reason, he failed to fathom..

Peter led her by the hand into the bedroom and, under instruction, helped her to undress. When she was curled up under the duvet, he joined her. There they lay, two naked bodies entwined without movement, appreciating the mutual warmth and stillness between them. Simone lay so still against his side, that he thought she must have fallen asleep.

As he pondered the new side of this usually sexy woman, demonstrated so graphically today, it came to him, with something of a jolt, that human relationships can very seldom be confined to one conveniently specific sphere of feeling. To put it crudely there was more to an association between a man and a woman than a good fuck, even if that's how it started out. They had hardly ever done anything other than spend time in bed together since he met Simone, yet now he would have been lying if he failed to recognise feeling a degree of affection for her, that was more than straightforward sympathy. Why wasn't anything in life ever simple?

The body beside him stirred, a face appeared above the duvet, fingers touched his lips. "I'm sorry sweetie, you didn't come round to hear my troubles did you?" She leant over him to kiss him tenderly on the lips. "You can make love to me now Peter, but take it easy, treat me gently."

Her smile made even her washed out face look beautiful, yet Peter was uncomfortable; the wild lust he had felt earlier had dissipated, he wanted to talk rather than make love.

"That's okay lover, we don't have to indulge today, why don't we just talk. You've never really told me about your kids, why it is that your ex has got custody." He brushed the hair back from her damp brow, returning the kiss, but prepared to leave it there, until her hand persuaded him otherwise.

After their quiet sex, they stayed closely entwined for some time before Simone, with an intake of breath and a stretch of her arms, sat up in bed, her smile stronger now with something of its usual element of mockery restored. "How about making me that cup of tea you we were going to have earlier, now you've had you wicked way with me."

Peter, astonished at Simone's change of mood, nevertheless went off to do her bidding anyway. When he came back, she smiled at his nakedness, touched his body before accepting the mug of tea proffered.

"Well, yes, I suppose I should tell you about the boys. You see I was having an affair at the time, so our breakup was really my fault, then there was my career, which was going well. Roger was left a lot of money by his father. He told the judge he was prepared to be a house-husband, not work, while they were young. So that was that: me a brazen hussy, not prepared to give up her job for the sake of her children, he the doting father betrayed, yet prepared to give up everything for his kids."

She laughed without much humour, there was a sigh to follow. "The old boy did say, he would review the situation when the boys got older, and could express their own sensible preferences but, by then, Roger will have thoroughly brain washed them, so I don't hold out much hope. Although," she paused, " I do love them very much, and I think at this stage, even though they're boys, they still need their mum."

Again the thought came into Peter's mind that this gorgeous woman was not quite the person he had assumed she was; for some reason that thought gave him pleasure. Nevertheless what he saw as this change of circumstances, left him feeling uneasy and, despite the protests from Simone, he made some feeble excuse for leaving the flat sooner than he might otherwise have done.

So with renewed guilt gnawing at his conscience, he was far from pleased when he reached the spot down the road where he had parked the car to find Mrs Benson sitting on a garden wall right alongside it. Dressed in her normal drab black, her face set in a grim scowl, she was not a sight to please his eye.

Peter decided to take the initiative; something had to be done about this damn woman. "Mrs Benson, please tell me what you hope to gain from following me about. I've said many times that I'm very sorry indeed about your little girl, but there is absolutely nothing more I can tell you about her." He spread his hands out in a supplication for understanding.

"I want to know what happened to Sharon. Who would want to kill a harmless little girl?" She got off the wall, moving towards him.

The injustice of this horrible woman's pestering, and the onset of possible physical contact caused him to flip. "For Christ's sake woman, I don't bloody know do I. The child was dead when I found her. I'm sorry, but if you don't leave me alone, I will go to the police, do you understand what I'm saying."

Most of these words were shouted over his shoulder, as he moved quickly to reach the sanctuary of his car. Once aboard, he hurriedly switched on the ignition, pulling violently away from the curb. He found he was shaking, whether from anger, or the fact that the woman made him extremely nervous, he wasn't sure which. As he calmed down, it occurred to him that Mrs Benson may well be in a position to make things awkward for him. She wasn't to know what went on inside Simone's flat of course, but mere mention of his visit would be difficult to explain if the woman happened to mention it to someone who knew him. Come to that how the hell did she know he was there, anyway?

When he arrived home, he half expected to see his black nemesis waiting on the opposite side of the road, spirited there on her broomstick. Of course there was no one around except the irascible Mrs Stackhorn, his next door neighbour, working in her front garden. His half-hearted wave of acknowledgement was ignored, as he might have expected.

She claimed to like dogs yet, ever since George had squirmed his way through the hedge between the gardens once or twice and, according to the lady, damaged her flower beds, the relationship with her had been less than amicable. She had seemed to find something to complain about every week; if it wasn't George, it was the shadow from the apple trees or the fact that the flower beds near to the boundary between the houses had not been properly weeded. Seeds were blowing onto her immaculate pride and joy. Peter put it down to the fact that she was a widow, hadn't got anything other than her garden, and anything affecting it, to occupy her.

He was earlier than usual, so decided to try and add a few words to the novel that he was slowly, and cumbersomely, writing. It had started when he had signed up for the writer's club course, initially as a cover for his Wednesday afternoons, but then he had found, as he engaged in his mythical homework assignments, he had gradually developed a real interest. This novel was the biggest thing he had, as yet, tried.

His involvement though was very spasmodic. What with the lack of time he put in and the difficulty he had making his words come to life, the progress was slow, but he had, at least, completed the first three chapters. The writing sort of cemented his Wednesday alibi, although now the danger of Mrs Benson spilling the beans might render that an irrelevance.

His concentration was not very high. Soon he saved and exited, intending to go into the kitchen to make himself a cup of tea. On the way he diverted to the sitting room, pouring himself an ample glass of whisky instead. It was too early in the evening to start drinking, but this evening his nerves were frazzled, the alcohol was necessary to calm him down. As he poured out a substantial measure it occurred to him, not for the first time, that he was drinking far too much, these days.

By the time the slamming of the front door, followed by a tramping on the stairs, indicated that James had returned, he was well into his second drink, already feeling sleepy. The boy was due to start at sixth form college in a week's time. Peter believed that would provide him with a sense of direction he seemed to lack at present. He only hoped that he and the teachers, had been right in suggesting James should go for Maths, Chemistry and Physics. The boy was as good at those subjects as any of the others, not really shining at any, but competent at them all, that was his James.

Peter had tried to interest the boy in sport, even taken him along to the squash club a few times, but his total lack of enthusiasm with anything other than that damn games console, made it such hard work that he had rather given up on him, as far as sport was concerned anyway. So different from his sister, who lived life at a gallop, appearing to cope with her school work with consummate ease. Such musings were put to flight by the sound of footsteps coming down the stairs and the entry of his sister in law. "Drink Rebecca?" he offered.

She smiled that toothy smile of hers, touched one of her breasts. "Can't can I, Peter, don't want the little chap to grow up an alcoholic do I?"

George was the next visitor. He laid his head on Peter's knee, gazing up into his eyes with soulful pleading. Peter sighed; still it would give him chance to ring Simone on his mobile, find out if she was alright, perhaps even ask her to look out for a woman in black, hanging about in the road outside the flat. "Come on then you bloody nuisance." When he heaved himself out of the chair, where he would have liked to remain, the dog frolicked about in anticipation.

"Peter, would you mind very much if I came with you, get a bit of fresh air?"

"Yes of course, but what about the baby?"

"That's okay. I'll get Charlie to keep an eye, or at least an ear out. He's only just been fed so he should be fine for hours anyway." She glanced down at the area of her bosom as though to confirm the point.

The sun was still shining when they reached the road outside. There was a soft warm breeze, making it very pleasant. Back to an empty house, he had thought, bit of quiet reflection, but all the time there had been people in their dens upstairs, and that was even before James clumped in that direction. The dog pulled eagerly at his lead, full of his usual impatience to reach the field. Quite why they had decided to buy such an energetic breed of dog like a Springer spaniel, Peter couldn't remember. Despite its exuberant nature he loved the beast. Rebecca laughed at the dog's antics, slipped her arm through his, presenting him with another of her easy smiles.

"You don't mind do you Peter?"

He cleared his throat. "No, of course not." But all that, for some reason, he felt uneasy.

"I really do hope that Willy and I aren't being too much of a nuisance. I think that Naomi would like to see the back of us, if the truth be known." She gripped his arm a little tighter.

"I'm sure Naomi wants you to stay as long as you like, you and the baby."

"I'm not sure you really know my sister like I do, but it was you I was asking anyway. How do you feel about having another female about the place, and a bawling infant?"

Peter had the idea she wanted him to say something flattering about her, part of some ill-defined and vague attempt at flirting. He was immediately serious. "You're welcome to stay as long as you need to, Rebecca. However, to be realistic about the situation, you will have to make long-term decisions, sooner or later, won't you?"

She stopped walking, the smile retreated, a tear hovered in the corner of her eye. "You're right of course, dear Peter, but that's easier said than done in my circumstances." She sighed, moving forward again, pulling her body closer to his. "I was hoping you could advise me. I trust you more than anyone else I know."

Exasperation welled up in Peter, he felt like shaking the woman. They had just reached the stile which led over into the field. "Sit down for a moment, Rebecca, I'll give you my best shot, but I warn you, you might not like it."

At the back of his mind lingered again the thought that she was flirting with him. He pondered whether, if Simone had not been in the picture, he would have responded. After all she was a sexy woman. New mothers always seemed to him to have a special sexuality of their own, as if producing a baby was proof of their sexual prowess, as it were. That didn't say much for his own moral backbone did it? Anyway Simone was around, so he stuck to offering the advice she had asked for.

"It seems to me, and I know this is what Naomi thinks too, that one slap is not worth throwing a marriage away for, particularly now you have William to look after." Sound advice maybe, but not what Rebecca wanted to hear.

She frowned, looked disappointed, then quickly climbed over the stile, walked on without waiting for him. When he caught up with her there was yet another sigh. "You're right of course, but no one clobbers me and gets away scot free."

After a short distance, they turned back the way they had come. Whether it was contrived or not, he would never know, but climbing back over the style, Rebecca slipped, spraining her ankle. It was so painful that she insisted that Peter go home to fetch the car, while she stayed sitting on the bottom step of the stile, nursing her foot and pulling faces. During the short journey to collect his sister-in-law, it did cross his mind that the accident could just be an excuse for delaying decisions about her future, the garnering of sympathy perhaps, but then again, it could have been genuine. He could only imagine what Naomi was going to say when she discovered there was one more reason she might be stuck with Rebecca, and the baby for a while longer.

Chapter 10.

The first few days at sixth form college weren't too bad, a bit like school, but less of the constant presence of authority. Although James knew some of the guys from his old school, there were some new blokes there, as well. There was a deal of laughing and messing about, a sort of excitement at having moved on from one stage in their education to another, no longer school kids, they were students now. The lecturers appeared to understand that, largely leaving them to their own devices when they weren't actually trying to teach them. He felt less out of place at college, and actually began to make friends, to join in with the foolish mockery of everything and everyone that surrounded the young people. There were girls there as well, but they still scared the living daylights out of him. Whenever the group included female students he tended to go back into his shell. James was surprised, even rather flattered, when Greg first approached him to ask about some chemical formula on which they had been working, that morning.

It seemed natural that they should afterwards go on to have lunch together in the canteen. It soon transpired that Greg had made something of a mess of his studies. The powers that be had decided he should start again rather than moving on to the second year with his fellow students. He may not have been the most assiduous student ever, but he was very much at ease with the other guys The fact that he appeared to want to cultivate a friendship with James, was a pleasant surprise. Nevertheless, he took it at its face value, rather liked the idea of having a close mate, something that had not happened at school.

A couple of weeks after the start of term, it seemed natural enough when Greg invited him home so they could tackle their homework together. "Won't be anyone there," he explained. "There's only my dad, and he doesn't get back until late most evenings." James didn't like to ask where Greg's mother was this early in their friendship. "Come on James make yourself at home." He led the way into the kitchen, opened the fridge, tossed a can in James's direction. James looked at the label on the can, smiled hesitantly over at Greg.

"Well I don't really…….."

He was cut short by Greg's shout of laughter, "Don't drink beer, that what you're saying, young James? Christ, man, where have you been?" Not wanting to appear to be some sort of wimp, James laughed nervously. He wanted this friendship; if that meant drinking beer then so be it.

"Not much, Dad's bought me a few shandies and that, but anyway got to start sometime." He opened the can and took a substantial mouthful, which caused him to splutter over the kitchen floor. It wasn't all that bad, but even if it had been poison, he wouldn't have lost any more face by admitting it.

When they finally got down to work, James was able to restore some of his credibility by taking the lead with the homework. Academically it appeared that his new-found friend was not all that bright, which suited James, as in all respects of social worldliness, his new friend was way ahead, which sort of evened things out a bit.

Once they had ploughed through the set work, Greg offered him another beer. They sat in the kitchen drinking, telling each other something about their respective lives. When it came to the question of the female sex, James felt himself redden when he confessed to having no girlfriend, indeed having very little knowledge of the subject. Greg came over to where he was sitting at the kitchen table and draped a sympathetic arm over his shoulder. "Not to worry mate, plenty of time for sex, you're a nice looking chap, the girls will sort you out in no time."

The physical contact might have been expected to have made

James feel uncomfortable, but he didn't at once shrug away from the casual embrace, taking it as a sign of their growing friendship. Anyway he went home shortly after, but as he walked towards his house he felt more cheerful than he had for a long time, flattered by the attention, happy that he had found someone he really liked, who apparently liked him.

Peter was surprised to say the least, when his son, having arrived home, came into the kitchen, smiled and said, "Hello dad, where's mum, what's for dinner, I'm starving," before going to the fridge to root around for something to eat. His usual arrival home was heralded by a clumping noise on the stairs followed by a slamming of his bedroom door, so it wasn't surprising that Peter was taken aback, although the rather inane grin that spread across James's face was a bit alarming. He wasn't used to his son being sociable.

"You alright, James?"

" I feel great dad, just great."

Charlie had arrived, just in time to hear her father's question. She took one look at her brother, sniffed scornfully, poked him in the chest. "For God's sake dad, can't you see the kid's pissed. Thinks he's grown up all of a sudden now he's at that college." She went over to the fridge to pour herself a glass of milk.

The grin on James' face vanished, to be replaced by a scowl, the euphoria of a moment ago, shattered. "Fucking bitch, what the hell do you know about anything." He swung an arm in her direction, catching the glass, which fell to the floor spattering milk everywhere. Brother and sister grappled for a few seconds, before the arrival of Naomi, and the explosion of her anger, brought about a cessation of hostilities.

"Just what the hell is going on here. I want that bloody milk wiped up now." She dumped her shopping bag forcibly on the kitchen table, and sat down. "For Christ's sake Peter, what the hell is going on here"

Annoyed at the way blame appeared to be gravitating in his direction, Peter returned the glare and got up. "Nothing to worry about, storm in a teacup, that's all dear." The 'dear' was delivered with an accentuated note of sarcasm, not lost on Naomi.

"Nothing at all mum, just your little boy is pissed, that's all," she grinned teasingly at her already maddened brother, hoping for a reaction that would divert any attention away from her.

"Charlie can't you leave the boy alone. Get this mess cleaned up will you."

"No, I fucking won't. The brat deliberately knocked the glass out of my hand, let him do it."

"Alright, alright, let's calm down shall we. Charlie you provoked the argument, please do as your mother says." Peter's intervention was all about what he saw as fairness.

His daughter banged about with the mop, managing to give the floor some semblance of cleanliness before slamming it back in the cupboard, then storming out of the kitchen, shouting over her shoulder as she did. "I'll get the fucking train to Durham dad, no need for you to put yourself out."

By then, James had already disappeared up to his room. The two parents remained, exchanging looks, each exasperated with the other, until Peter, at risk of further attack, beat a retreat to the lounge. He stood at the French windows looking out at the garden watching the greenfinches squabbling round the bird feeder, seeing an analogy of sorts for his own argumentative children.

His reverie was interrupted by Rebecca limping into the room, bleary eyed and tousled, her usually long sleek hair, tangled and lack lustre. Her physical appearance, taken together with the old grey cardigan, and the faded print dress she was wearing, seemed to be saying that she was a distressed woman. Peter was learning. His thoughts might have agreed with Naomi's in-so-far as it all seemed to him rather like a part she was playing. "What on earth was all that shouting about Peter, woke me up, and the baby."

Peter's first reaction was to ask what on earth was she doing asleep at this time of day, an even more deeply hidden thought was, when would the damn woman go back to her own home, play the part of a normal wife. Of course he expressed none of this, instead explaining tersely that there had been an unimportant altercation between his beloved children. There wasn't time for much more, before Naomi's voice could be heard from the kitchen. "Don't mind about me, you two have a nice chat, while I get on with the dinner."

"Sorry, darling, be with you in a minute, just got to feed the baby." As she left the room she directed a last soulful look in Peter's direction. He turned his eyes away, stood a little longer staring out into the garden before making his way to the kitchen to receive his punishment, and be allotted his tasks for the evening.

"Peter I hope you're going to be a bit more use when we have this bloody party, if we have the party at all, that is." She did look tired. Peter felt genuinely guilty for not helping more around the old homestead. He made a half-hearted attempt at a hug, from which she shied away like a frightened filly, her body busy and tense, her face averted. "Look I'm shattered, go and find something in the freezer will you, have to make do with whatever's there." As he went through the door into the garage, where the freezer lived, she added, "and then, dear husband, you can go and pour me a fucking great gin and tonic. That bastard, Clarkson, is driving me right up the wall."

Naomi gulped at the drink Peter gave her, before sitting down on the chair with an audible bump. "You think we should still go ahead with this party thing, no one seems keen?" She felt, indeed looked unusually tired this evening. The thought of organising a party, even though it was supposed to be a sort of farewell do for Charlie leaving home, seemed an impossible mountain to climb.

"Well, I've already mentioned it to Robbie, and you said yourself that Sue and Murray Clark had accepted. Tell you what, we could invite Simon." He smiled at the thought, but then after reflection it didn't seem such a bad idea, that was before Naomi had her pennyworth, though.

"You can't be serious Peter. Can you just see my dear sister agreeing to that?"

"Don't tell her then. Make it a surprise. Never know, it might work, anything to have that dear little Willy doing his crying at home for a change." Naomi ran her fingers through her hair in a distracted way, pursed her lips.

"That would be a relief, I admit, but it's a hell of a risk, might backfire completely, ruin the party, even make sure they stay on here forever and a day."

One thing was certain, she could do with at least one of her worries out of the way, so she could concentrate on her battle with Bill Clarkson. She absolutely hated the way she was treated like some damn secretary, when it came to policy-making or decisions affecting the finances of the firm, yet when there was a difficult case, the man had no qualms at all about unloading it on her. She couldn't say it was sexism because she knew that other junior partners were treated that way too. Ivan Campion, for instance, had mentioned only yesterday, that he was thinking of getting out. In fact now his name came to mind, she remembered that she had invited him to this wretched party, which was one more reason for not cancelling.

"Alright, Peter, we'll go ahead, but I'm getting someone in to help with the catering, and the kids can get off their arses, lend a hand when it comes to passing round the drinks, and stuff." She knocked back the remnants of her drink, holding her glass out to Peter to be refilled.

When Peter told James about the party, that he would be expected to give a hand, he was amazed at his response. He appeared almost keen, only asking if he could bring along his friend Greg to help, to which his father readily agreed. Charlie was less enthusiastic, but when both her parents stressed that it was really her going away party, and with her knowing that this was the last family thing she would be involved in for some time, she accepted her fate quietly.

The party wasn't going to be a big affair, although Naomi had decided to invite Rosalind as well as Ivan and his wife Margaret. The biggest surprise was when she mentioned they were having a party to Mrs Stackhorn, their unfriendly neighbour, as a sort of apology before the event, and then thinking it only polite, sure of the negative response, she added that the lady would be very welcome if she wanted to join them, the old dragon accepted.

Murray and Sue were old friends. She had been at university, in Manchester, with Sue. They would give a nice normal balance to the evening. They might be needed when Robbie Barkworth arrived with that whirlwind earth-mother figure of a wife of his, spreading joy and advice to all around. She wasn't looking forward to seeing that pompous old ass Michael Jackson, who she had met before at company functions, but Peter thought it might serve his ambitions to invite him and his wife.

On the Saturday in question, James brought Greg along early. He seemed a nice enough boy, not raising any objections, when Naomi asked if he would mind not wearing his baseball cap which was emblazoned with the words 'no shit'. She even went along with the fact that they were both wearing destroyed looking jeans and tee shirts outside their trousers printed with the words 'this is a war zone'. It was par for the course with youngsters these days. She asked them to be polite, to lay off the booze, to which both nodded their heads vigorously. She was actually rather pleased to see her son apparently happy, enthusiastic about something, as opposed to his usual introverted self.

When the two boys came into the kitchen to get some brief instruction on how to serve the wine, Mrs Tate frowned at them, before turning her back to take two more trays of vol-au-vents out of the Aga. Charlie joined them. Looking only slightly less outrageous herself, she nevertheless, scoffed at the lads' gear. Naomi stepped in at once to say there would be no rows on this particular evening. No rows among the kids perhaps, but what was going to happen when Simon suddenly put in an appearance at the party?

Mrs Stackhorn arrived ridiculously early, asked for a dry sherry, which was about the only thing Peter didn't have in stock. After some negotiation she finally opted for a gin with a large proportion of bitter lemon, then took a stance by the French windows, frowning, looking out at the Shadbolts' less than immaculate garden, while Peter desperately tried to sustain a conversation about the only thing he knew she was interested in, which was gardening, all the while longing for the doorbell to ring so he could be released to welcome other guests, any other guests.

Finally it did. He bustled off only to find Charlie had beaten him to it. She had already opened the door to his boss and Marjorie, his lovely wife, as he always called her. Peter hadn't seen his daughter since she dressed, if you could call it that, for the evening. She too was wearing frazzled jeans, the expected tee shirt with some outrageous slogan. He felt slightly uneasy though, at the way she had squeezed herself so tightly into this evening's top, that her breasts appeared to be unusually prominent, probably no bra. Peter eventually succeeded in dragging Michael Jackson's eyes away from his daughter's bosom. Once he and Marjorie were supplied with glasses of wine, he took them off to meet Mrs Stackhorn, who had remained at her critical vantage point by the French windows.

Doorbell again: there on the doorstep were three people he didn't know, who he assumed Naomi had invited. His wife came downstairs opportunely at that moment, to introduce him to her friend Rosalind, who had arrived with Ivan Campion, a solicitor from work and his wife, Rosemary. Before Peter could close the door again, he was relieved to see Robbie and Wendy, although surprised to see they had brought Justin with them. He had thought it was all over between the two youngsters, but you could never tell these days. His earlier conclusion was born out when a few minutes later Charlie hissed in his ear. "What the fuck's he doing here dad?"

Naomi liked to organise. This evening would be no exception. When she was sure everyone had had arrived, all except Simon that was, she rang a little bell. When the guests stopped talking to see why, she explained that each time she rang the bell they should move on and talk to a different group of people. She wanted them all to mix, not stay talking to the same people all evening. Peter made a face at Robbie. In truth he was pleased that his wife had taken over control. When the bell rang next time he obediently moved on to talk to his boss, and the excited Marjorie, who kept saying how wonderful it was that he should have such a capable wife.

The two lads were perfect waiters, quiet and polite, constantly offering food and wine to the assembled guests, although without anyone noticing they were helping themselves to the odd glass of wine, when they retired to the kitchen to replenish supplies. Mrs Tate saw what was going on, but her work was finished now; it was none of her damn business anyway, so she quietly slipped away, leaving them to it.

They weren't the only ones who were making the most of opportunity. Mrs Stackhorn had accepted the offer of a top up from Charlie, who rather switched the proportions between the gin and the bitter lemon her father had poured earlier, with the result that the old dear not only talked with great enthusiasm about the iniquities of the town council, but ended up with a bout of the hiccups, which in turn had her giggling almost to the point of hysteria.

When the bell rang again, and it was Peter's turn to chat to his neighbour, the old dragon, instead of complaining about the dog or the state of the garden, had become maudlin, maybe the gin getting to her. "I envy you your family, Mr Shadbolt. I would have liked children, you know, but somehow we never got round to it, and then Henry died quite young, so I don't have much in the way of family myself. Do you mind if I sit down for a moment." She almost fell into the nearby armchair.

Peter, relieved from having to listen, looked round at the noisy hubbub surrounding him wondering what life was all about. Him and Naomi, rebellious kids, the sad Mrs Benson, and her lost child, ambition in the work place, his lust for Simone; where would it all end, was any of it worth it. Just what was it all about, a depressing sense of futility swept through his mind..

The figure in the chair at his side grunted, or that's what it sounded like and, when he looked down, Mrs Stackhorn was fast asleep, her great face slack, mouth slightly open, and a faint rattle in her throat every few seconds.

He was about to move on to another group, without waiting for Naomi's signal, when he heard a shout from the next room. It quickly became clear that Simon had arrived, that Naomi's hopes that, given the circumstances of the party, the two of them might just pretend to be civilised, had come to nothing. When he reached the scene, Rebecca was in tears. She was shouting something about betrayal, at her sister. Simon hovered, his hands raised in exasperated surrender, while Naomi, her party in danger of ruin, attempted to put her arms round the distraught young woman to calm her down, without much success. Rebecca angrily shrugged her off, and with a last venomous outburst of, "You fucking rotten bastard," she crashed out of the room, apparently in no way impeded by her injured ankle.

Peter admired his wife's aplomb as she reinstated her smile, raised her shoulders in a dismissive gesture, implying, through sheer force of personality, that everyone should get on with the job of enjoying themselves, ignore minor domestic upsets, which weren't anything to do with them anyway. In no time at all, she was again deep in discussion with her legal clique. Peter was about to return to the other room when Charlie came up to him, grinning broadly. "Someone at the door to see you Dad."

There she was, she hadn't changed since the first time he had clapped eyes on her, even looked like the same black dress. "Mrs Benson this really…"

"Having a party are we Mr Shadbolt? I'm pleased for you, glad you can put your guilt behind you so easily. you bastard," she added, as an afterthought.

Peter noticed one or two of the guests glancing through the open doors to get a glimpse of what new bit of excitement was emerging. "Mrs Benson we've been through all this. You have my utmost sympathy, but I can tell you no more, now I must ask you to go. The last thing I want is to involve the police but if you insist on stalking me you leave me with no alternative."

To his amazement the woman stepped through the door. Before he could bar her passage, she had brushed past him into one of the rooms where the guests had just settled down again to talk and drink. In a strident voice, which immediately had everyone's attention, she started to address them. "This man, your charming host, says he found my daughter dead, just found her like that, in the woods, can you believe it, then wouldn't talk to me, her mother, wouldn't tell me what happened."

Wendy Barkworth was the first person to move. She quickly put her arms round the agitated woman, pulled her into her chest, patting her gently on the back as she did so. "Look dear, no one's going to go to the police, but you must understand that Peter here, had nothing to do with the death of your little girl, other than find her. Alright he should have talked to you, but that doesn't mean he harmed her. Come with me sweetie, let's go and get a cup of tea shall we?" Naomi came forward to help, but Wendy waved her away as she guided the now crumpled figure, out of the door towards the sanctuary of the kitchen.

James wasn't feeling too hot. He and Greg had retired to his room with a half-full bottle of red wine, and had taken turns swigging it out of the bottle. Now James was feeling rather sick, mainly because the room wouldn't keep still. Earlier they had both drunk a good number of half glasses during their waiter duties, so it wasn't surprising that he felt that way. Greg came over and sat on the bed next to him, put his arm round his shoulder and pulled him close enough to him so their cheeks met. Something told James that this wasn't right. He tried to pull away, yet part of him rather enjoyed the intimacy.

"Take it easy old son, we're mates aren't we, no harm in a manly hug now and then." James felt silly at his overreaction.

"Sorry, course not, feeling a bit queasy, that's all, sorry Greg." The last thing the boy wanted, was to lose this newly-found friendship. He needed to be best mates, and Greg was his best mate. When Greg replaced his arm, James went along with it. Even when he kissed his cheek he made no move to resist. In fact he felt rather excited by the intimacy that was developing. However when he realised that he had a full erection, he turned bright red, trying to cover it up with his arms.

"Feeling a bit frisky are we old son?" Greg gently took away the protective arms and placed his hand on James's thigh near to his crotch. James knew he should punch the guy in the nose, fucking queer, but he seemed to unable to move away. Then, when Greg reached inside his open fly, he was overcome by an overwhelming desire for sexual contact.

It was dark when James woke up. At first he couldn't understand why he felt so uncomfortable in his bed. Then with a start his hand encountered naked flesh, not his own. His mind reeled with shock as he remembered something of what had happened earlier that night. A deep sense of shame engulfed him, his head ached, he felt sick. Then, practicality taking over, he wondered how he was going to smuggle Greg out of the house, past his parents, and more importantly, past Charlie.

As he lay there quietly panicking, his breath ragged with nerves, he was alarmed to find himself in a state of rigid tumescence. He started to ease himself out from under the duvet, thinking to distance himself from his shame, but as he sat on the side of the bed, wondering what to do, how to act, he became aware that his bed fellow was stirring. At once he got to his feet fearing some sort of physical approach. The bedside light came on, and through bleary eyes he saw Greg actually smiling at him. He pulled the duvet back over himself to cover his embarrassing erection, but not before Greg had seen the state he was in.

His friend grinned widely at his confusion. "Always a bit of a shock the first time."

"It was a mistake, I was drunk, fucking hell how are we going to get you out of the house."

"Calm down Jimmy, these things happen, no harm done, and don't tell me you weren't up for it last night, like a fucking animal you were I'm telling you, like a wild fucking animal." He was lying there calmly, his hands cupped behind his head, almost laughing out loud at James's confusion.

"Don't be disgusting. I didn't know what I was doing. I'm not a fucking queer, you bastard." He wanted to blame someone for his sense of shame, to lash out at the grinning boy in his bed.

"The term is gay, old boy, and whether you admit it now, or sometime in the future, you are most definitely gay. Why don't you come back to bed, and we'll have a little chat about it."

Long before James was getting into a tizzy about his sexual orientation, the party downstairs had petered out. Even though the gate-crasher was no longer on the scene, and despite Naomi's strength of personality, the party was over. Mrs Stackhorn slept on, but most of the others offered thanks before making subdued departures. Wendy was still in the kitchen with Mrs Benson, Robbie accepted the glass of whisky Peter thrust in his direction, Justin had gone too, Charlie was drinking a glass of wine and looking amused.

"Sad I know, but that woman's stalking you Peter, can ruin your life if you're not careful, go to the police."

"Well that went well." Naomi did not look pleased. "I'll have one of those, Peter, if it's not too much trouble that is." She couldn't really give a damn about the party as such, but did resent the fact that her conversation with Ivan Campion had been cut short. He was just as fed up as she was with the cramped nature of Bradford, Lang and Oldfield, and what, they both regarded, as the patronising attitude of Bill Clarkson. They had been tossing the idea around that they might just break away, perhaps start something themselves. Rosalind had been eager to go with them but there was much to consider. Naomi would have like to explore the ramifications further, while Ivan's enthusiasm was bubbling. Her own fault of course inviting Simon, but then the Benson woman would have put the damper on things anyway.

A snort from deep in the armchair. "My God where's everyone gone, don't tell me I dropped off, how terribly embarrassing, do forgive me, Mrs Shadbolt." She struggled to her feet, waving away Robbie's efforts to help her. "Thank you so much, and once again please accept my apologies for my deplorable manners." As Naomi saw the old woman to the door, Peter couldn't help musing that his neighbour's embarrassment might prove useful in the future when she thought about complaining over boundary issues.

As Naomi left the room, Wendy came in with Mrs Benson holding her by the hand. What a contrast, Wendy, large and expansive, untidy and warm. Mrs Benson black and grim, her face set like a mask, although she appeared calm now despite the frown.

"Look Peter this lady knows you had nothing to do with her daughter's death, but she wants to talk to you about it. Apparently you gave her the brush off the other day. She says she saw you in Norfolk Street and that you threatened her with the police." Wendy offered a look that half-expressed sympathy, while at the same time implying that he should have been more considerate towards this unhappy woman. "So what about it Peter, can you help her?" She led Mrs Benson to the sofa. The two of them sat down, two sets of eyes turning to him expectantly.

His heart felt again a small lurch of regret, of pity, whatever it was, when he thought about that little girl lying there so silently in the woods. Now when it came to the black widow, her mother, all his sympathy had been used up.

If the truth were known, Peter's main worry at that moment was that someone might ask what on earth he was doing in Norfolk Street. Luckily Naomi hadn't come back from seeing Mrs Stackhorn out, nevertheless he didn't want the location to be raised again, so his cooperation with any questions that might be asked was eagerly offered. He didn't even bother going over what he had said so often before, that there was nothing he could tell the woman, but instead left it to her to ask away.

When it came to it, given absolute freedom to ask her questions, Mrs Benson covered her face with her hands, and started sobbing, a harsh sound that was heart rending, although, Peter thought impatiently, hardly going to get them any further forward. Wendy put her arm round the distraught woman, tried to encourage her to explain what she wanted to know. Naomi came back and raised her eyebrows at Robbie, who gave a little shrug in reply.

Eventually the questions came, stuttered and emotional, but covering the ground Peter had been over on previous occasions. Finally Wendy gently led her away and to the front door. She refused a lift home with her and Robbie, before slowly making her way down the drive, and into the road. Peter was relieved that no further mention had been made of Norfolk Street, relieved that he had seen, what he hoped, was the last of the woman in black.

"You hungry? What happened to James and his friend Greg?" Naomi wore a frown, as she often seemed to do these days.

Peter had picked up the Times, attempting to take in the details on the front page, but his mind was wandering elsewhere.

He had come to the conclusion that he no longer loved Naomi, yet in a direct contradiction of that feeling, he badly wanted to have back the woman with whom he had shared most of his early life.

Unfortunately, perhaps for both of them, that wasn't the woman frowning across the room at him.

On the other hand this thing with Simone wasn't any sort of replacement love; it was unadulterated lust: great in its own way but not what, in his heart of hearts, he wanted. God, he was a mess, didn't know what he did want, that was the trouble.

"No, I don't know." Thinking that sounded unnecessarily rude, he adopted a milder tone. "Sorry about the interruptions to your party, but I think your guests rather enjoyed the excitement, don't you?"

"I thought it was our party. The Simon bit was my fault anyway. At least, maybe now you've finally seen off your stalker. I'll have a glass of wine please."

Chapter 11.

Charlie was off on her big adventure. She just couldn't wait to get away to university. "Dad you really don't have to bother taking me all that way, I can just as easily catch the train." Peter, though, had other reasons for offering to take Charlie up to Durham. One, straightforward enough, was that it was about time he visited his mother, bit of a detour, but also in a northerly direction, the other was that being away for a couple of days would enable him to fit in an off-schedule, call on Simone, see how her boy was, see how she was.

"But I would like to see you settled. Anyway I want to call in and see your grandmother either on the way up or on the way back. You've got a mass of stuff to shift, be a bit difficult carting all that on the train." His smile met Charlie's post-shrug smile. He realised for the umpteenth time how attractive she was, and how proud he was to have a daughter that looked like she did.

"Fine, Dad, but give me a break, go and see grandma on the way back. I love the old thing, but my mood right now is not geared to family reminiscences." As soon as she said it, she knew how heartless it sounded, but she so wanted to get on with this university thing, to meet new people, to escape from families for a few months. Of course she loved them, even that little shit James, but Christ did she need a rest from this suburban claustrophobia.

Peter shook his head, tut-tutted, yet he could understand something of her impatience to spread her wings, to move on to the next stage in her life. She went upstairs, he sighed, slumped down in the chair with yet another glass of wine, his head already fuzzy from the intake of alcohol. What the hell was going to happen with him and Naomi? They didn't appear to have much mutual affection these days; should they be thinking of splitting, The kids were growing up, James at college, Charlie may be gone from the nest for ever, as a permanent base anyway. It was a big step, lots of practical things to consider, but they both had well-paid jobs, so the problems were not insurmountable. Should he raise the possibility, or let matters drift for the time being?

"You hungry? What happened to James and his friend Greg?" Naomi wore a frown, as she often seemed to do these days. Peter had picked up the Times, attempting to take in the details on the front page, but his mind was wandering elsewhere. He had come to the conclusion that he no longer loved Naomi, yet in a direct contradiction of that feeling, he badly wanted to have back the woman with whom he had shared most of his early life.

Unfortunately, perhaps for both of them, that wasn't the woman frowning across the room at him. On the other hand this thing with Simone wasn't any sort of replacement love; it was unadulterated lust: great in its own way but not what, in his heart of hearts, he wanted. God, he was a mess, didn't know what he did want, that was the trouble.

"No, I don't know." Thinking that sounded unnecessarily rude, he adopted a milder tone. "Sorry about the interruptions to your party, but I think your guests rather enjoyed the excitement, don't you?"

"I thought it was our party. The Simon bit was my fault anyway. At least, maybe now you've finally seen off your stalker. I'll have a glass of wine please."

"God you've got some junk here Charlie, and you thought you could travel up by train. You'd have needed the bloody train all to yourself." Pretending to be annoyed with one's offspring was a father's prerogative. Actually Peter was looking forward to the long trip up to Durham in the company of his ebullient daughter. She had made it abundantly clear that she couldn't wait to get away from her family, but that in no way prevented his feelings for his pretty daughter, welling up inside him in a rather disturbing way.

"You wanted this, Dad, so stop moaning about it." She grinned, leant across to kiss his cheek. "Wagons away, we've got a long way to go." She snuggled, cat like, down into the passenger seat, as Peter drove out of the driveway.

Charlie was excited, eager to resume her acquaintance with the glories of Durham University. Michaelmas Term didn't actually start until the 4th.October, but she wanted to get there a couple of days early to get her bearings, perhaps meet a few of the guys.

She had loved Josephine Butler college, when she had travelled up to look the place over, had been impressed by the pristine looking accommodation with its en-suite bathrooms, the easy atmosphere that pervaded the place; eat what you like and when you like. This was what she wanted, independence and freedom from family constraints.

Judging from her mother's rather matter of fact goodbye, before she rushed off to see yet another important client, that might be what she wanted as well. Work, yes, she might work, but that would come after she had settled in to appreciate glorious independence, fresh ambience. She was down to study for a BA (Hon) in Sociology, yet she was far from sure why she had chosen that subject. Already she was having thoughts about possibly changing courses once she had talked to a few people. For the moment work was secondary to freedom.

It was an early start; over three hundred miles in a day. Charlie had made it clear there would be no visiting granny on the way, no breaking the journey with an overnight stop. As he drove, Peter couldn't help glancing across at his daughter every so often, appreciating the image she presented. Jeans today, as usual, but with a less provocative sweater in terms of design, although tight enough to attract any red blooded male, and that included her father. Fatherly affection, yes, but there was, it had to be admitted, a sexual element in his feelings for his daughter, which she appeared to reciprocate at the permitted level. Several of his glances were caught by her teasing, understanding smile, which seemed to Peter confirmation of his speculations. An exchange of messages which could never be specifically acknowledged.

"Wouldn't be surprised if James was off next, wanting his own place, seems to get on well with that new mate of his, Greg, or whatever his name is. Then you and mum will only have Rebecca and Willy for company. When she eventually goes home to Simon there'll be just the two of you. Chance for a new start, second honeymoon, that sort of thing." She opened the window half way, enjoying the flow of air through her long blond hair.

Peter ignored the suggestion that he and Naomi needed time to themselves, not a subject he wanted to discuss with anyone right now. He did wonder what Charlie would think, if she knew about his thing with Simone; probably find it amusing, if he were to hazard a guess. "I'm just glad he's found a friend. He's certainly a lot brighter since he started at college. Can't see him setting up on his own though, even with a couple of mates. Can you just imagine him, cooking and doing the washing up; I don't think so." That's what Peter said, yet the idea of his son living elsewhere was not an unattractive one. He was fed up of the boy's rudeness and total lack of communication. He might just appreciate him more if he saw less of him, at least until he had honed up on his social skills in the company of other people.

Charlie's response was to give a little snort of derision. "It wouldn't be a problem Dad. He could bring his laundry home for Mum to do, eat takeaways and easy stuff like that. What does it matter of they only wash up once a week. Boys of his age don't seem to notice dirt until it starts moving."

Of course she loved her younger brother, but he was one more aspect of family life she would rather appreciate from a distance, at least for the foreseeable future. Putting James out of mind, she turned suddenly serious. "What about you and mum Dad? As far as I can see you don't show much affection for each other, these days. We used to have some fun as a family yet lately, I never see you and her having a laugh like you used to. What's up between the two of you? Not having a bit on the side are you Dad?"

Peter hadn't been paying much notice to what Charlie had been saying over the last few miles, just enjoying the cheerfulness of her company, but he heard the last bit alright. An involuntary start, a momentary look of horror, that flashed across his face, were obvious indicators that his daughter's unintended thrust had struck home. He hoped she hadn't being paying enough attention to notice. "Of course not, don't be ridiculous, Charlie. There's nothing wrong between your mum and me, that a bit of peace and quiet, won't cure."

He gripped the steering wheel, staring at the road ahead, while his daughter, having understood the situation with easy feminine nous, retreated into her own thoughts, saying absolutely nothing. In fact neither of them did for several miles. They were both relieved when Charlie switched on the radio, tuning in to some classical music.

They stopped for something to eat in Alfreton, before joining the A1, preferring the old world hostelry to the alternative motorway eating facilities, that would be available later on. When their conversation had restarted both father and daughter were careful to stick to neutral topics, rather obviously avoiding any reference to family matters In the interval both of them had had plenty of time to think. Peter wondering if his reaction to Charlie's comment about a bit on the side, had been a dead giveaway, Charlie vaguely excited by the thought that her dad might be having it off with another woman, excited and, she would have had to admit, if she was being honest, amused at the thought. She should have been feeling sorry for her mother, if what she suspected was true, but for some reason she wasn't. Anyway, she may be barking up the completely wrong tree.

Charlie suspected that this was the last time for a while she was going to be spoilt when it came to eating out. She determined to make the most of it. Garlic mushrooms, a steak, that even Peter would have had difficulty getting through, strawberries and ice cream, together with half a bottle of Hock, would keep her going for the rest of the journey, and well into the evening.

"You won't be eating like that for a while young lady, " Peter smiled across at Charlie, when she sat back with a sigh of contentment.

"That was great Dad, set me up for week. Reckon I'll have to get used to baked beans on toast from now on," she laughed, "Couple of days, then it's me, nose to the grindstone, no time for fancy food."

"Glad to hear it, not that I believe a word. To be serious though Charlie, I hope you'll make the most of your time at uni, not go too far off the straight and narrow."

Charlie's brow furrowed. "Don't be so fucking pompous Dad, you sound like some Victorian father giving advice to his stay-at-home daughter. I take it you mean the dreaded trio, sex, drugs and alcohol. Well for your information, I know how to take my booze, I only smoke a bit of pot now and then, and I'm certainly no innocent virgin, so that takes care of all those doesn't it?" Before he could react to her straight talking, she got up from the table to pay a visit to the cloakroom, flinging a grin over her shoulder as she went. "Better have a pee before we depart, don't want to hold you up later on."

Peter waited in the Wheatsheaf car park, enjoying the bright sunshine that had now replaced the earlier overcast skies, his spirit elated by the sheer vitality of this precocious daughter of his, over whom he had no control, but in whom, for some reason he had absolute trust. She had an integrity personal to her alone, but very strong, and he admired that. Thinking back to what she had said a few minutes ago he realised that, if asked to voice an opinion, he would have guessed that his daughter was no longer a virgin, indeed Naomi had supported that probability, but to hear Charlie affirming it so openly, without embarrassment, had taken him aback slightly. Now reflecting on her words, it seemed all part of that integrity, and indeed of the world .today.

For no particular reason he walked to the car park entrance, glancing casually up and down the road that ran past the hotel. Not many people about, but one couple caught his eye; a little old man walking his little old dog, some kind of wire-haired terrier, stiff legged, white muzzled but still moving with jerky energy, eager for his exercise. His master was dressed for the rain, despite the pleasant sunshine. Peter couldn't help but notice the contrast between his tatty trousers, and the pair of brand new trainers, he wore on his feet. It amused him to speculate that the pair appeared to illustrate the opposite end of the life spectrum from that of his nubile daughter, so bursting with life and potential.

"Come on dad, let's be on our way, never mind the day dreaming."

Durham was great, the university campus was great, taking Peter back to his own college days, and the easy camaraderie that prevailed then. Charlie booked in before locating her room in Josephine Butler college. Peter helped her unload the numerous boxes and bags that would enable her to turn her smart looking room into a junk shop. She sat down on her bed, bouncing up and down, grinning at her father, pleased to have arrived, eager to go and explore.

"Well Charlie that's you for a few months, do you fancy a drink before I go and find somewhere to sleep tonight?"

Charlie had been told by someone in the admin office that accommodation was available on campus for parents at this time of year. Feeling very guilty, she didn't pass that information on to her father. "Look, Dad, it was great, you driving me up and all that, but I would like to settle in, if you don't mind, look around, meet some of the guys, perhaps." She knew her dad would be hurt, but hell, this was the start of a new life, and if there had to be a few casualties so be it. She loved the man, but he had to be put back in the family niche, for the time being, while she investigated a whole new world.

Peter pretended he didn't mind being sent on his way. When they hugged, he felt love, disappointment and loss, while putting a brave face on it. Charlie, for her part, felt affection and impatience. After leaving his darling daughter to get settled in, Peter quickly found a Holiday Inn, booked himself in, used room service to order a sandwich, made use of the mini bar in his room, felt unreasonably depressed.

Kids grew up, kids left home, kids had their own lives to lead. They would continue to move away from their parents, if not for the rest of their lives, at least for some years to come. There was no reason to feel depressed about the natural way of things, but he did. He wished Simone was here to relieve his loneliness or even Naomi which he hastily realised was an unworthy way of thinking about his wife, as some kind of secondary resort for support.

He watched some crummy police drama on the box, drank more whisky and went to bed early, still with the burden of depression weighing him down. Tomorrow he would visit his mother to spend some awkward time with her, which rather bore out his earlier thoughts about children moving away from their parents.

Chapter 12.

In the morning he felt better, indulged himself with a full English breakfast, then made an early start towards Cheshire, and his Mum. In the brightness of the day, his pangs over Charlie leaving home for the first time, his shadowy guilt about cheating on Naomi, seemed less pronounced, something he was able to deal with.

Driving comfortably along, it came into his mind that the old favourite about weather and mood was undoubtedly true; it did have a very real effect on a person's feelings and emotions. That morning it was nippy, but bright enough to sustain his improved mood. He enjoyed driving at a moderate speed, not over-eager to arrive too early, perhaps catch his mother before she had made ready to receive him. She didn't like surprises, liked to be in control, to have everything in its place, everybody dancing to her tune.

He had promised to stop the night, take her out for a meal in the evening, which promise would involve her in day long preparations. The sort of process that had made his father so mad when he was alive, but which Peter accepted was part of the woman she was then, and still was today.

Mrs Shadbolt, from what Peter could see, was very happy being a widow, not seeming to miss her husband to any great degree, enjoying her circle of friends, her coffee mornings, her Saga holidays, the occasional visits from the vicar. She had a private pension thanks to Brian's company scheme, and was now getting her state pension, as well, so she didn't want for money. She lived in a neat little house in a neat little cul-de-sac in Hartford, just out of Northwich, bought outright with the proceeds of Brian's life insurance policy and his pension scheme, plus the money from selling the town house they had lived in when Peter and Margaret were children. There had been money left over to invest. Meeting her broker, and chatting about her modest investments, was another of her pleasures. She kept in touch with her family, albeit less so, now her grandchildren had become teenagers. To all appearances she seemed happily self-sufficient. Peter sometimes wondered if she would notice if he and Margaret vanished from the face of the earth, but that would be doing her an injustice.

Peter pulled into his mother's driveway only to find a Mondeo parked there instead of the expected Renault Cleo, which, when he last spoke to his mother, was what she drove. He had little time to think about this sudden change of vehicle, and was just about to ease himself out of the driving seat, when a dapper-looking man appeared at the side of the car, took hold of the door and held it open while he got out.

Not surprisingly, Peter was rather taken aback by the presence of a strange man in his mother's driveway. His immediate thought was that there was some kind of emergency, but that was quickly dispelled by the man's opening words. "Hello young man, so glad to meet you at last, we've been expecting you."

Peter took the proffered hand, exchanging a wan smile for the wide show of teeth aimed in his direction, while remaining totally at a loss as to the identity of this man who projected an aura of rather forced, and certainly precipitate, friendliness. "Liz and I have been looking forward to your visit ever since we heard you were going to call in."

Liz, who on earth was Liz? His mother was Elizabeth, but she had never in his hearing ever permitted anybody to call her Liz. "I'm sorry but who are you?"

"Bit of a surprise eh? I'm Gerald, friend of Liz's. We met on a Saga coach trip to Norway a few months ago, hit it off straight away."

Well why not, people made new friends, but why she'd invited him here on the day of his visit was a bit of a mystery. He had no time to speculate further because at that moment his mother made her appearance, looking vibrant, hurrying forward to bestow, what to Peter seemed to be unusually eager, kisses on his cheek and mouth.

They all went inside. While Peter and his mother settled down in the lounge, Gerald departed, probably tactfully, to make them all a cup of tea. The door remained open so Peter whispered "Who the hell is this Gerald chap. What on earth did you invite him round today, for God's sake, when you knew I was coming?"

His mother looked faintly embarrassed. To Peter's surprise she actually blushed. "He's a dear friend, and I didn't invite him round, he lives here."

The look she gave her son was anxious, almost pleading, as though she knew what his reaction to the news that she was living with a man, would be. Peter's first thoughts were along the lines of vulnerable widows being taken for a ride by plausible predators, although he didn't know what 'lives here' actually meant; perhaps he was some kind of lodger. "For God's sake mum, what have you got yourself into," he mouthed, frowning his disapproval.

That was it for the time being, because the bright and very breezy Gerald returned bearing the tea tray. They chatted about family matters for a while, but then when the conversation turned to topical news items such as the Iraq war, it became rather laboured Eventually during a break in what had now become stilted conversation, his mother asked. "Are you still taking your old mum out to dinner love?" adding before Peter could respond "You don't mind if Gerald joins us, do you dear?"

"Oh no, I wouldn't want to intrude on a family occasion."

The protest appeared half-hearted to Peter, but in any case before he could think of anything to say his mother came back at once. "Don't be silly Gerald, you're as good as part of the family now." The look she directed very deliberately towards her son was defiant. He had no alternative but to accept that there would be three for dinner. Gerald, for his part, smiled rather smugly as though he had been sure of his ground, all along. On the way to removing the tea things he stopped to squeeze Elizabeth's shoulder with a show of overt affection, maybe designed to show Peter how strong was his position in the house.

For the rest of the time until they left to go to the Bluecap for their scheduled meal, Elizabeth was never alone with Peter, denying him any chance to quiz her about this new man in her life. She spent most of that time upstairs in the bedroom or bathroom, beautifying herself as Gerald described it, while the man in question regaled Peter with stories of his time in the army, keeping him constantly annoyed with his suave manner, and his over-ebullient chat.

The long-standing invitation to take his mother to dinner had been Peter's, but when they arrived at the restaurant the obnoxious little shit, as Peter already thought of him, took charge, and when he protested, insisted, supported by Elizabeth, that he, Peter, was the guest. Gerald's manner was ostentatiously pompous, particularly in the attention he showed to Elizabeth.

It wasn't until the fussy seating operation had been concluded, that Peter could settle back to really loath the man smirking at his mother. She loved it, simpering her delight through her war paint in a way that made Peter almost physically sick. This dapper little man, with his immaculately groomed white hair and his bristling moustache, had his mother absolutely in his thrall; Peter was very worried. After all, she had some small funds. This guy could be a kind of con man out for what he could get, well aware of the vulnerability of ladies of a certain age.

The conversation round the table veered in the direction of Naomi and the children every so often, but not for long as Gerald concentrated his attention on Elizabeth. Why on earth his mother couldn't see that the man was playing her for a fool, that his extreme consideration was part of an elaborate game. He was shocked at his mother's naivety It was all so blatant, sick-making to an observer, but apparently real to her. It did cross Peter's mind that it could be genuine, a late blossoming love, but then he dismissed that as the evening wore on. The flattery and little secret exchanges continued, in a nauseating way, that he couldn't believe was authentic.

Peter was relieved when it became clear that the embarrassing experience was nearing the end. The waiter brought the bill, and was about to place it near to Peter, when Gerald snapped at him "Give it here man." and reached out for the plate. In his hurry, he knocked over a half full glass of wine.

"For Christ's sake, now look at the mess." He glared at the waiter with barely controlled fury, half getting to his feet, then sitting back down again. As the waiter covered the stain with a napkin, Peter observed his mother looking on nervously, unsure how to react to the outburst. Gerald reached inside his jacket but his hand came away empty. "My God, I've forgotten my wallet, how bloody embarrassing. Look, old boy, do you mind taking care of this, give you a cheque the moment we get home."

"Don't worry, Gerald, Peter will pay, won't you dear. After all it was his invitation in the first place."

"Won't hear of it, Liz, my apologies to you both, cheque at home." He helped Elizabeth into her coat, which the solicitous waiter had brought over, while Peter handed over his credit card. All he wanted to do was to get the hell out of that restaurant, escape the curious looks from other diners that were still being directed towards his little party.

Later that night Peter lay in the spare room bed without having had the chance to talk to his mother about Gerald, thinking of the two of them in their own bed, and what that pompous little bastard was planning for his mother's future. The previous night's depression visited him again, attempts at prurient thoughts of Simone, failed to shift his mood. When he eventually dropped off, his sleep was scattered with fragments of images of people, mostly strangers, about whom he was deeply worried, although he had no idea why. When he woke in the morning, unrefreshed, the remaining picture in his mind left over from the dreams was of a vaguely threatening figure in black, undoubtedly Mrs Benson, come to continue her haunting. The one consolation he found, as he struggled to replace the remnants of his dreams with waking thoughts, was that in real life, he hadn't seen that sad women since Wendy had taken her in hand on the day of the party.

The night's sleep hadn't done him much good, leaving him feeling jaded, even after a shower. When he went downstairs, he found his mother in the kitchen at the stove singing quietly to herself, with Gerald, in his dressing gown, reading the paper.

"Morning darling sleep well, bacon and eggs suit you?"

"Just toast for me, Mum, and a cup of coffee." He exchanged greetings with Gerald, an exchange of glances between them was ambiguous.

"Oh go on, make the most of a bit of home cooking. Gerald nearly always has a cooked breakfast, got to keep his strength up, haven't you dear." She smirked. Her lover, if that's what he was, smiled uneasily back at her, maybe having the grace to feel embarrassed by Elizabeth's open show of affection.

"No really Mum, just toast please." He sipped his coffee, declined the offer of the newspaper, while Gerald started work on a substantial plate of fried food. He felt uncomfortable sitting there hating Gerald, both for sleeping in his mother's bed, and for the way he had insinuated himself into the house, obviously planning some form of financial scam. That cheque for last night's dinner had not been forthcoming, which was just as Peter expected. Obnoxious little bastard maybe, but his mother was smitten, so he would have to be careful how he went about his warnings. Of course it was just faintly possible that he could be wrong.

"What do you think of our new Prime Minister then Peter?"

There was some desultory conversation before Gerald took his plate across to the sink, kissing Elizabeth on the back of her neck, on the way.

"Mum, I want to make an early start, but before I go could we have a word please, in private."

"Anything you've got to say, you can say in front of Gerald, Peter, we have no secrets from each other."

"No, no, that's alright, quite understandable. I'll just pop up and have my bath." He planted another fleeting kiss, on Elizabeth's forehead this time, then hurried away upstairs.

The frown on his mother's face when the two of them were left alone, spoke of storms to come. "Right Peter spit it out. I suppose you think Gerald is some kind of predator out to fleece a poor widow of her savings." Before Peter could say a word, on she went. "Well let me tell you this, he pays more than half our household expenses. He's got his army pension, an occupational pension, and it won't be long before he gets his state old-age pension, he's got absolutely no need to steal from me."

"So why does he need to move in with you then?"

"If you must know he rented a small flat before. This place is much more convenient for two people, no other reason than straight forward common sense. Anyway what kind of fool do you take me for Peter? Whether you like it or not, we are fond of each other, enjoy each other's company, what's wrong with that?"

Said like that, what could he say? There was absolutely no reason why two people, whatever their age, shouldn't live together, if that's what they wanted. Gerald might not be his cup of tea, but it wasn't him living with the guy. Yet he still didn't like it, even though he could summon up no reasonable argument against it.

"Alright Mum, I was just worried about you that's all."

Elizabeth snorted. "Worried about me, how often do you or that sister of yours ever come near me, I've got my own life to live you know."

Peter muttered something about her always being welcome at his house, but there was truth in what she said. Since the kids had got older, they had rather forgotten about her, always assuming she lived a full and happy life, without much attempt to check it out. Anyway the discussion was over. Whatever he thought, there was nothing to be done about it. He left about half an hour later, his mother all smiles again. As he was about to get into the car, Gerald handed him an envelope. "Don't forget your cheque old boy."

He should have felt better, admitted he was wrong about that anyway, but somehow he still couldn't help but see Gerald as an intruder, a stranger insinuating himself into the Shadbolt family fold.

As he drove away, he wondered how Margaret would react, when she found out about their mother's new domestic arrangements. Thinking of his sister, he realised how their two families had also grown apart. She and Sebastian had four children, and when Charlie and James were young, they had delighted in visits to the shambles that made up their cousins' house and surroundings.

Both Margaret and Sebastian were potters, operating out of a disused railway station near Goudhurst in Kent. That was only their place of work. They actually lived in an old building that had been some kind of chapel at one time. They had stripped it inside, rebuilt it with a huge central living room, with a gallery above running right around, leading off to the bedrooms. The garden was about an acre of largely unattended jungle, which the children all adored.

Chaotic it might have been, but the two potters had appeared to make a good living out of their craft. Peter could remember them all going off for holidays to exotic places like Mexico and Indonesia. In fact the two families had one or two holidays together, a hired farmhouse in Provence, and then on another occasion in a Norwegian lodge deep in the forest by the side of a lake.

Good memories, but now all the children were doing their own thing, university, college, gap years and all that. Their parents seemed too busy, or not interested enough to exchange visits.

Life these days seemed less enjoyable. Peter missed the children being young, felt dissatisfied with his way of living, although he knew he had absolutely no need to feel that way.

The family had split up, and would probably, from now on, only meet when there was a wedding or a funeral.

The elements of Peter's family would go on to form their own family groupings.

Somehow, this morning anyway, he found that sad.

Chapter 13.

Naomi was feeling stressed, a not unusual state of mind these days. Better go to Tesco's after work, she sighed to herself, Peter due back this evening, though why on earth Rebecca couldn't get off her arse and do something, she couldn't imagine. Young babies did take up a lot of time, but if she was living in her own house she would have had to find time to do other things than look after the baby so why not here where her help would have been appreciated.

Charlie had gone, leaving a gap – a gap between rivals in a way, rivals to be the dominant female around the house. Of course Naomi loved her daughter, but the older she got the more frequently she got on her nerves.

When she had driven off with Peter, a couple of days ago, she had felt unreasonably jealous. There had never been the intimate relationship between her and Charlie that some mothers and daughters had, shopping together, sharing clothes, and so on. Even as a very young girl, Charlie had had a spirit of independence that had precluded anything like that – and, of course, every time she misbehaved she had an instant apologist in the form of her father. Seeing them drive off, left her feeling excluded, Charlie so excited and eager to be away, Peter so proud, almost like a couple in the teasing way they behaved towards each other.

Naomi didn't look forward to going into the office these days. Bill Clarkson was always on her back lately, with his constant mantra, billing, billing, billing. Yet the work she was doing was frequently tedious, often reducing her to little more than a legal clerk. She knew that Ivan felt the same. They had discussed the prospect of leaving Bradfield, Lang and Oldfield several times, but it wasn't easy to flit from one firm of solicitors to another, particularly as the senior partners of the various local firms had a sort of self-protective lunch club, guarding against rebellious employees.

All this divorce work, fighting for your side, knowing that every point won meant the other party losing. Even then, her own winning clients were seldom satisfied with what they had achieved in court. That, and bloody conveyancing, occupied too much of her time in the office. Efforts to seek other types of work were met by Bill's patronising flattery that she was so good at her work, that client's asked for her by name.

"Got your husband back yet Naomi?" Rosalind was always cheerful, despite what Naomi knew was an unsatisfactory personal life; an on-off boyfriend who was just using her as far as Naomi could see, weight problems and regrets about the kids she had never had.

"He'll be there by the time I get home, I expect. Done his duty, depositing his daughter at college, calling in to make sure his mother is still alive." The pursing of her lips and raising of eyebrows made it fairly clear what sort of mood she was in.

She collected her mail before moving into her office, to sit disconsolately at her desk, sifting through the tedious correspondence. All routine, until she came to a blue, unopened envelope marked 'personal', which raised her interest a degree. Inside, written on matching blue paper, was a brief note in spidery handwriting addressing her as Mrs Shadbolt. In rambling sentences the letter asked how her husband's literary course was going, whether he had had any work published yet, and that was it. There was no signature, or any other indication of who might have sent the letter.

Of course Naomi recognised the implication that maybe, just maybe, Peter was not spending his Wednesday afternoons in quite the way he claimed, but why bother with the innuendo, why not come out and say that her husband had got a bit on the side, if indeed, that's what the writer was saying. Perhaps she had missed the point but, if it wasn't that, then she couldn't think what was the point of the message.

She drank the coffee the girl had brought in, while she was still pondering the strange letter. She was surprised to find she wasn't particularly shocked. Yes, she minded in a hurt pride sort of way, but there was no sense of devastation in the thought that Peter might have gone astray. They had drifted very much apart in recent years with little sign of affection between them, for the most part. Perhaps they had really both been working too hard to notice what was happening to them.

As she sat there, at her desk, she considered quite calmly and objectively whether she still loved Peter. Twenty years of marriage must mean something she mused, but then she realised that that in itself didn't mean anything at all, if there were no mutual feelings left to cement it. She knew only too well that many marriages carried on as a matter of a habit, which it wasn't worth the hassle to break. She was also of the opinion that only one in say ten thousand marriages was sustained by continuous romantic love. My God what an old cynic she was becoming.

"Naomi, Mrs Bakewell is here for her appointment."

Another distraught woman, another shattered marriage, more evidence to support her cynicism. She would do her best for Mrs Bakewell, persuade the judge of her client's rights and needs, but what wouldn't she give for some commercial work or defending some underdog against the power of a corporation. At lunchtime she went out to the pub with Rosalind, thought about mentioning the blue letter, then thought better of it. There was no hurry, she might do a bit of detective work on her own, shouldn't be difficult; if she then found what she suspected to be true, what then?

There was no sign of anyone in the house when Peter arrived home, but the smell of baby excesses lingering in the air told him that Rebecca, at least, was still in residence. George was there to welcome him, running round in excitement, at first exuberant with real love, and then turning that into an appeal to be taken for a walk, which was just about the last thing Peter felt like doing.

He managed quite easily, to set aside the little pang of guilt at not responding to the dog's unstinting affection. He had thought of going round to Simone's, right then, after all no one knew exactly what time he was due back. She might still be working, he was tired, and if he did go round he would not want to leave for considerable time, might want to curl up entwined with that soft body and sleep all night through, so he stayed at home..

In an effort to do his bit, he searched in the freezer for something to cook, did a few vegetables. Might as well earn a few Brownie points, if he was going to stay in, put Naomi in a good mood, you never know what might happen. It did cross his mind that there was something vaguely immoral about his willingness to have sex with whatever woman happened to be available, when he felt randy. To hell with it, he was too weary tonight to philosophise on the subject. He poured himself a large Scotch, slumped down in the armchair then promptly fell asleep, unaware of the whisky spilling from his glass as it dangled from his hand by the side of the chair, before dripping to the floor.

"For fuck's sake, Peter, look at that bloody carpet." The words edged through the fog of his waking, only slowly becoming comprehensible.

He looked at his wife through misted eyes, saw an angry woman standing in front of him. "What's up then?" He rubbed his face, slowly banishing the strange dreams, heavy with sleep, unwilling to deal with whatever was upsetting Naomi.

"Your whisky, look at it, all over the carpet."

He sighed, shook his head. "Welcome home Peter, nice trip, so glad to see you." Not a good start, she could at least pretend she was glad to see him back.

"I'll get a cloth." She made to move away, then seemed to change her mind, stopped in her tracks. "Alright then, how was it? Settle Charlie in O.K? How was your Mum?" It was becoming a sighing competition. "Sorry, Peter, but I've had one of those days. Seeing you spark out there with whisky all over the floor, set me off"

Peter dragged himself to his feet, kissed Naomi's unreceptive cheek, an effort now might produce dividends later. "I'll clean it up, don't suppose whisky'll do it any harm though, nice sort of air freshener."

There hadn't been any rushing into each other's arms, but then again Naomi didn't stamp out of the room. Peter answered her tersely worded questions in a civil way, including his worries about the horrible Gerald. Truce, unspecified, but a truce nevertheless. Polite behaviour was on the cards for a few hours anyway. Curiously, with that unspoken resolve, both felt better, glad the evening would not be one of conflict.

"Where is everybody?"

"James is probably with that mate of his, hardly ever see him these days, treats the place like a hotel. Rebecca went into town to buy more clothes for that baby of hers, expected her back before now. I wouldn't mind a drink if there's any left in the decanter." Said with a smile that cemented the peace, for now.

In bed that night they did have sex: sex, but not love making, unsatisfactory to both of them. Naomi made a decision to accept Peter's sexual approaches, but when it came to the physical process, she could summon little enthusiasm, kept finding fault with his foreplay. In the end just lay back, allowing herself be fucked rather than start a row by saying that she had changed her mind, and didn't want to have sex after all.

There were all sorts of reasons, the blue letter with the suspicions it brought, for one, but it was the overall relationship with Peter that was the main thing. As far as she was concerned sex or making love, which was what she wanted, was the result of continuing affection, little ways of being paid attention, and, yes, she would have said, romance, all that stuff. Of course she realised that the feelings that two people had for each other in the early, exciting, days of a relationship was bound to wane, yet as far as she was concerned, in their case, it had dwindled to nothing but habit. The effort needed to maintain their marriage in some sort of shape was substantial.

Peter had wanted sex, but he too was disappointed. He was sure he was doing all the things that used to get Naomi excited, yet after some initial feeble response she just flopped there, seeming to exclude herself from the process, wanting nothing but for him to get it over with so she could go to sleep. In the end it was more like some form of up-market masturbation, than love making. Afterwards he felt resentful, certainly not grateful for her begrudging contribution to the act.

Lying there, with Naomi stolid by his side, he too, thought back to the early days of their relationship, when they made love at every conceivable opportunity. Then it was love and boy did she participate, indeed often initiated their sexual encounters. Not unnaturally, that brought his thoughts round to Simone. He wondered whether his affair was affecting what happened in bed between him and Naomi, but no, it wasn't that, or so he told himself. He had only accepted what Simone had on offer because of the lack of intimacy between him and his wife. Thinking of Simone after what had just taken place was making an invidious comparison, which he realised was unfair, but it was there, like it or not, one woman drove him wild with the lust, the other wasn't interested.

In the morning the crying of a baby woke Peter from a troubled sleep, full of dreams which melted away with his consciousness but left a sense of uneasiness behind. He lay there for some minutes. Saturday morning, lie-in time, but he was restless and eased himself from under the duvet. He looked down at Naomi sleeping, felt guilty, touched her shoulder. "Would you like a cup of tea?"

"Later, I'm asleep." She turned away, eyes shut tight, snuggling deep beneath the duvet.

Downstairs in the kitchen, he found Rebecca wearing her usual alluring nightdress, feeding her baby. She made no attempt to cover the substantial breast, at which the child was sucking voraciously. As Peter turned his eyes away from the feasting, they connected with what seemed, to him, to be a slightly mocking smile playing round his sister-in-law's lips. He got the impression she was enjoying the sensual tugging at her nipple, the open display of her ripeness, and indeed the discomfort all this was causing Peter.

"Morning Peter, I hope young Willy here didn't wake you up, little bugger's got one hell of an appetite."

Peter's thoughts ranged from the prurient, to the exasperated. She should be at home with Simon, not flaunting herself in his kitchen. She had had her pound of flesh, now was the time to accept her husband's abject apologies and give him another chance. In that, at least, he knew he and Naomi were as one. "No I was awake anyway, and you can't stop babies crying can you. Just going to make a cup of tea, fancy one."

"You and Naomi have been so very kind to me; I don't know where we would have been without you, isn't that right Willy?" She bent down to kiss the red face still working hard at his breakfast. "Love a cup, if it's no trouble."

Kettle on, Peter turned again to face Rebecca. He would have had to be made of stone not to be stirred by the image, she presented. Hair tousled, face still faintly puffy with sleep, but somehow voluptuous, everything about her spoke of rude health, of new motherhood, of nature fulfilling its roll. That image certainly turned Peter on, making him think what a bloody fool Simon was to have risked losing all that for some petty argument, but then again he wasn't the one resisting reconciliation.

"I really should start thinking about the future, got to make decisions." She saw Peter's slight frown. "Okay, I know what you and Naomi think, but violence has no place in a marriage."

Same old mantra that Rebecca had been repeating ever since she had arrived; it was beginning to wear thin. "Of course not, Rebecca, but you have to make the punishment fit the crime. Let's face it, he made one mistake. He's been saying sorry ever since. Don't you think it's time to give him another chance?" The kettle boiled, he made the tea, she changed the baby over from one breast to the other, causing the child to give a little yelp of protest, at the interruption to his meal.

"I'll have that tea after all, Peter, while you're at it." Neither of the other two had heard Naomi's come into the kitchen. The look she gave her sister made it quite clear that she thought that nursing should take place elsewhere, certainly not half-naked in front of her husband.

Rebecca knew what that look meant. "Had enough Willy," she said, putting the sleepy baby over her shoulder, patting him on the back, unworried by the milky dribble that ran down her nightdress. Peter collected the newspaper from the doormat before going back upstairs, leaving the sisters to antagonise each other in peace.

Chapter 14.

Glad to get back to work, Wednesday to look forward to, Peter was in a cheerful mood as he turned into the company car park. That was until he saw his nemesis standing next to the name sign indicating his parking space. Mrs Benson was one worry he had thought had been dispensed with after Wendy had had that serious talk with her, on the night of the party; he hadn't seen her since then. The brightness of the day dulled. He clambered out as soon as the car came to a halt, resignedly waited to hear what the sad woman had to say. Still dressed in her usual black, her face gaunt, an air of distraction, which it seemed to Peter, bordered almost on madness.

"Mrs Benson, I thought we had agreed there was nothing more I could tell you. When you came round to my house that evening, Mrs Barkworth explained that none of us could help with your grief. It just isn't fair to persecute me like this." He spoke in a business-like way, hoping against hope, that she would get the message, and walk away.

"They still haven't found out who killed my Sharon, Mr Shadbolt. You found her, you held her, you're the link with my living child. Don't you understand, I've got nothing else."

He wanted to scream, *what the hell can I do about it,* at the top of his voice. Of course he didn't, instead he said quietly. "I'm afraid she wasn't living, when I found her. There was nothing I could do. I'm deeply sorry, as I've said many times, but it isn't helping to harass me like this. You need counselling Mrs Benson, you really do need someone to help you come to terms with your loss." His tone was gentle now. He was impatient to get away, yet felt an obligation to exchange a few words rather than give her the brush off.

"Not a mark on her."

Peter put a hand on her shoulder. "I'm sorry, but I have to get to work now. You really should go and see your doctor." As he walked towards the office entrance he heard her voice behind him. "Doctors, doctors, what do they know, they can't bring back my Sharon."

He sat at his desk, his mood unsettled by the encounter in the car park, glad when Kylie brought the mail in to give him something else on which to focus his mind. Then before he could even get started on the day's work, Michael Jackson put his head round the door. "Settle Charlie in alright then, Peter?" Without waiting for an answer, he added. "Can you spare me a few minutes later on, my office at about eleven, okay?" and he was gone.

It really was about time the old bugger retired. What now? Some hair-brained scheme to justify his continuing presence on the board. This wasn't how Peter's Monday morning had begun. His earlier cheerful mood was now replaced by niggling petulance at the way things were turning out. The meeting at eleven o'clock did absolutely nothing to enhance his state of mind. "For Christ's sake Michael, it's an integral part of the commercial department, we've always bought the wood pulp. What is this, a leaving present to production?"

Jackson sighed. He looked uneasy to Peter, might even have said downright shifty. Why on earth should the old fool have agreed to give away part of their department's function, when he was due to retire in a few months' time. That was it, of course. He was going to retire, could afford to do a few favours, when they weren't going to affect him. "Take it easy Peter, it's one small part of the operation, always was a bloody headache anyway. Production made a good case and I, well the board, decided it was for the best. You'll have quite enough on your plate when I go, without bothering about damn wood pulp."

"That's not the point Michael, you've conceded a point to

production. Before you know it they'll be taking over the whole department. Thank you, thank you very much." He was seething, saw his future sphere of control being snatched away from him without him even being consulted.

"Well it's done, and that's all there is to it." It was very unlike Michael Jackson to use such a tone, his words were dismissive. He looked old and worried, sitting there at his desk. Peter left his office wondering what the hell was behind this unexpected, and definitely unwanted shift in power. He was irritable for the rest of the day, unfair to Kylie, refusing the offer of a lunchtime drink with Norman, leaving early.

He needed to talk to Naomi about what had happened at work. Curious how, in a crisis, one turned to a long-standing partner for advice, even if that relationship had worn thin. She wasn't home yet, so he took George for a walk. It wasn't until he clambered over the style that he remembered his encounter that morning with Mrs Benson. It struck him then, that his concern with the woman had been to get her off his back. He had hardly thought about the little girl he had found in such tragic circumstances, for quite a while now. He supposed it was a relief in a way, although now there was a twinge in his conscience..

George ran back towards him, checking to make sure he was coming, wanting a reassuring pat, before he dashed off again, chasing shadows through the woods. Hours later, Peter lay awake in bed listening to the silence of the night, broken every so often by the sound of a passing car, the hoot of an owl and once by the brief barking of a dog, to which George answered, from his basket in the kitchen, with a low growl and one sharp bark of his own, He knew Naomi was still awake, because when he farted, he felt her move, in annoyance, further over on her side of the bed. After all these years of marriage, she still found his farting in bed, a distasteful habit.

He was thinking about that old fool Jackson, and why he had agreed to the wood pulp change, then about Gerald living with his mother, remembering as well that he hadn't yet rung Margaret to tell her about it. He thought about the woman in black, about him and Naomi, about Simone, and about his children, and he wasn't happy. His thoughts sped from one worry to another, growing hazier as he slipped in and out of sleep, still awake enough to hear the clock strike one o'clock, but eventually falling into troubled unconsciousness.

Another Wednesday, another lying in bed, this time resting after an exhausting session with Simone, but still with an overriding sense of dissatisfaction with life. The sex had been glorious but now, lust satisfied, body satiated, his damn mind would keep returning to this unsettled state. An involuntary sigh caused Simone to raise her head from his chest her blue eyes smiling, but at the same time asking a question.

"What's up Peter, not losing my touch am I, failing to give the client satisfaction. That's an indictable offence."

"No lover you were great as usual. It's me, bit unsettled with things at the moment, you know, things on my mind." He licked his lips, sighed a soft sigh, shrugged his shoulders in apology for his mood. She kissed him sympathetically on the forehead. For a while left him in peace, but once was never enough for Simone. After a decent interval, she reached down between their bodies to coax him back into tumescence, before kneeling astride his supine body and with every increasing movement dispelled, for the moment, thoughts that shouldn't be in bed with them anyway.

Despite her lover's willing response, Simone sensed his earlier mood had returned, once she had finished with him. Was he getting fed up with their little romance? Was the spark going from their affair? She had gone into this thing with her eyes wide open, without demands or expectations. The thought came to her now that she would be devastated if Peter decided he had had enough. It might look like casual sex, but his Wednesday visits had provided a focus in her life, something to cling onto besides her absent children, and her life at work. She needed affection. These Wednesdays seemed to her to provide that. It was then that it came to her, like a flash of lightening; she loved the bastard, the thought of losing him was earth shattering.

Simone knew very well that to start asking Peter if their

relationship was cooling off, would be just about the worst tactic, she could apply, so she eased herself out of bed, pulled on her dressing gown, and went into the kitchen to make them both a cup of coffee.

Later that same day, Peter did finally get round to ringing Margaret, only to find she knew all about Gerald. Her attitude towards the situation between their mother and her new man was good luck to them, she was a big girl, and all that. From what she could see there was no exploitation going on, just two people coming together to exorcise loneliness. Anyway she had worries of her own.

Alistair, away at Manchester, studying graphic design had admitted to taking coke. He had assured his mother that it wasn't a regular thing, but she was worried, which to Peter seemed a bit hypocritical. The Darling household had always been pretty freewheeling. During the time when the two families used to see each other on a regular basis, all the adults had smoked some cannabis from time to time, when the kids were in bed of course, but nevertheless the attitude of Margaret and Sebastian had been that mild drug-taking was less harmful than alcohol. It was reasonable to argue that if a family had a culture of drugs, was it any wonder that the children would follow suit.

Margaret's revelations brought Charlie to mind. He put the phone down from speaking to his sister, then immediately dialled his daughter's mobile number. The conversation was brief. She gave the impression that chatting to her father was taking up time that could be spent much more enjoyably doing something else. He did manage to elicit that everything was fine, that she might soon have to get down to some work after the hectic settling in period. Naomi came into the hall just then. Realising he was talking to their daughter she took the receiver from him, but there again the conversation was short. She put the phone down with a little frown of annoyance.

Peter thought it would not be auspicious to mention Alistair's little problem, so confined his answer to Naomi's questions about the Darling family to generalities. One thing did occur to him however, once Naomi had returned to the kitchen to help Rebecca with the evening meal, and that was the strength of the bond that all parents, or at least most of them, had with their children. Of course children loved their parents but that tended to fade as they started their own families while the emotional tug of parent for child seemed to continue for always.

Upstairs, Willy started crying, Naomi's raised voice could be heard from the kitchen. It was time to pour some oil on troubled sisters. As he went in, Rebecca dashed out, shouting over her shoulder. "Alright Naomi you've made your point, you don't have to go on about it, Willy and I will pack our bags tomorrow. I take it you can put up with us for just one more night."

Naomi was red faced, sighing, and Peter thought, looking pretty whacked. "Look whatever you need doing I'll do, go and sit down, pour yourself a gin and tonic or something." His concern was genuine, part of a realisation that she did always end up doing more than her fair share round the house The presence of her sister should have helped, but instead it only appeared to make things worse.

His offer, genuine though it was, was thrown back in his face in no uncertain manner. "Isn't that fucking typical. You always come on the scene offering to help when the work's done. You and that bloody sister of mine you're two of a kind, token offers to do something useful when you know it's too bloody late." Peter moved to put an arm round her shoulder, but she shrugged angrily away.

"Why don't you piss off Peter, just let me get on with it." If the truth were known the letter she had received, virtually accusing her husband of infidelity, was almost certainly at the root of her irritability. She had been on the point of blurting out some comment about how he spent Wednesday afternoons but held back, not ready yet, if ever, for such a confrontation. She had thought of following Peter to check up on him but, again, unwillingness to learn what might be the truth, had made her hesitate. Her marriage might not be in a prime state, nevertheless, the thought of a complete breakup scared her. She wasn't quite sure why that should be, except that the upheaval and complications that would entail were singularly unappealing.

James was happy, embarrassed, but happy. He rejected the slightest show of affection from Greg in public, but when they were alone, he seemed to relish the physical contact. When he wasn't with Greg he had an almost permanent erection thinking about what they did together. They had plenty of opportunity as Greg's father hardly ever seemed to be around, yet despite the sex, James was finding it very difficult to come to terms with the situation. He didn't want to be queer, didn't think he was queer, most certainly didn't want to be part of the gay community.

His feelings for his friend were ambiguous, the lust thing was clear, yet when it came to affection, he was far from sure. The boy was confused to say the very least which was spoiling the happiness, he felt some of the time. He liked talking to Greg, liked being his mate, but any show of post coital affection caused him to shy away. The thought of love between two guys was anathema to him causing him to resist his partner's attempts at non-sexual touching. Kissing and cuddling without the constituent of sex was something to be resisted, something effeminate, something guys didn't do. All this drove Greg wild. He told James he loved him, even threatened to end the relationship if he failed to make an effort to respond.

They were drinking beer at the kitchen table in the flat, when Greg returned once more to the unfeeling attitude of his friend. "You know Jimmy you can't have it both ways, you can't want to fuck someone one minute, then not want them to touch you the next. You've accepted that you like it up the arse, we're friends so why can't you show a little bit of affection for me. I'm not asking for anything soppy, just the odd hug and the occasional kiss."

"I do like you Greg, of course I like you, but it feels odd kissing a bloke, just like that." In fact, although James was worried by this aspect of their friendship, he couldn't do without the sex. The thought that Greg might walk away filled him with dismay.

"Why the fuck not. You like it well enough when we're on the job. I mean if all I am to you is a convenient arse I'm not sure there's any future in this for either of us." He got up from the table, went round to the other side, to put an arm round James's shoulder. James tensed, but with an effort, he didn't pull away. He was going to have to try and meet Greg halfway, or lose him altogether. The arm stayed, he relaxed a degree or two, the kiss was accepted, it made him feel randy, so was that part of the non-sexual deal or not? He was still confused. On this occasion it didn't matter what it was, because it soon became sexual. The two of them went upstairs with a very common purpose, that made discussion about love something to think about at another time.

Chapter 15.

Charlie was coming home for Christmas. She had rung to ask if she could bring her boyfriend to stay for a few days, including over Christmas itself. Curiously Naomi and Peter were as one in agreeing. Perhaps they both saw a full house as a way of avoiding any awkwardness between them. That agreement appeared to lead to a wider truce, with the two of them actually going shopping for presents together, and later discussing what they would have in the way of food, with Peter offering to help in that direction too.

It was a surprise when a couple of days later Rebecca took Naomi to one side and, rather red faced, asked her if she would invite Simon over for Christmas day. The long rebellion looked as though it might be over.

"Mum, you know this mate of mine, Greg, well his Dad has got this new bird, and he wants to spend Christmas with her, so I was wondering if he, Greg, I mean, could come here for the day." Well eight was a nice round number, and the dining room table was designed to seat eight It appeared that the numbers at the festive feast had been ordained by the furniture, was how Naomi, jokingly agreed.

It was a cliché of course that fathers don't like their daughters' boyfriends, but Peter felt justified in the case of Rupert, who in his eyes was an ignorant arsehole, who treated the whole family with condescending attitude, that bordered on the arrogant. Maybe his attitude was something to do with the fact that his father was a banker, and had produced a rhyming offspring. The first couple of days had been bearable, mainly because he had taken Charlie out most of the time. Apart from breakfast, which amounted to little more than coffee, the couple had not joined in with the family routines.

Christmas day was a different matter, however, particularly when James's friend Greg arrived. Rupert and Greg not only came from different backgrounds, had a different attitude to life, they also had no intention of compromising their opinions of each other, Christmas, or no Christmas. Before Greg arrived, Rupert had already produced a couple of bottles of Moët et Chandon champagne, which he said his family always had as a light accompaniment to the festive turkey. When Greg handed over his bottle of Tesco's Chardonnay to Naomi, Rupert's mocking smile was a put-down, which straight away registered powerfully with Greg..

Peter glanced over towards his daughter. She understood at once what the little pursing of his lips intended to convey. Her only response was an almost imperceptible shrug of the shoulders, as if to say, *"what can I do about a couple of males of the species who might be about to lock horns."*

Naomi understood the undercurrent as well. "Thank you Greg, that's very kind of you, we'll appreciate a glass of that later on."

Attention was diverted by a wail from Willie, followed immediately by a fluttering around of his very recently reunited parents. For one horrible moment Peter thought Rebecca was going to offer the child her breast right there in the living room but, small mercies, she and Simon retreated upstairs, where no doubt both her men would appreciate the exposure. Still, Peter thought, maybe that's one strand in the web of his life's complications, that might soon be resolved, permanently.

"Charlie, would you like to give me a hand in the kitchen?"

"What can I do to assist, Mrs Shadbolt, we can't have you overdoing it can we?" This from Rupert, sounded to everyone in the room, like the patronising offer it probably was.

"That's alright Rupert, Charlie and I can manage, thank you." Peter caught the brief expression of distaste on his wife's face as he concentrated on setting the table. It pleased him that Naomi's view of her daughter's boyfriend appeared to coincide with his.

Once safely in the kitchen, out of earshot, Naomi could no longer contain herself. "I'm sorry, darling, but your Rupert is an arrogant sod." She was only firing an opening shot, appearing in no way angry, just mildly annoyed. The look she gave her daughter was quizzical, wondering perhaps what Charlie saw in this latest addition to her life.

"Alright, Mum, I know he comes over as a bit full of himself, but he's good fun, really he is, anyway I like the bloke."

Back in the sitting room, Peter was handing round the drinks. The baby's parents had re-joined the throng, Rebecca opting for an orange juice, using her usual excuse. "Don't want the young man to get tiddly do we?" Simon smiled indulgently, and asked for a Scotch and Canada. The boys opted for beer, while Rupert asked if he could mix his own dry Martini, for himself and Charlie. Peter took a long gulp of his own whisky, before sidling into the kitchen to ask the girls what they wanted.

Naomi started to say that she had too much to do without worrying about drinks, but then changed her mind, smiled instead, and asked for a gin and tonic, Charlie said she'd have one too, not realising that her beau was already preparing a drink for her.

Naomi could feel the tension rising, cooking a big meal always had that effect on her, but she was programmed to keep calm, not snapping at her husband was part of that seasonal determination.

Charlie rather surprisingly kissed her father on the cheek. She too was in a peace-making mood, must be the festive spirit. "He's alright Dad, really, once you get used to him."

"I didn't say a word my darling daughter." He gave her a little hug before leaving the scene of frenetic preparation, for the potential minefield of the sitting room..

As Peter re-entered the room, he caught the edge of a giggled whisper from Greg to James, something about him thinking he was James Bond. Willy's parents were taking turns to dangle their son, pretty much oblivious to the others in the room.

"How do you occupy your time then, Greg?" Innocent enough,

but Greg was immediately on the defensive.

"I'm at college with James, if you must know."

"Doing what at college?" His tone was peremptory. It was immediately obvious that Greg resented the interrogatory manner of the question.

"Sciences if you must know, same as James."

"Thought about which Uni you going to apply for yet, got to get in early these days." Greg hadn't even decided whether he wanted to go to university, even if he could scrape sufficiently high grades.

"What is this, fucking third degree, or something? Sorry Mr Shadbolt."

"Keep your hair on old chap, only asking a friendly question."

"I'm not your old chap," he glared across the room, "Just lay off alright, stow the questions."

James put his hand on Greg's shoulder, a calming gesture, but also one to assure his friend what they both knew, that Rupert was a stuck-up shit. He shouldn't let the wanker get to him.

Peter stepped in to pour oil on the bubbling waters, by asking Rupert what he was reading at Durham, while Rebecca went out to the kitchen mumbling something about helping out. Simon continued to be completely absorbed with his newly-recovered son. The rest of them were regaled for several minutes by Rupert giving forth about the advantages of archaeology, as a study subject.

Peter's thoughts turned to Simone, who he knew had the kids with her for Christmas day, to be returned to her ex-husband promptly by midday on Boxing Day. He pondered on the joys of family life. Just for a moment or two, he wondered what Christmas Day would be like if he and Simone were shacked up by themselves. Not much attention would be paid to the feast, he concluded.

Any further thoughts about his lover were cut short. There was a buzz of activity, as the three women appeared carrying various dishes on their way to the dining room. Naomi asked Peter to go and collect the turkey as it was very heavy. Rupert with something of a proprietorial relish set about opening the champagne. James was about to tell him to stuff it when offered a glass until a look from Peter changed his mind. He took the glass with ill-concealed reluctance. Willie was already dozing, so was taken away by his doting father for a sleep upstairs.

Finally they all settled down to Christmas dinner with the conversation shifting from praise for Naomi for her organisation of the meal, to the economic conditions in the country, and what effect they had had on the festive season. The two lads were very quiet although neither stinted themselves, when offered refills of champagne from the second bottle.

Peter felt good, the champagne helped, but the day was going well despite Rupert's attempts at needling Greg. The prospect of Rebecca going back home was a pleasing one. He exchanged smiles with Naomi indicating peace on that front, the baby was asleep, so all was well. When everyone had stuffed themselves silly, Peter announced that he would do the washing up, and if anyone cared to help they would be welcome.

"No, Mr Shadbolt, me and James will do that, won't we mate, you go and put your feet up." As he addressed James, he casually draped an arm round his shoulder, just a friendly gesture, you might think. James reacted sharply, shrugging away from his touch as though he had been stung..

"Great idea, let the two old pals contribute to the day, they'll enjoy washing up together, won't you boys?"

Whether Rupert intended any implication with those sneering words, would never be known. Whether or not, James exploded in immediate fury. "What the hell do you mean, you stuck up bastard, why don't you fuck off back to Durham. Trust you Charlie to find some chinless wonder to fuck around with."

The scene that a moment ago had seemed so peaceful, erupted into action. Rupert made a move towards James, intercepted by Charlie's restraining arm, Naomi shouted at her son that she wouldn't have language like that, Greg ushered James out to the kitchen, Rebecca and Simon looked embarrassed.

Peter, watching from the side-lines, was left with some

worrying thoughts about the nature of the relationship between his son and Greg. James's reaction to Rupert's fairly mild comments had been way over the top. It seemed to him there had to be a reason. He was normally a live and let-live kind of guy, yet when it came to his own son, he didn't like the obvious conclusion that came immediately into his mind.

Peter would have described himself as a liberal, yet as far as homosexuality was concerned he had always seen it as abnormal, being vaguely repelled by the whole idea. Not that he wanted anyone persecuted, or given less rights, but if the truth were known, he didn't want to have anything to do with gays, in any context. Now there was a suspicion in the air that James and Greg might have a gay relationship; he didn't like it one little bit. Naomi must have been aware of his unease because, when he looked across at her, she immediately understood his mouthed suggestion that they go upstairs to talk. She was well aware of Peter's views on most subjects, and knew, before he opened his mouth, what was worrying him on this occasion.

"Is it me or did you get the impression that James's reaction to that oaf Rupert's comment, was way over the top. Do you think our son is ….?"

"Yes, Peter, I do, but what does it matter if he is. I think what is much more worrying that he's still ashamed of the fact, that's going to make his life very complicated."

"But doesn't it bother you, that our son might be an arse bandit?" The words were ugly, ill chosen, driven by emotion, his tone incredulous, angry. Not for one single moment could Peter begin to understand why his wife was taking it so calmly.

"Do you have to be so bloody crude." Naomi's face was a mask of distaste, not with her son, but with what she saw as, her stereotype husband, with his prejudiced views on life .

"These things happen Peter, it's no one's fault, James can't help his sexuality. Right now he's having his own battles coming to terms with the fact that he's gay. He probably doesn't want to be gay, worried by his attraction to Greg, worried about how the outside world will react. Things are not as bad as they were, but there are still plenty of people around only too ready to mock. What your son needs now, and for some time to come, is sympathy and understanding. You, as his father, have got to be there for him, through all the misery he will probably have to endure." Quite a speech, but it was important that she brought this throw-back of a husband of hers, into line, not for her sake, but for the sake of their suffering son.

Of course, Naomi was right – or at least would have been had her comments applied to anyone other than his own son, but it was James she was referring to. Peter was struggling with the facts before him, struggling with how he was going to look the boy in the face the next time they were together, struggling with what his feelings towards his son were going to be, now he knew he was gay. It was hard because, try as he might, he hated the idea that his son was a homosexual. Naomi could reason all she wanted, but reason was one thing, feelings and long and deeply held opinions, were quite another. How was he ever going to adjust to this new image of his James.

He kept assuring himself that he still loved him, whatever he was, but did he. Could he love a son who was going to have male partners for the rest of his life. Naomi recognised Peter's gigantic struggle with his feelings. She had been married to him long enough to be well aware of his views as applied to the public in general, and could see what a strain it must be to reconcile his love for his son with his views on homosexuality. She came over and put her arms round her disturbed husband in a real gesture of affection, sympathy for the conflicts that were raging in his brain.

Whatever their differences, and there had been many over recent months, the many years of marriage had created a bond of intimacy, when it came to sharing problems, that was strong. Her attempts to reconcile her husband to their son's sexuality while sympathising with his reactions failed lamentably. He broke away from her tentative embrace to announce he was taking George for a walk, always the palliative when things went haywire in the Shadbolt household. .

Outside in the fresh air, it was cold and cloudy, the exercise was doing nothing for his mood. He shouted at George, who couldn't understand what he had done wrong. The walk was short, in no way therapeutic. He returned to the house with his thoughts still in turmoil.

The rest of Christmas day rather petered out. The usual television repeats, sandwiches, and more alcohol. The two boys weren't seen again that day, Rebecca and Simon clucked over their child, while Rupert and Charlie went for their own walk. Naomi paid solicitous attention to her husband all day, without succeeding in cheering him up. Peter got rather drunk, eventually falling asleep in his chair during some over-familiar film on the box that failed to hold his attention.

Later on, in bed, Naomi made it clear that she was offering the solace of sex, but Peter turned her down, trying instead, to go to sleep. He didn't sleep though, despite his intake of alcohol. After tossing and turning for some time, he got up and, taking his dressing gown from behind the door, went downstairs, leaving his wife sound asleep in the marital bed, no doubt exhausted by hosting Christmas, while at the same time trying to get her recalcitrant husband to see sense with regard to their troubled son, who so badly needed family support, not rejection from his father.

Peter made himself coffee and, with much running of hands through hair, sighing and blowing out his lips, tried to make some sense of the stream of thoughts running through his brain. Had his marriage ended, could he start again with Simone, how would the kids react if he did, would it be fair to Naomi, of course it wouldn't, would he ever be able to look his son in the eyes again, or feel the same way about him. Then there was work, what other surprises had that fool Michael Jackson got up his sleeve. On top of all that, always hovering in the background, there remained the obnoxious black presence of Mrs Benson. Alright, he shouldn't think of her like that, but there was nothing he could offer. Like the nursery rhyme ...*Oh how he wished she'd go away.*

He even went on to wonder about his mother shacked up with that smug little man. Despite, his sister's assurances, he still felt uneasy about that relationship. Then there was Rupert, what if he and Charlie got serious, could he ever accept that pompous twit as his son-in-law? Christ what a mess my life is in, he thought.

He knew full well, when you got down to basics, looking from the outside in, in comparison to many other people, his life would be considered to be privileged. That made him feel like a spoilt brat who didn't appreciate the advantages he was lucky enough to have. On and on it went, thoughts invading his mind like unwelcome spectres, until he finally fell asleep in the chair, no nearer to deciding what, if anything, to do with his life.

While his father was engaging in his soul-searching, James was fast asleep in Greg's bed. They had gone back to his place after his post-Christmas-dinner outburst, James being too embarrassed to face the family again. Eventually Greg had soothed his agitation to the extent that James accepted his advances resulting in a bout of hectic sex. Afterwards lying in bed, sated and very comfortable, Greg tried to persuade his friend that he should be open about his sexuality, with his family and the rest of the world. He was gay and that was that, why fight it, why be ashamed of it.

"Listen mate, there are always going to be some ignorant slobs who think gays are an inferior breed, but prejudice against us is fast becoming a thing of the past. Most gays these days come out openly, and declare their sexuality. Look at those people on the Weakest Link, they have no problem announcing to the world that they're gay, and that's on television."

"You're right of course, but I'm not sure I am gay, really gay I mean." Greg burst out laughing.

"Well if you're not my friend, you were giving a damn good imitation a few minutes ago."

Even James had to smile at the inconsistency between his actions and his words. He sighed, didn't resist when Greg put an arm round him to hug him close, yet still there remained an element of unease about this intimacy with another man. It would take some getting used to, even if he accepted that he really was gay. Would he ever again be able to look his Dad in the eye. He fell asleep, thinking about his next meeting with his father, most definitely dreading it.

James didn't sleep well, the bed was too small with two of them in it, the beer he had drunk on top of the champagne the evening before, the turmoil of this gay thing. He dreamed about walking out of a railway station to pass the time presumably waiting for a train, then, when he tried to find the station again he couldn't. He spent ages walking down street after street, turning corner after corner but still couldn't find the railway station. All through that seemingly endless search he was getting more and more anxious, and frustrated.

In the morning he emerged from sleep depressed, with a heavy weight bearing down on his chest. The depression stayed with him, but he pushed off Morgan, Greg's cat, who had decided to use James as a warm place to take an early morning nap. Greg was still sound asleep, so he edged out from under the duvet as carefully as possible, so as not to wake him. He shivered in his nakedness, hurrying to pull on his shirt and trousers. He paused before leaving the room, to look down at last night's sexual partner, wondering what he was supposed to feel. Was he attracted to Greg's looks, did he feel any sort of affection for him? Sex, yes, OK, but was that all, was that all there was between them?

In the kitchen, James boiled the kettle to make himself a mug of tea, the thought of taking one up to Greg didn't occur to him, although plenty of other thoughts crowded into his brain, the principle ones revolving around whether he was really gay or not, what that meant in real terms. Would he still go to bed with a girl if the chance arose, the answer was probably, yes. What did that make him, bisexual or what, someone who wanted to satisfy his lust in whatever hole made itself available.

He didn't like that image of himself, but had to admit that sex featured hugely in his thoughts almost all the time. He concluded that he didn't like himself very much, couldn't find any redeeming features. Christ he was mixed up; how was he going to carry on his friendship with Greg, feeling like he did, when Greg had apparently accepted the fact that he was gay without any problem.

Hunger was one thing he understood. He found the bread bin, set about toasting several slices which he liberally spread with peanut butter. The solace of food did something to improve his state of mind. Then came the problem of what to do next. It was Boxing Day, but he had no intention of going back home knowing that chinless wonder, Rupert, would still be there. Anyway how could he face his dad after his outburst with all its implications. His mum would be alright, whatever he was or became, but he was worried about his dad, particularly after having listened to his father's views in the past. If he stayed here with Greg there would be more arguments about his sexuality, but where else could he go. A long walk perhaps, more thought, decisions to be made, but the rest of his clothes were upstairs in Greg's room.

He made his way as quietly as he could upstairs, tiptoed into the bedroom, started to collect his clothes scattered around the room, when he realised that his friend was awake, looking at him from the bed, an amused smile on his face.

"Doing a runner mate?"

"Just felt like a breath of fresh air. By the way I helped myself to some breakfast, OK?"

"That's cool, James, but before you go home to mummy, you might just bring me up a cup of tea, okay? Unless you feel like coming back to bed that is." He lifted the duvet up to reveal a rampant penis gripped in his other hand like some kind of votive offering.

James felt a spurt of anger partly at his own tentative feeling of arousal at seeing the seeing the naked body in the bed, but mainly at his own state of indecision. His upbringing was still part of who he was, so instead of responding to the sexual invitation, or telling his friend to fuck off, he said quietly. "No problem."

As he made his way down stairs he could hear Greg's voice from the bedroom... "You are something else James, do you know that?" ...and then a burst of laughter, which appeared to James a bit over the top.

Chapter 16.

The after-Christmas return to work for the Shadbolts, found the couple in very different states of mind. The Christmas break had passed without anything else significant happening, drinks at the Barkworths on Boxing day, Rebecca and Simon taking Willy home the day after. Then Rupert and Charlie left as well, apparently having had enough of family life, for the time being. His parents had seen little of James over the last few days and, although he did sometimes turn up for meals, he barely spoke, scooting up to his room as soon as he had eaten.

Peter hadn't discussed the delicate question of his son's sexual orientation since that unsatisfactory bout of words with Naomi on Christmas day. There had been no sign of the black widow spider, which was how he had cruelly come to think of Mrs Benson, over the holiday, another thing for which to be thankful. Peter had also received a reassuring report from Margaret, who had made a flying visit to their mother over the holiday, confirming that the old dear was very happy with her Gerald. She told him he should stop worrying about her, so that was alright then – perhaps.

Nothing to do with resolutions and all that, but Peter was pleased to be back at work. The New Year, with the prospect of a seat on the board, once that old fool Michael Jackson had finally removed himself from the scene, looked bright with promise. The matter of the wood-pulp question still rankled, but you never knew; once he was completely in charge of the department he would be able to show that he could run the commercial department standing on his head, quite able indeed to take on additional responsibilities.

He believed the only reason for the functional changes between his department and production had been because of the weakness of his boss; if he had been in charge he would have been able to fight off the incursion.

Kylie didn't look too pleased to be back at work, although she was quick with the first cup of coffee of the day. Peter jollied her along so that by ten o'clock she was already tackling the morning's mail, when the internal phone rang. "Mr Jackson says can you go and see him please as soon as possible, urgent he said."

Peter sighed, made faces at Kylie, before reluctantly making his way upstairs to his boss's office. "Come in and sit down Peter, good Christmas?" The enquiry seemed rather automatic, as though it was beside the real point for which the man had asked him to come and see him. Jackson's office was large, the mahogany desk impressive, all the accoutrements of power To Peter's eyes all this was wasted on the man for whose ability, he had little respect. It was he who ran the department, supplied the reports, made the contracts, negotiated and so on, while his boss merely signed off on the work he undertook. The sooner reality was established, leaving him to take his rightful place in the company hierarchy, the better.

"Peter I have something rather important to discuss with you." The man's large, fat face was moist with sweat, something was bothering the stupid old fool. Peter waited to hear what mess, he would be asked to deal with. "The company's been going through difficult times, as you well know. You've always done your very best to ensure that this department has made its contribution to the effort to keep our heads above water. You've always worked hard and I, well I think, you know…"

Why didn't the old fool just come out with it and tell him he was handing over the reins, that he was retiring, nothing new, why all the histrionics? Jackson's voice cut through his musing, bringing his attention back to the here and now. "It's really no reflection on your work, or your ability, Peter, but as I say, we're fighting for survival, sacrifices have to be made."

Jackson got out of his chair, walked over to a bookcase, but did nothing but fiddle with the glass doors when he got there. He was distinctly agitated. Peter was beginning to get the feeling that this involved more than a straightforward handover of responsibility. He didn't like the word sacrifices, but that wasn't going to involve him directly, so why was the old man talking about it now.

Suddenly the director turned round from his preoccupation with the bookcase, sighed heavily, before blurting out. "I'm afraid they're making you redundant Peter, merging the commercial department with production, my job too, of course, but I was going anyway, and yours will no longer exist. I'm so sorry. I'd hoped to pass the reins to you, but the Board have made their decision, and that's all there is to it, I'm so very sorry, must be a shock for you."

To say Peter was stunned was to greatly understate the effect Jackson's words had on him. He could not believe what he had just heard, gazing open-mouthed at his discomforted boss, completely at a loss for words. "The good news is that your severance package is very generous, far above the statutory requirement for redundancy, notice and so on, but they do want you to leave straight away." He spread his hands in front of him, as if offering a child a present, to make the acceptance of bad news more palatable.

"Good news, my God, Michael, you fucking bastard, how long have you known this was in the offing?" He was angry enough to throw something at Jackson's head but, even in the midst of his absolute dismay, he had a sense of his own arrogance being punished for taking life for granted, not that it made his situation any easier.

"I admit I did know about this a couple of weeks before Christmas, but didn't want to spoil your holiday. What could I do Peter, they were all in favour of the move, I was a voice in the wilderness." He was almost whining. now, his tone pathetic, seeking sympathy. Peter was out of his chair.

"Why the fuck should you care, you're off anyway."

"Please don't take it like that Peter." The man was almost wringing his hands, "these things happen, it's life in business, survival and profits have to come first." Jackson badly wanted his protégé to recognise that he had fought for him. The 'powers that be' had overruled his objections, had been stronger than him. He came forward, making a clumsy effort to shake Peter's hand, which the other man deliberately ignored. Why should he make it any easier for the old bastard, yet he knew that what his boss had said about the Board was probably true, not that he cared a damn about what was fair at that moment.

Jackson then produced a large brown envelope, proffering it to Peter. "All the details of your golden handshake are in there Peter, I think you'll be pleasantly surprised." He hovered close to Peter, still hoping for that handshake.

Peter took the envelope, laughed sharply devoid of any humour. "Oh, I'm surprised alright Michael, you can be sure about that, shattered might be a better word. I thought I was here for the rest of my career. Now here I am, a forty-eight-year-old unemployed man out on the street."

"I know Peter, really I do, I'm so sorry. I don't know what else I can say."

"I think you've said enough Michael. I'll go and tidy up a few loose ends and then say my goodbyes."

"Ah, no Peter, I've been asked to see you off the premises. You can collect stuff from your desk but that's all."

"Oh for God's sake, what do you think I'm going to do, sabotage the company?"

The next few minutes were painful. Kylie looked on in shocked silent wonder as he cleared his desk, and broke into tears when he said goodbye. The next thing he knew he was sitting in his car in the car park, trembling with angry emotion. He couldn't take it in, his whole life gone in a moment, his expectations shattered by a distant boardroom decision. Yes there were some tears as well, but his next thought was to get the hell out of this damn place, where he had been stabbed so cruelly in the back.

He switched on the ignition, revved the engine violently, some sort of expression of his anger, still not quite taking in what had happened to him over the last half-hour. One moment he was set to be running his own department without interference from above, now he had been unceremoniously dumped. The last twenty minutes had changed his life, ruined his fucking life; he hated the world, accelerated out of the car park, with tears streaming down his face.

He never even saw her, but he heard a thump, felt the small impact on the car. Straight away dread replaced his anger, dread that he had hit something or somebody. Things had suddenly got even worse. He stopped and got out to see a black clad figure lying on the pavement. He must have cut the corner and hit her with the wing of the car.

When he reached Mrs Benson, she was already struggling to her feet. She looked at him in that self-same way that had haunted him over many weeks, that accusation that he had been unable to refute. "Are you alright Mrs Benson, I'm so sorry I just didn't see you." What had he done to deserve this, could things actually get any worse, he was thinking, when in fact he should have been worrying about what, in his careless anger, he had done to the poor woman.

"Yes I'm alright, but I'm going straight to the police. You deliberately ran me down, wanted to get me out of the way, not satisfied with keeping back things about my little girl, you want me out of your life. My life is over. You have a nice family, good job, children and yet you won't help me." She brushed herself down, flexed her right leg. Her words were a cruel irony given the circumstances of a few short minutes ago.

"Let me take you to the hospital, get them to check you over, make sure there's no damage done." He reached towards her, a feeble attempt to make up for what he had done, but she moved sharply aside.

"I'm alright I tell you, but I'm serious about the police." It's true, she didn't seem to be badly hurt, but you never knew with impact accidents.

"Alright, I accept completely that I'm at fault, let me drive you to the police station. I'll explain what happened."

Curiously there was no anger in her face. Her manner appeared resigned, resigned that she would follow a course of action without any expectation that it would do her, or anyone else, any good. She would go ahead anyway. "Do you really think I would get in your car, I'll walk,. I'm alright physically no thanks to you, but you have to pay for what you tried to do."

Peter watched his nemesis limp down the road, his anger now turned to bitter misery at what the fates had thrown at him, this bright Monday morning. It was all so damned unfair. He found it difficult to feel sorry for the woman, almost as though he blamed her for the accident. Her behaviour had been so bizarre ever since he found her little girl, that it didn't seem too far-fetched that she had deliberately walked into his car. That couldn't be true he rationalised, but in his emotional state he wanted to blame someone.

There was some guilt in there too, guilt that the initial sympathy he had felt for someone who had lost a child had dwindled, guilt that, however she reacted, he should understand and make allowances. He watched her walking down the street until she passed out of sight round the corner. Of course he had no option but to go to the police himself, but should he get there before the mad woman or give her time to get there first.

In the end he decided to bite the bullet and go straight to the police station. At least inspector Goddard would remember the case, perhaps be sympathetic, being aware that the woman he had knocked down was indeed a strange creature. He drove a different route from that taken by Mrs Benson, not wanting to overtake her on the way.

While Peter had been facing his morning of trauma, things were going slowly at Bradford, Long and Oldfield after the holiday. None of the partners had arrived, when Naomi got there. People were milling about, unwilling to get noses back to the grindstone. Legal secretaries, junior solicitors and various administration staff were exchanging their seasonal experiences over the holiday period. The words 'marvellous' and 'terrific' could be heard emerging from every conversation, hiding the traumas and tensions that had actually occurred over the period of goodwill. Naomi greeted Ivan Campion on the way though to his office, before getting into a huddle with Rosalind, eager to hear how she had navigated the break, whether she had seen the illusive Jeremy.

In fact Rosalind had spent Christmas day with her mother, as she usually did. She confessed rather sheepishly that she had met Jeremy, briefly, on Boxing day, when he had used the opportunity at home, when no one else fancied a walk, to drive to Woodbury Common, where, in a response to his call to her mobile, Rosalind came running, or at least driving to meet him. She grimaced, spared Naomi the details of what went on when she joined her occasional lover in his car. As usual she was mildly depressed, happy to hear that Naomi's family Christmas had passed without serious ructions, but fed up with her own stale way of getting through the break.

As Naomi listened to Rosalind's description of her holiday, she watched her friend's face, saw the pursed lips, heard the self-deprecating laugh, recognising, only too clearly, the terrible futility of her association with that sod, Jeremy. A sadness came over Naomi with the realisation that the poor woman would probably never have anything else by way of a relationship for the rest of her life. It was so unfair; she was a nice woman dealt a lousy hand by fate, most of the time putting a brave face on it.

During the Christmas break, Naomi had given quite a lot of thinking time to her position with Bradford, Lang and Oldfield. She thought about looking elsewhere for a job, even following up the idea of setting up her own firm, possibly with someone like Ivan Campion. Peter was earning good money, so the family could survive financially until she got established, was her line of thought. Her inclinations in that direction were reinforced later that morning by a visit to her office from Bill Clarkson.

All smiles, he asked her how she had enjoyed her Christmas, even asked individually after the members of her family. "The partners have been giving some thought to our pro bono work, my dear, and we have decided that it would be a good idea if one person in the firm concentrated on that area of our work." He was still smiling, it was quite obvious what was coming next.

"No way Bill, we agreed a long time ago that it would be good for all the solicitors to play their part, good for them, as well as good for the clients. There's no way you're getting me to see all the free half-hours. You know damn well they seldom result in follow-on business apart from the few legal aid cases, and that's going to show up on my record of billing."

"Naomi, we would of course make allowances for that situation, but I have to say if you refuse outright, it would reflect on you as a member of this team." He wasn't smiling any longer. "Please give it some thought my dear, we'll discuss it further at a later date."

Then he was gone, leaving a disconcerted Naomi unable to continue with her work for several minutes, not surprisingly taking her thoughts back to the question of leaving. For some unaccountable reason, she thought of that strange blue letter received weeks ago now. The inference had been obvious, but she had not followed it up, asked no questions. She wasn't sure why; was she frightened of what she might find out? Her relationship with Peter rocked from time to time, but then what marriage didn't, and the thought of a split filled her with fear. Did that mean that if there was something behind the letter she was prepared to tolerate it for the sake of preserving her marriage? Maybe she thought that if she just ignored the possibilities, they would disappear of their own volition. Christ, she didn't know what she thought; anyway the time had passed. She was going to forget that she had ever received the blue letter.

She had lunch with Rosalind Makepiece, naturally raising the matter of the pro bono work during their conversation. They both agreed that Bill Clarkson was a bastard, but that was a given anyway, so got them nowhere. Naomi talked about her ideas about moving on, the on the spur of the moment asked her friend a question .

"Rosalind, you know I've mentioned before that I have thought about looking for another job, well I'm thinking again, or..." she hesitated, and stared into her beer glass, before looking up at her friend, "...or trying to start up on my own, perhaps with a partner. What do you know about Ivan Campion's financial background?"

"Nothing really. He gives the impression of being comfortable, nice car, pretty exotic holidays, lives in a nice house in Countess Wear. I went there once with some papers, met his wife, no kids. I believe she's a school teacher, but that's about all I know. Why? Are you thinking of asking him to join you if you decided to set up on your own? Hell of a risk for you and him. It would be lovely to tell Bill Clarkson to stick his job up his arse, though." She giggled, not quite sure how serious Naomi was about her plans.

"Well Peter and I are financially pretty secure, small mortgage, he gets bloody well paid. If I did make the break, we could manage without my salary for a while, until I could attract some clients of my own but look, don't get too excited, I'm only thinking."

"Well if you did decide on the adventure, please take me with you. I'd work for nothing until you got established, it would be exciting. I could even invest some money if that would help. That's if you want me, of course." She shot a look across the table, a look requiring immediate assurance.

Naomi reached for Rosalind's hand, squeezed it tightly. "Look love, I'm sure it would be great to have you on board although, as you've already said, the risk would be high. Anyway I'm only thinking aloud at this stage. I haven't even discussed it with Peter apart from an occasional moan, which I'm sure didn't register with him. He's too involved with his own position at work, expects to go on the board in charge of his department, once his boss retires this year." The two women were late back. The euphoria generated by their lunchtime conversation with its exciting possibilities kept both of them buoyant for the rest of the day.

Waiting to see Inspector Goddard, gave the shell-shocked Peter

Shadbolt, time to think, something he was doing a lot of these days. Every time he tried to rationalise about what he might do with the rest his life, his thoughts digressed into bitter accusations against Michael Jackson, what he regarded as his betrayal, and against that fucking woman who had blighted his life for absolutely no reason, he could understand. He knew only too well that feeling sorry for himself wasn't going to change anything. Despite that, he couldn't rid himself of the feeling that life was treating him unfairly. The bitterness worked on him like a disease eating away at his soul; a deteriorating marriage, a son who might be a homo, a boss who had sacrificed him to economic niceties, a woman in black who persecuted him for no good reason.

He needed Simone, he needed the solace of her bed. It wasn't Wednesday but he had to see Simone, to pour out his tale of woe, whatever the cost. Once he had got over this interview with Goddard, he would camp on her doorstep until she got home, or ring her on her mobile, get her to cancel whatever she was doing, tell her to come home straight away. Why wait, there was no one else in the room. He dialled her number and got a curt "yes" for his trouble. That put him off for a start, then before he had even begun to tell of his disastrous morning, Simone cut in. "Sorry Peter I can't talk now, I'll ring you after lunch."

His immediate reaction was to tell not her to bother. If she couldn't at least listen to him, then she could fuck off, but he didn't. He needed her. To fall out with Simone now would have been like cutting his last lifeline to sympathy. He switched off, ran his fingers through his already tousled hair, was about to engage in another bout of despair, when Inspector Goddard came into the room, shaking hands before sitting down at the other side of the table.

"Well Mr Shadbolt you don't seem to be having a lot of luck with our Mrs Benson do you? By the way she's in another office right now giving us a statement about the accident. Perhaps you'd like to tell me what happened, then we can decide what to do about the situation."

Peter went through his version of events. His redundancy, his anger, his carelessness, his lack of memory as to what had actually happened. He really didn't know how he had come to hit the woman, he was desperately sorry, but one thing he was adamant about, there had been no intention to harm her. He hadn't seen her anyway, only became aware of her, when he felt the bump, then knew he had hit something, or somebody. Even then he had no idea that it was Mrs Benson until he got out of the car only to see her scrambling to her feet.

The inspector thought he recognised in Peter Shadbolt a law abiding citizen, someone who would help the police if a situation demanded it, as indeed he had done over the investigation into the death of Sharon Benson, and his abortive attempts to help the girl's mother afterwards. All that aside, there was no getting away from the fact, with which both parties agreed, that he had hit the woman. Goddard hadn't read Mrs Benson's statement yet, but had heard her shouting the odds when she had arrived at the station.

"Yes I see Mr Shadbolt. I'll need you to put it all down in a statement please, then you'll be released on police bail to return as and when required." Peter's dismayed expression made him continue. "Look, the lady's not hurt from what I can see, but she'll have a medical examination to check her out. Once she's calmed down she may modify her side of events. I wouldn't worry too much if I were you. I'm sorry about the job, sometimes it seems to be a rotten world doesn't it?" He smiled and put a hand on Peter's shoulder. "Now that statement please, Mr Shadbolt."

Chapter 17.

Back home, despite the ecstatic greeting from George, he felt utterly desolate, worn out, and it wasn't lunchtime yet. Before Christmas he had his worries, but not about his job, which he thought of as safe, with great prospects for the coming year. Now here he was out of work, shocked to the core. The rest of the day spread out bleakly before him. He was agitated, at a loss to know what to do, impatient to get a call from Simone, although even that was uncertain. He knew he should have called Naomi, but he couldn't bring himself to tell her the news yet. He needed to think about how he presented the facts, both about the job and the accident, knowing how she always had to have the most minute details of things. He wasn't ready for that yet.

As usual, at times of crisis, he took the dog for a walk, not that it did much to alter his mood, the woods bleak, still dripping from the overnight rain, reminded him of that sad little girl he had found all those months ago when the world for him, at least, was brighter. As though sensing something of his master's mood the dog's behaviour was less manic than usual. When Peter called him to put on his lead on he came straight away without the usual need for repeated shouts to return. Back home he opened a can of soup, eating it while watching the news on television. He must have nodded off, because he was startled by the sound of his mobile. It was Simone returning his call, bless her.

Alright he should have told Naomi first, should have telephoned her wife with the dramatic news of his redundancy, she had a right to know after all. Why the delay? A softer reception from his lover perhaps. When his wife heard the news he expected there would be an element of blame in her reaction, and he wasn't ready to face up to that yet. A lengthy marriage often resulted in support of one party for the other in the event of a crisis, but at a price. That price often included an examination to discover whether the spouse had contributed to the crisis in question. His sacking and the accident with Mrs Benson had shattered his confidence. He had been frightened that should he ring Naomi, she would rush home and start the inquest, which in turn could well escalate into a row. He wasn't sure he could take that without saying things which he would regret later.

Simone listened, in silence, as he spilled out the facts of the day. She could get home in an hour she said, suggesting that he should go to her place and wait there, try not to worry too much, troubles shared, and all that. Peter understood only too well that he would have some explaining to do later, when he got back home again to face Naomi; what had he been doing all day, why hadn't he phoned and so on, but here and now was what mattered, and now he needed Simone. Unusually, there was no sexual element in what he needed from her, just her unadulterated, undemanding, sympathy: someone to listen to him ranting about the fates, without pressurising him for too much detail, or what he intended to do about it.

She was as good as her word, as far as timing was concerned. It wasn't often that he saw her dressed for business. In her severe business suit, she came over in a different way than his expected image of her. He himself must have looked rather dishevelled because, when she got out of the car, she stood back, looked him up and down, raised her eyebrows and shook her head slightly. "My God Peter you look like shit, you'd better come inside, I'll make you a cup of tea."

Once inside the flat, they paused, looked each other in the eyes, before falling into a strong hug, therapeutic for Peter, understanding from Simone, which lasted until she eventually broke free with a laugh. "You're crushing me to death, lover." She kissed him lightly on the lips, but no electricity was generated, his current so low that even the thought of Simone's bed, could not lift his spirits.

"What the hell happened with this woman you hit, are they charging you, was she badly hurt, what on earth happened Peter? What does Naomi think about the situation?" Somehow Simone's questions came over as sympathetic rather than inquisitorial, which was what he expected from his wife.

"I haven't told Naomi yet, she's bound to blame me in some way, then come out with list of things I should do. I need to think first before I face my dear wife." He was only too aware that he was being very unfair. Naomi would, in fact, be understanding, sympathetic, at least at first, but she wouldn't allow him to be sorry for himself. That's why he was here, wanting to feel sorry for himself, to cry on an uncritical shoulder, away from responsibility and explanation.

Simone took his hand and led him through to the sitting room, gently pushing him down into an armchair, where she put her arms round him, kissed the top of his head. "I'll go and make that tea, then you can tell me as much as you feel like doing."

Peter slumped in the chair, anger fighting with depression for dominance in his mind, head in hands, feeling like crying, feeling so very sorry for himself, knowing that he had to pull himself together before going home to face Naomi. He heard Simone coming back into the room with the tea, raised his head, made an effort to smile. He was so angry inside, he felt like kicking someone to death, maybe that stupid old bastard, Michael Jackson.

As he sipped his tea, with Simone sitting on the arm of the chair gently massaging the back of his neck, he started to talk, kept on talking for several minutes, without stopping, about his betrayal at work, his shattered career hopes, his on-off relationship with his wife, his worries about James, and of course that stalker, Mrs Benson, for whom he could no longer summon up any sympathy .at all.

Platitudes maybe, but she had to say something to make her wrecked lover feel better. The James thing is probably just a phase, even if it isn't did it really matter, they surely couldn't charge him over the collision given that the woman had been pestering him for months, he was still a young man with plenty of possibilities in the job market, and finally Naomi, well as far as that went, he had to decide for himself. Did he still have residual love for her, did he want to separate, or divorce with all the upheaval that would involve. If he did would a certain lover want a permanent arrangement. At that point she laughed, and ruffled his hair.

Her words made sense, her kiss was soft and delicious, but he couldn't bring himself to accept the obvious invitation behind it. They talked on through the afternoon until, by four o'clock, Peter had begun to feel less stressed out, the blackness had grey at the edges, even if the light at the end of the tunnel was very dim indeed. Simone came out to see him off. "I see you've still got the Volvo."

"Part of my generous severance package," he laughed grimly. His kiss goodbye was one of gratitude for her patience, although it very nearly made him turn round and take up her ready offer of sexual solace. No, he had to go and face the fireworks at home. He owed that to Naomi, and it would be difficult enough anyway explaining why he hadn't rung her, leaving it until she came home, to break the bad news.

He started up the engine ready for the off. Looking through the open window at that beautiful, if slightly anxious face, he was tempted again to say to the hell with his marriage, to go back inside, and make frantic love. His sense of duty prevailed, leaving him to drive away with a sad wave. As he watched her in his rear-view mirror standing on the pavement, waving until he turned the corner, he experienced gut-wrenching regret; all his troubles came flooding back, his coming meeting with Naomi leading the pack.

Pulling up in his drive, he saw Mrs Stackhorn coming out of her front door. He waved but she ignored him, probably would have said she hadn't seen him, not that he cared. He had far more important things to worry about than a recalcitrant neighbour. To hell with Mrs Stackhorn, how was he going to break the news to

Naomi? How was he going to explain why he hadn't rung her with the bad news earlier in the day? He fed the dog, poured himself a whisky, tried to read the Telegraph, but couldn't concentrate, found himself sighing again, cursing the fates, and yet impatient to hear the sound of Naomi's Clio arriving in the drive, so he could get it all over with.

"Got the dinner on then?"

"Would you just sit down first before you have a go at me, I've got some bad news."

"It's Charlie isn't it?' Naomi didn't sit down, instead standing over him in a display of anger. "For Christ's sake tell me what's happened to her?"

"No, there's nothing wrong with Charlie or James for that matter. Calm down. Let me pour you a drink, then I'll tell you everything."

She did sit down, did take the proffered drink. "You do like a good drama, Peter, don't you? Now will you stop fucking me about, tell me what's happened." She was tired, angry at her husband's procrastination, impatient to hear the worst.

He looked at her, sitting there on her accusing arse, demanding answers, and wondered, not for the first time, why he had married a dark-haired woman when all his life he had been attracted to blondes. Before he could start to explain the day's events the telephone rang. It was Robbie Barkworth suggesting squash. Peter didn't say anything about the job, instead making some excuse to get out of playing. He sat down again, ready for the inquisition, looked directly at his wife. "I've lost my job."

Naomi stirred uneasily in her chair, her face genuinely concerned now that she knew Peter wasn't just making a mountain out of a molehill. "Lost your job? Go on Peter let's have it, why have you lost your job?"

As various thoughts scudded across her mind, one stood out ahead of all the others. If Peter was out of work, her half-constructed ideas of leaving Bradford, Lang and Oldfield were blown to pieces. She pushed that selfish thought aside, concentrating on being sympathetic towards her husband's plight.

She listened as he went through his story in detail, understanding his anger while adding her own. When he got to the part about hitting Mrs Benson, her manner changed. "How could you not have seen the woman, for God's sake Peter?"

He sighed and threw up his hands. "I honestly don't know, but if you're implying that I was angry enough to hit her on purpose..."

"No, of course I'm not, Peter. What did that inspector say when he interviewed you. After all the woman has been harassing you for weeks, he might just have thought you had reached the end of your tether and..."

"Nice to know that my wife's support can be relied on at all times." Peter got up and poured himself another Scotch, it was going to be a long evening." Goddard was very reasonable, seemed to accept there was no intent, if you must know."

"Peter I'm sorry, really I'm sorry, didn't for a moment think you ran her down on purpose." She went over to sit on the arm of his chair, making a clumsy effort to put consoling arms round him.

She was his wife, they had been married a long time, the habit of shared problems had been established. Tonight he needed her sympathy, affection, residual maybe, but there anyway. He pulled her down onto his lap, burying his head in her breasts, while she stroked his unruly hair. They stayed like that for some time before Naomi, ever the practical one, lifted his head and kissed him. "I don't suppose you got any lunch, I'll go and put some food on."

As she walked out of the door she suddenly stopped. "Sorry, Peter, but what I don't understand is why you didn't ring me at work."

His explanation about being too embarrassed and upset, didn't ring true even to him. Naomi, whatever she really thought, let it go, continuing out to the kitchen, leaving her husband to stew in his self-pity. She would have been lying to herself if she hadn't recognised that any plans she had for breaking away from Bradford, Lang and Oldfield, and her nemesis, Bill Clarkson, were scuppered, at least for the time being. Not the time to mention her own frustrations though, was it?

Husband and wife ate, drank, and talked on, into the night. Money would not be a problem for some time, given that Peter's redundancy package amounted to nearly a year's salary, and then there was the car. Mrs Benson hadn't been hurt so neither of them could envisage a serious charge arising from the accident.

Peter would get another job easily enough, although the state of the economy would limit the number of vacancies around. By the time they decided to go up to bed, Peter was feeling better, grateful for the wifely support, guilty that his first call in the crisis had been to Simone, now surprised to find in himself, a renewed affection for Naomi.

Peter lying in bed, reading, glanced up to see Naomi coming out of their bathroom, naked, something she had not done for a very long time. She slipped under the duvet beside him seeking the warmth of his body. For once their love-making was mutually considerate and satisfying.

When Peter awoke in the night, the memory of their encounter was still strong, Naomi was still lying close. She sleepily accepted his renewed, but gentle rather than passionate caresses. It had been years since they had had sex twice in one night. Peter fell asleep, wondering if he still loved his wife after all.

Chapter 18.

The first day of unemployment for Peter was strange. He got up at the same time as usual, went through the same routine as usual, bath, shave and so on, but at breakfast, the feeling came on him that he should be getting a move on, was at once deflected by the realisation that there was nothing to be in a hurry for, which he found confusing, unsettling and unpleasant.

Naomi was solicitous, quietly making suggestions about signing on, looking for jobs but pushing nothing. When she kissed him goodbye there was affection there, sadness in her eyes. She had earlier offered to cook him egg and bacon, which he turned down with a touch of irritation at what he regarded as her slightly over- the-top attention to his needs. As he heard the front door close, he wanted to run after her, call her back, say he was sorry, hold her in his arms, but he didn't.

With Naomi gone, the day loomed long and empty. George was happily restless with his master's unexpected presence, hoping there was a walk in the changed circumstances. Peter decided that a walk would give him chance to think about what he was going to do, so the dog got his way.

Later on that first day, Peter tried to write down a plan of action, contacting people he knew in the industry, getting trade papers to look for jobs, signing on at the Job Centre Plus. It wasn't long before he got fed up with that. When he tried to read the newspaper, he couldn't concentrate for five minutes at a time, so switched to watching some quite awful day-time television, before ringing Simone to apologise for his stressed-out visit of the previous day. She was busy and, he thought, a touch dismissive, leading him to another of those unfair comparisons between the two women in his life. When he tried to ring Margaret, there was no reply. He didn't leave a message.

The day dragged on. Finally he decided to walk down to the Red Fox, only to find the pub virtually empty, apart from a few strangers sitting at tables away from the bar. Henry Robson, behind the bar, had time to chat. "Not often we see you on a weekday lunchtime, Peter."

He was not about to discuss his woes with the landlord, it was none of his business. In truth, he felt rather ashamed, a feeling that came upon him suddenly and unexpectedly. "You're right Henry, a few extra days holiday, taking it easy, thought a couple of beers might go down well. How's trade with you then?" He ordered a pint of Otter, found himself drinking it rather too quickly, too soon ready for a refill.

After two pints, Peter could have easily managed another, but it seemed somehow decadent to be drinking beer on a weekday lunchtime. What's more he knew too much beer in the middle of the day would make him sleepy later on. He had chattered to Henry about the state of the country, what a mess the government were making of things, yet that feeling of restlessness continued to plague him. After that second pint, he left the pub, still wrapped in a mist of indecision about what to do with this sudden surfeit of time on his hands.

Back home he determined to be positive, sitting down with his laptop, to work on the neglected novel. After half an hour he hadn't written one word, his imagination stifled by a massive sense of inertia. The norms of his life had been shattered and he couldn't cope with the changed circumstances. He started to watch some film on the box, which was showing for the umpteenth time, but again couldn't concentrate. He got up to make himself a cup of tea and wandered round the house looking at objects he and Naomi had acquired during their married life; the time passed slowly.

At one point he shouted at George who, unused to Peter being home on a weekday, had been seeking attention to a degree that got on his master's nerves. The dog slunk away leaving Peter to feel regret well up in his stomach like antacid. He had to follow the animal into the kitchen where he had retreated to his basket, to pat him apologetically.

He woke up to the sound of Naomi's car tyres crunching on the drive shortly followed by the sound of her key in the front door. He hadn't meant to fall asleep: felt wretched now, realised, with a guilty start, that he hadn't done anything useful about the place, like starting on the evening meal. Now he readied himself for Naomi's onslaught. He hurried out into the hall, kissed her cold cheek, before taking away her coat. She stood back for a few seconds looking at her husband's crumpled face, understanding without being told, something of what he must have been going through during the day.

Her day had not been very enjoyable either, but it was Peter who must have suffered more. She was strong enough to make any allowances that might be required, put her own problems to one side, for this evening at least.

Naomi got some chops out of the freezer, while Peter peeled potatoes. The atmosphere between then was subdued to say the least, yet without animosity. By the time they sat down to eat, they had managed to start a mutually sympathetic exchange, helped by a bottle of Chardonnay. He asked what devious schemes Bill Clarkson had been hatching, she asked how he had spent his day, cautiously throwing in suggestions about going to the job centre and the best ways to look for work.

There had been no sign of James, not even to be fed, until about ten o'clock when the front door crashed open, followed by noises from the kitchen indicating a search for food, then the noisy retreat up stairs. Peter looked across at his wife. "He still seems to be in the land of the living then."

What he meant was that perhaps they should discuss their son, the possibility that he was gay. Naomi switched off the television, reading her husband's mind she said,. "What does it matter if he is gay, Peter, as long as he's happy."

"He doesn't show much sign of being happy though does he?"

Peter might have said a lot more .He didn't for one moment like the idea that his son might be homosexual, couldn't rid himself of those long embedded ideas that homo sexuality was an unnatural phenomenon. However he was very well aware that Naomi's thoughts on the subject were far more liberal, so he kept his views to himself.

"Peter you've said what you think about the gay scene often enough, but this is our son we're talking about now; you might want to modify those ideas in the circumstances."

Peter gave an exasperated little sigh, threw his hands up. "Do you think I don't know that. He'll always have my support whatever he decides he is."

"And your love Peter." She got up, intending to offer some slight show of affection, hand on shoulder, kiss, or whatever, but the look on her husband's face caused her to change her mind, so instead she collected the coffee cups, before making her way out to the kitchen.

The next day dawned. The prospect for Peter was for a day similar to the previous one, long and probably tedious. In fact the call at the police station was a welcome break in that tedium.

"And have you seen or heard from Mrs Benson since the accident, Mr Shadbolt?" Whatever the outcome of today's meeting, it was a relief to be away from his immediate environs, talking to an outsider, for a brief time at least.

"No inspector, I haven't seen her at all since then." He had been tempted to add "Thank God.'' but in the circumstances thought better of it.

"Given all that went on before with the lady, and your tolerance of her somewhat unusual behaviour, brought on by her sad loss, it has been decided to charge you with the lesser offence of careless driving. You will still have to go to court, but a fine and points on your license will be the probable outcome." Goddard was acting the part of an understanding policeman, dealing with a normally upright citizen in the community, who had momentarily gone astray, and doing it well.

"That's a relief. I hope she's still showing no ill effects from the bump." It's true, Peter was relieved, yet it was only now that he realised that he hadn't been worried either way. The shock of his dismissal had been the much greater worry, that was the one that had left him in this state of daily inertia.

"Yes she appears to be completely unhurt, although it's only fair to warn you that she still believes there's something about her daughter's death, that you haven't told her. I've done my level best to assure her that that isn't the case, and to warn her, as gently as possible, that she must leave you in peace. Any luck on the job front Mr Shadbolt?"

The interview was over. Peter walked out of the police station with no idea of how he was going to spend the rest of the day. He had already taken the dog for a walk, his attempts to restart his neglected novel, had founded after a couple of paragraphs. He couldn't remember what he had written earlier, or even the names of some of his characters. The only thing he had to look forward to was his Wednesday afternoon visit to see Simone. After their last meeting he wondered how that would go, especially as his mood was little improved since then. One thing had surprised him was when Naomi had said in the morning, "I suppose you're off to your writing class tomorrow are you?"

There was something about the look she gave him as she posed the question. In view of her lack of interest in his writing in the past, the question had come as a surprise, but then he put it down to her being solicitous about his welfare in general. Any thought that she might suspect he was doing anything other on his Wednesday afternoons than learning how to create his masterpiece, was dismissed before it even took root.

Back home Peter decided to ring the job centre to enquire about signing on for unemployment benefit. He had never been unemployed before, but if he was entitled to some kind of benefit, then he might as well apply, take up some of the time that was now so abundantly available. To his surprise he was told that he could apply there and then over the telephone for job seekers' allowance, although he would be asked to attend the job centre for a follow up interview, which was also arranged, there and then, for the following Friday.

He felt somewhat better after that, a sense of taking action, no matter how slight. George had another walk, longer than usual, the Red Fox had his custom for a short while, then he watched some of that awful day time television. In a better frame of mind, he determined to surprise Naomi by having the evening meal ready and cooking, by the time she got home.

Chapter 19.

When she first arrived, college life had been a breath of fresh air for Charlie, giving her the chance to blossom, away from the stifling atmosphere of her family home. At least, that's what she would have said if anyone had asked. At first she did feel a touch of home sickness, missed the cut and thrust of life of family life, but all that soon passed as she morphed quickly into the college scene, and the hectic pace involved. She found that there was a huge range of activities taking place with something new, and different happening almost every day. There were sporting events, concerts and recitals, public lectures, hops, gigs, plays, dance performances, exhibitions, and so on.

She was glad she had chosen Josephine Baker College, the newest college in the university, only having opened in 2006. Everything still had that air of comfortable newness, yet in the background there was the history of the university itself and Durham as a place. The en suite rooms were of a high standard, and she liked the idea of self-catering.

The college bar was always teeming with students ready to meet new people from their own college, and from other colleges, paying visits. That's how she had met Rupert, at first impressed by his confident charm, and the fact, she had to admit, that he was apparently well-heeled enough to give her a good time. Christmas with her family had revealed an invidious comparison between him and her father, which dimmed her enthusiasm, once she was back in Durham. There was more to life that owning a sporty BMW, and being the first to buy a round of drinks. She had noticed a reaction against Rupert from some of her new friends, which appeared to support her own changed feelings towards the boy.

Life was hectic, with or without Rupert, but his constant presence began to feel like a restriction on her freedom of action. He showed signs of irritable jealousy if she talked too long with any other male animal. She got the impression that by keeping her well topped up with alcohol each evening when they went out, he could assume a role of protector, when the booze began to have an effect. Added to which, she was easy prey to his sexual demands, once she was tired and inebriated.

One evening she had arranged to meet Rupert in the college bar at seven o'clock. It was teeming, as usual, with thirsty undergraduates, all eager to get their alcohol fix. A hand on her shoulder. She turned to find Phillip grinning at her, pint of beer clutched in his fist. "Thought any more about it Charlie?"

Actually she hadn't thought any more about it, because the theatre club was just one of the many opportunities that had been thrust her way, when she first arrived at college, none of which she had yet taken up; the excitement of the social scene had been quite enough to keep her busy thus far.

She remembered when she met Phillip for the first time thinking he was attractive, but that was before Rupert came on the scene, sweeping her off her feet with all that he could offer. "Drink," he offered, and scuttled off to get her a glass of white wine, thinking that now was his chance to get a convert to his club. His club, that's how he thought of it, anything else at college was imposition on his real purpose in life and that included his degree course in Russian and Italian, which had seemed cool at the time. He had his As, found languages a natural, although Russian was a new challenge, and one he had neglected badly in his first two years, the theatre bug possessing him and his time, to an exorbitant degree.

"Hello sweetie, you look gorgeous, want a drink pet." Rupert had arrived like a sudden rain squall on a sunny day, pushing his way through the throng, as though he had some special right to occupy the bar.

"Thanks, but Phillip's fighting his way to the bar to get me a glass of wine." Inwardly resigned to a relationship that was beginning to wear thin, she accepted his kiss, smiling at his less than friendly frown.

"Who the fuck is Phillip? Anyway sweetie we can't wait I've booked a table for supper at the Tranto, that Italian place in town. We really don't want to be late, they might let our table go, it's bloody popular I can tell you." He took hold of her arm possessively, in an attempt to hurry her along. A shadow of annoyance clouded Charlie's face as she shrugged out of his grip.

"We can't just go like that when someone's kind enough to fight the mob to get me a drink. The Tranto will just have to wait." At that moment Phillip arrived with her wine. "Great, thanks, do you know Rupert, my boyfriend?"

All the while they were being pushed one way or another by newcomers shouldering their way through to the bar, the noise was deafening. "Hello Phillip, great to meet you, sorry we can't stop, just on our way into town, bit of supper." It suddenly came to Charlie that now was the time to make some sort of point, a small assertion of her independence as it were. She put her hand on Rupert's arm.

"Look lover, do you mind if we don't go into town tonight, I'm a bit bushed and I should anyway make a start on an essay that is long overdue." Rupert's face expressed his anger only too clearly. Phillip looked on, faintly amused by the coming storm. Charlie sipped at her wine, still smiling her apologies, determined to carry on making that point.

"For fuck's sake Charlie, the Tranto, don't you know what a job I had getting a booking, best fucking place for miles around." He took her arm again in a further attempt at physical coercion, but once more she shrugged out of his grip.

"Sorry Rupert. What's all the fuss anyway, it's only a restaurant." Then turning away from Rupert towards the other man, she said, " Tell me something about this theatre club then Phillip." She was still smiling, although her question to Phillip must have appeared dismissive to Rupert. He wasn't used to being given, what amounted to a brush off. His petulance rose swiftly to the surface. "You ungrateful bitch, I'm sure I can find another bird who would jump at the chance of a meal at Tranto's." He turned sharply away, pushing his way through the mob, making for the exit. He hadn't meant to show such anger, but he felt put down in Phillip's presence, forced to react to Charlie's show of independence. Even before he reached the door, he recognised how pathetic and immature his outburst had been, but by then it was too late. There was no turning back without losing even more face, and he wasn't going to do that. To Rupert the evening was a setback, but he was confident that he would be able to buy his way back into Charlie's favours, the next time they met. Apologies and treats was all that would be needed.

As the two of them watched Rupert striding towards the exit, Charlie made a little grimace, shrugged her shoulders. "Don't think he's too pleased do you?" She sipped her wine, listened to Phillip going on about the theatre club, while her thoughts dwelt on Rupert's over-the-top reaction: perhaps aware that the end of their relationship had arrived.

As the evening wore on and the white wine continued to flow, Charlie was glad she had turned down the trip into town. She found Phillip's ease of manner charming, his enthusiasm for the theatre quite beguiling. He explained that what he was doing at university was just practice for when he started out on his real career. What he did was to download plays off the internet to suit the number of players he had at his disposal at any one time. He often opted for farce on the grounds that even if the actors weren't up to much, the sight of their fellow students making fools of themselves, made for good audience response. "I've made a few short films as well,. although that's more difficult to find a structure with a real meaning."

"So what are you rehearsing for now Phillip? It's my shout by the way, I can't let you buy me wine all evening." He handed over his pint mug with another of his engaging smiles. As Charlie elbowed her way to the bar, she was already thinking that she might have found a sudden enthusiasm for theatre. It also crossed her mind to wonder whether this theatre fanatic already had a girl friend or not. She was amazed at how quickly her loyalties appeared to be switching, but then she was hard-headed enough to recognise that she had been looking for an excuse to ditch Rupert anyway. She wasn't a romantic by nature, but as she fought her way to the bar her heart rate indicated a certain excitement at the evening's turn of events.

"It's a farce called 'Off the Hook' by someone called Derek Benfield. Okay, you've never heard of him, well neither had I, but it's the kind a silly romp that goes down well, not too demanding on the actors as far as getting their lines right. They just need to know the gist of the plot, say roughly the right thing, and we're away. The audience will love it." It was hot in the bar. Phillip took out a grubby looking handkerchief to wipe his sweaty face, grinning his enthusiasm at Charlie. "Complete bore aren't I? What about you, what turns you on?"

Charlie found out that her new friend played squash, so they agreed to meet up for a game the next day. The evening rushed by, becoming pleasantly hazy as the alcohol took effect, not that there was anything new in that sensation. Phillip took her back to her room. Apart from a soft kiss, he made no predatory moves. Was she disappointed, or was it refreshing to find a bloke that didn't want to get in her knickers the first time they met? In all truth she wasn't sure, but she was sure that she was looking forward to seeing him again, even if it was only on the squash court.

She had no idea what time it was. The loud knocking on her door had to be dealt with, or her head would split in two. Charlie shook her head, blearily rubbed her eyes, before dragging on her jeans and a tee shirt, and staggering over to remonstrate with the intruder. If she had thought about it, she might have known it would be Rupert, and there he was. With a deep intake of breath, hoping this wouldn't take long, she opened the door wide, gestured him inside.

She yawned and dodged aside, as Rupert made a clumsy attempt to kiss her. "You look as though you had a good evening, anyway."

"It was okay thanks."

Not full of his usual confidence, indeed looking decidedly sheepish, Rupert made a few false starts, before finally blurting out what he had come to say. "Look sweetie, I was out of order last night, bit upset about the Tranto booking, and that, I'm sorry. Can we just forget it, and by the way I didn't take anyone else."

"That's a pity Rupert because I think you and I should call it a day." Apology and humble pie turned, in a flash, to anger.

"What the fuck does that mean, call it a day? You can't dump me over one stupid incident. You're my fucking bird." His initial bland expression had changed into an angry grimace, to go with his furious words. Charlie sighed, spread her hands, moved a step towards him. She knew he was hurting, but she had gone this far, had to complete the execution.

"I'm sorry Rupert, it's nothing to do with last night, I want us to split. We've had some good times, but now I'm sorry, but it's over." His face distorted with fury, Rupert spat out.

"You fucking bitch, you can't just walk out on me after all the money I've spent on you, all the attention I've paid you. We're a couple, you can't do it." She was frightened by the violence of his reaction, frightened to say much more in case it angered him further. "I'm sorry Rupert," she repeated, "but there it is."

The man looked shocked, uncertain what to do next, just couldn't believe this bitch had the fucking nerve to throw him over, it wasn't on. His anger blotted out reason. Charlie, ready for further verbal recriminations, was totally taken by surprise when Rupert took a wild swing at her, his fist glancing off her cheek. Dazed, she staggered, falling over as the back of her knees hit the edge of the bed. The next thing she knew, Rupert was leaning over her, tears in his eyes. "Charlie I'm so sorry, I would never hurt you, it was an accident, really an accident."

She wasn't hurt to any degree, but the display of violence had shocked her to the core. After a moment or two, while she gathered her senses, she pushed herself up from the bed. Any feelings of guilt she might have harboured about ditching the guy were pushed aside by her own anger, she went to the door, stood there holding it open. "That rather shows you in your true colours Rupert, don't get your own way and you lash out. Now just piss off out of my sight, and out of my life. You haven't heard the last of this you bastard." She was trembling in fear, and rage.

Rupert started to slink out of the room, stopping halfway to plead his case and make further apologies. Charlie didn't listen, slamming the door on him with a sense of relief. She couldn't believe that he would have reacted like that.

Her first thought was to go and see one of the college counsellors to report the assault, but then, standing under the consoling shower, she changed her mind. The blow was more shocking than damaging. She didn't fancy the repercussions that would follow an accusation of violence. After her shower she looked at her face in the mirror. There was red mark where Rupert's fist had caught her that glancing blow, a bruise would no doubt follow, but still she decided against taking matters further. She couldn't bother with the furore that would inevitably follow..

As she finished dressing, she remembered that she was due to meet Phil, who had promised to take her to see a rehearsal of his play, before their game of squash. She had been looking forward to it, and to seeing Phil again. Now in the aftermath of the spat with Rupert, she was left with a sense of unease. She hated quarrelling with people; it always left her with a distasteful sense of regret, no matter who had been at fault. That's how she felt now, yet she decided to keep the date, hoping her mood would improve with the change of scene.

Chapter 20.

Another Wednesday, another visit to Norfolk Street. "I hope you've perked up from the last time you were here." Simone answered his welcoming kiss with equal fervour. Impatiently they made their way into the bedroom and undressed. Simone broke away from their naked embrace saying that she must go to the bathroom, she needed a pee. She went into the en suite leaving the door open behind her. Peter waited a few seconds, before following her. As he leaned against the doorpost, already in a state of arousal, the sight of a naked women sitting on the toilet caused his blood to boil even further. Simone just grinned, finished what she had come for, dabbed at herself, washed her hands before coming over to where he stood by the door, pressing herself against him, her hand between their bodies taking a firm grip on his stalk.

She hadn't objected to her lover's prurient interest; in fact, him standing there watching her piss, had rather excited her. Now the two of them fell in a tangled heap on the bed, both eager to a degree that would result in an early culmination. Later they would make more studied love, taking their time and pleasing their partner, but their first fuck had to be dealt with straight away, as a matter of extreme emergency.

Simone pulled the duvet over them where they lay sweaty and satiated. As usual she was reluctant to let Peter doze off, as he was wont to do, after a bout of sexual athletics. She leant over him, brushed bedraggled hair from his face and kissed him gently on the forehead. "Well, lover, back to my original question before I got diverted by your randy attentions. How are things working out, the job and the phantom woman in black and all your other troubles?"

The sex and the quiet solicitous attention were the kind of therapy that Peter needed, indeed relished. Naomi had been kind and considerate, yet behind her all her actions, he felt, was a practical imperative. He had a family to maintain, he should get on with doing something about his situation, whereas here in Simone's bed, he was under no pressure, or at least not the sort his mind was focussing on right then. He explained about his meeting with Inspector Goddard, mentioned his forthcoming visit to the job centre, and then felt rather inadequate in explaining that boredom was his worst enemy.

"I guarantee that you won't be bored for the next half hour," Simone moved to straddle him, a position she liked because she could work on her lover for some time without him coming, whereas if he was leading the action there was always the fear that his impatience would get the better of him.

Peter equally loved his prone position, with its continuous temptation to push her off, take control himself. He loved to caress her breasts as they dangled over him, nipples engorged, loved to move his hands around her bottom and the rest of her slim supple body, and most of all loved it when he felt her shudder into orgasm. He was impatient today and after that first shiver of culmination he pushed her aside and took his own pleasure thrusting roughly in to her from behind, demonstrating, perhaps his overriding anger with the world.

His kiss as they lay back on the bed was one of gratitude. Once again he wondered whether he ought to say to hell with it, give up his marriage to live instead with this gloriously sexy woman, permanently, but that was a huge step. Life didn't revolve entirely around sex. He was realistic enough to recognise that the excitement of his illicit meetings with Simone would not be the same if they were together all the time.

Simone eventually slid off the bed with the announced intention of going to make them a cup of tea. As she walked across the bedroom floor to gather her robe from the hook on the door the sight of her slim naked form caused a renewed flutter of Peter's libido, despite all the action that had so recently taken place on those crumpled sheets.

When she returned, was snuggling down affectionately at his side, she started to tell him about her goings on, about her weekend with the children, about her successes in her business world. That brought home to him what an absolutely selfish bastard he was, not only this afternoon either. His own worries and his sexual lust had been his only concerns. Other people had their problems too. He was using Simone, and although she seemed to accept the situation without any problem, he could see now in his post coital rationality, that he was using her as a form of release therapy, call it what you will. How could he ever think of ditching this woman, who he was sure he loved, or was it what she gave him that he loved?

Much too big a problem to deal with now. He extricated himself from his lover's arms to take a shower and dress. He wanted to be home well before Naomi to make a start on the evening meal. Reluctantly he tore himself away from the lingering kiss that Simone bestowed as he made for the door.

As he left the block, Peter glanced up and down the street half thinking perhaps to see his black nemesis hovering around. He hadn't seen the woman since the accident but the memory of her suddenly appearing in all sorts of places had stuck with him. There was no sign of her, which was something, but nevertheless his mood had slumped. The euphoria of sex with Simone evaporated quickly. The thought of seeing Naomi and making polite conversation, after the way he had spent his afternoon, made him uneasy to say the least That combined with the worry about his job situation, accounted for a distinct change of mood.

He was later than usual, so when he got home, he hurried into the kitchen to start peeling potatoes, and search in the deep freeze for something for supper. George wanted his food too. He had just put the dog's bowl down, when he heard the front door go. As he turned to face Naomi, he raised a smile, hoping there were no signs on his face or person to suggest how he had spent the afternoon. "Hello Peter, had a creative afternoon while the workers have been at the coal face? You look rather flushed, what have you been doing to exert yourself?"

Was that innuendo. Peter sometimes suspected that Naomi knew he was having an affair. Her words as she came into the kitchen might well have confirmed his suspicion. He ran his hand through his hair, mopped theatrically at his brow. "Just slaving over a hot stove you know. How was your day with the Clarkson beast?"

She sighed and shrugged her shoulders. "Much the same, not that Bill was there today. We did have some excitement though. Rosalind has had a win on the lottery. She's talking already about handing in her notice, telling Bill what he can do with his job."

She paused to look across the kitchen table at her husband. Was there something in his demeanour this evening, it was Wednesday after all, the day of suspicion as she might have called it, that spoke of guilt, she wasn't sure. Anyway she was tired. Such thought were put to one side in favour of the proffered gin and tonic. Then a civilised dinner, without James, followed by an evening watching television, a normal happily married couple you might say.

Their domestic evening was interrupted at one point by the ringing of the telephone. It was Robbie Barkworth again, still after that game of squash. Peter's first reaction was to put him off, then he realised that sooner or later he would have to tell his friends and relations about his redundancy. A beer after a game of squash might just be the time to start, so he agreed a time two days hence.

Thursday was the day of his interview at the job centre, so despite feeling the unpleasant aftermath of another night of bad dreams, a regular occurrence these days. He got up at the same time as Naomi, dressed smartly in suit and tie, not knowing what to expect, feeling downbeat about anything good coming out of his visit.

He had been right to have low expectation and wasted his time bothering about appearance; he might just as well have gone in his gardening clothes. They were busy, a production line of form filling. It took twenty minutes or so for him to be told that because of the terms of his severance package he would not be able to claim job seeker's allowance for some weeks, but they would very kindly allow him national insurance credits in the meantime. The chances of finding a job at his management level were slight, they said, but offered some practical advice about how to search for jobs, and prepare for interviews.

When he came out of the job centre it was raining hard.

Well that fits into the general pattern of my life at the moment, he thought to himself.

He started to run towards the car park, then thought what the hell, and slowed down to a walk; he was soaked anyway, why get out of breath as well. In the car he used a handkerchief to mop his face and hair. He hadn't expected anything from his interview, yet the deadening process had left him deeply depressed.

George was glad to see him, depressed or not, but he found it hard to respond to the animal's show of affection. He switched the kettle on to boil while he went upstairs to get out of his wet clothes. Then he sat morosely at the kitchen table drinking his tea, reading the headlines in the morning paper, political corruption, economic chaos, wars and murders, just the news to lift his spirits.

Finally he came to a decision: couldn't mope about all day. So despite having had one soaking, he found his boots and dressed in rainproof gear and loaded up a delighted George in the car, before driving over to Woodbury Common. There would be nobody stupid enough to be around on a day like this, which suited him fine. The therapy, if indeed therapy it was, involved hard walking, going nowhere, seeking solace in the mechanical process of moving one foot after the other.

The rain continued to fall, then intermittent lightening and loud thunder claps added to the natural drama. Even with his rain gear the water was beginning to penetrate. The dog's initial enthusiasm had waned, now he skulked along miserably close to his master's heels.

Despite of the discomfort, Peter kept going, determined to bring about a change in his mind set through exhaustion, if nothing else. He might have carried on further but for the sudden appearance of a figure out of some kind of ruined building. That triggered a déjà vu-like memory of a few weeks earlier, when there had been a similar confrontation on the common, probably the same mad man. This man was dishevelled in the extreme, wild eyes, hair all over the place, shouting something Peter couldn't make out. It might have happened before, but still the shock was enough to drive man and dog back to the shelter of the car.

Squash was alright, he enjoyed it, but the less than subtle way he violently attacked the ball left him easy prey to Robbie's more controlled play. "Seemed like you wanted to take it out on someone tonight, Peter, none of your usual guile on show."

Peter took a long swig at his beer. "You're quite right, Robbie. Look I might as well get it off my chest, I've been made redundant, out of work, that's me." He grinned rather stupidly at his friend's surprise.

It was something of a relief to tell someone other than his lover and, of course Naomi, about his redundancy. "The bastards screwed me over, something terrible, amalgamated two departments, which meant my job was scrapped. From what I could see, my boss, Michael Jackson, didn't put up much of a fight, he was going anyway, so why should he care. No discussion, generous financial package, nothing to be done, my job no longer exists so they are able to make me redundant." It all came out in a rush, a torrent of indignant words.

"I'm really very sorry, Peter, but are you sure you really are redundant. I mean the work is still there isn't it. Perhaps you could take them to a tribunal. Go and get some advice, CAB or somewhere like that, see what they say about it."

Robbie's face showed his concern, but inwardly was there a vague feeling of relief. Not to be articulated of course, but in the current state of the economy to feel secure was a gift, a vantage point, from which to look down and sympathise with those less fortunate. There would be no redundancy for doctors particularly in his practice, given the pressure for their services that existed.

They sat for a while not speaking, although Robbie had obviously been thinking. "Tell you what, Peter, why don't you and Naomi come round for a spot of supper sometime soon? I'll get Wendy to give Naomi a ring and fix a date." A token maybe, but a kind thought nevertheless.

Peter got home to find Naomi sitting at the kitchen table with a pile of papers spread out before her. He kissed the top of her head as he passed by to make himself a cup of coffee. "Want one?" Naomi blew air out through her mouth, hunched up her shoulders, looked tired, nodded her acceptance of the offer.

"Good game? How was old Robbie then, still making his fortune, tending the sick?"

"You work too hard for that firm of yours. When are they going to offer you a partnership?"

"I wish. Trouble is that sod Clarkson always has to have these deadlines. Every Monday, at the weekly briefing, we have to set a time scale for our cases, then he's always pressurising us to reduce those times. You just can't work like that in the legal world. We deal with human beings, circumstances are changing all the time. As far as Clarkson is concerned the quicker we process, the quicker the billing; I tell you Peter I'm fucking fed up with it." She slammed some of the paper she had been working on down on the table to illustrate her frustration. Peter put her coffee down in front of her, massaged her shoulders.

"What about looking around, see what other openings there are in the market place?" If only he knew. Now was not the time to raise the possibility of going to alone. so she contented herself by replying with a deep sigh.

"Oh yes, you out of work, kids at university and college, economic meltdown, just the time to go looking for another job." Her momentary anger subsided at once. "Sorry love, but I'm just fed up with working for that bastard of a man. Anyway I'm done for this evening, let's go in the other room, watch the news, not that that's likely to cheer us up."

Later in bed they lay side by side in the dark, neither asleep, both knowing the other was awake, each concerned with their own worries, not in a state of mind to offer comfort to their spouse. Despite the mutual words of sympathy and support earlier in the evening there remained a sort of resentment between them, not to be expressed in words, a selfish philosophy summarised perhaps by the view that I've got enough problems of my own without worrying about yours, very unfair, hardly connubial but that's how it was on that sleepless night. Sleepless that is until both of them eventually dropped off, still segregated at the extreme sides of their large bed.

Peter didn't want to go to the dinner party. There were only going to be six of them with Murray and Sue Clark completing the guest list. They would all be sympathetic, full of helpful suggestions, stories of other folk who had found that losing a job had been the best thing that ever happened to them.

As it was nobody mentioned anything about his redundancy until right at the end of the meal. He began to hope the evening would pass without discussion of his plight, but then the ever-concerned Wendy, in the middle of pouring coffee, suddenly said, "Have you thought of voluntary work while you're looking around, Peter? I mean boredom must be a problem, you have to keep your brain ticking over don't you." There was something of a hiatus round the table while everyone considered what they should contribute, but it was left to Peter to respond, however reluctantly.

He lied, he hoped convincingly, explaining that having time to himself was a great relief, a break in the rat race, a chance to think about his future, chance to do some writing and so on, all offered with a smile, to show his unconcerned confidence to his unconvinced fellow guests.

He drank some coffee, hoped he had diverted attention away from himself, but Wendy, always concerned for other people, wasn't going to let it go at that. "Well I'm pleased to hear that Peter, but if you do get bored, there are organisations that can put you in touch with charities and so on who are looking for volunteers, Involve for instance, just type 'Involve' and search, you'll be surprised what they can offer, all sorts, bound to be something you would enjoy."

Naomi, recognising that Peter was already gritting his teeth, tried to change the subject back to MP's expenses, something that they had been discussing earlier, but Wendy hadn't finished yet. She was entirely well meaning, always full of suggestions to improve people's lives but, as Robbie knew from experience, was sometimes like a dog with a bone, when the bone really didn't want to be chewed, any more. He offered brandy as a diversion, but that didn't stop her.

"Please don't think I'm trying to interfere, but I know how terrible it must be to find yourself out of work. Keeping yourself occupied is important, you know."

He was a guest, Wendy was only being kind, but Peter had had enough. "Wendy do you mind if we change the subject, I'm not interested in the third bloody sector as you call it. I need to work for a living, not ponce-about helping the less fortunate among us, worthy though that may be." He couldn't stop now he had started. "You are a lovely lady, Wendy, but do you know how fucking annoying it is being preached at, about what someone should do, or not do. I'll deal with my own problems in my own time and I ..."

He ran out of steam, shook his head, spread his hands wide in apology. "Sorry love." Peter had spoken with undue force, for which he was immediately sorry. Again there was silence round the table for a few leaden moments, then everyone began to talk at once, each hoping to gloss over Peter's outburst, pretending that nothing had happened, while Wendy looked at her husband in mute appeal.

Peter got to his feet. "Look Wendy that was unforgiveable, I'm so sorry, put it down to nervous tension or something. Anyway now I've ruined your dinner party, I think it's best if I go. Murray would you mind giving Naomi a lift home? Don't want her evening spoiled because of my rudeness."

Of course Naomi didn't accept the offer. She hugged Wendy tightly, as they said their good byes. Sue and Murray stayed on, no doubt to speculate on Peter's state of mind. Robbie saw then to the car, squeezed Peter's shoulder, as he continued to offer apologies.

Naomi drove home, it was her turn anyway. There was silence in the car, weighted silence, silence heavy with repercussion, sympathy laced with an element of criticism The atmosphere was heavy with the need for words to be said to move them on to a new position, to have it out, as it were.

Peter sat, dull with distress, his eyes closed for most of the journey until, as they turned into their driveway, he suddenly sat up straight, turned round in his seat, to look back over his shoulder. He looked as though he had seen a ghost. "She was there, across the road, that damned woman, come to haunt me some more." He opened the door before the car had come to a halt, scrambling out and running back up the drive, out onto the road.

It was very dark, but Naomi could just about make out the form of her husband in the road, running first one way, then another. After locking the car, she put the key into the front door, with a feeling of exasperation with her husband's behaviour this evening, and indeed ever since the redundancy blow. She had seen no one lurking at the side of the road. While her sympathy instincts were strong, she had had enough of her spouse for one night, she just wanted to go to bed.

She left the front door open, delaying going upstairs to make herself a cup of coffee, then sitting at the kitchen table until her overwrought husband came back into the house. She looked up quizzically. "Well did you find your woman in black?"

"You might find it funny Naomi, but I could have sworn I saw her. She's often before stood just there across the road, so it wouldn't be unusual. No, I didn't find her, I must have been wrong on this occasion." He shook his head, sighed, then sat down opposite his wife. He felt sorry for himself, yet at the same time disgusted at his reactions over the evening as a whole. What on earth was happening to him? "OK love, I'm sorry, made a fool of myself, no excuses. I'll put things right with Wendy, give her a call. You fancy a nightcap?"

There had been too many nightcaps of late. She shook her head, said she was off to bed. Peter went to pour himself a large Scotch, then changed his mind, following her upstairs. He could have spent a couple of hours with the whisky bottle, but had enough sense to realise that in the morning a headache would be of no help when he came to putting his mind to the next stage of looking for a job. It was another night of two people lying side by side awake for some time before sleep overtook them.

Chapter 21.

"You don't seem to find that stuff difficult, James ...isn't it?"

They were in the college eating hall filled as usual with a mass of hungry students, when a young girl from his group joined him in the queue. He recognised her, of course, but being approached so directly took him by surprise, leaving him tongue-tied, as he usually was in the presence of girls. He shrugged his shoulders and managed a smile as he responded, "Well I wouldn't say that."

She seemed a pleasant enough girl. He couldn't just ignore her, although thinking of what to say next was a worry. She solved his problem for him by continuing to chat. "Where's your mate, Greg, today then? You two seem to be great pals. I'm Kirsty by the way. Here let me get that, then perhaps you wouldn't mind answering me a few questions about that lecture we had this morning." James docilely followed the girl to a nearby table, where they sat down with their coffee. She chattered on, apparently unconcerned by the lack of response from James. For his part he found he was enjoying being with a good-looking girl, but somehow uneasy as he fleetingly thought about his relationship with Greg.

Despite all he had been up to in bed with his friend, he still didn't regard himself as gay, ridiculous as that would seem to a third party. His libido could still be stirred by a sexy female, and this Kirsty was certainly that. Before he met Greg all his sexual fantasies had featured girls and not boys. His reverie was interrupted by a direct question from Kirsty. "You got a girlfriend then?" Once again her forthrightness put him into a state of confusion.

"Well I, well no, actually, not at the moment." When he looked at her smiling face beneath a rather untidy shock of fair curls, it occurred to him that she might just be gently teasing him.

She produced a throaty little laugh which James found very sexy. "It's alright don't look so worried I'm not trying to pick you up. You're a serious boy though, James, aren't you? Relax a bit, let it all hang out. Anyway I must go, nice to chat, see you in class." She was off before James could think of anything to say, witty or otherwise.

That brief interlude had stirred his senses though, made him think again about his sexuality. Girls had always been a mystery to him with their monthly bleeding, their constant attention to appearance. Charlie had always bullied him for as long as he could remember, mocking his immaturity, so full of confidence herself. And yet girls had always been the object of his early desires, pictures in girly magazines had excited him, sexual fantasies involving girls had accompanied his masturbatory sessions, so why the hell had he ended up in a sexual relationship with a bloke.

As he drained the dregs of his coffee, he glanced up to see Greg standing over by the self-service counter looking at him in a strange way. When he saw that James had clocked his presence, he came over to the table and sat down banging his drink on the table hard. "What's with the bird then?" He seemed to James, to be mad about something.

"That was Kirsty, she's in our class, you must have seen her."

"Right, so what did she want?" he interrogated. Greg was most definitely out of sorts this morning. James was frowning now. Surely his mate couldn't be jealous could he?

"What the fuck are you getting so uptight about Greg? All she wanted was some advice about that last session in class."

"Nothing, nothing at all." Greg got up without finishing his coffee, striding off with a muttered, "See you in class."

He really must be jealous concluded James, how bloody ridiculous, a bloke jealous of another bloke speaking to a girl. He and Greg had been living close to each other for the last few weeks, with him staying overnight at Greg's place on several occasions. They had begun to recognise each other's moods. Today had been the first time one or the other of them had reacted in the way Greg had just done.

James collected his work papers, then made his way out of the hall, having decided on the spur of the moment to go home tonight, whatever the alternatives on offer, maybe renew his acquaintance with his parents. He knew about his dad being chucked out of his job, felt rather guilty about the lack of interest he had shown, even recognising his mother's accusation about him treating the house as a hotel as being pretty justified. For once, he determined he would show some familial interest.

In class, Greg appeared back to his normal self, making the class laugh with crass comments, giving all the appearance of being in a good mood. As they walked together afterwards, Kirsty came running after them, inserted herself between them taking an arm on either side. "What about that bit of tuition you promised me, James, you still up for it?"

"Sorry Kirsty, me and James have already arranged to study together tonight." He wasn't smiling, seemed fidgety about the girl's arm being entwined with his.

"You're both in for a disappointment then. I promised my mum I would be in the house for dinner, some special family thing."

Greg broke away from the other two, turned to face James, ignoring Kirsty. "Got piazzas in didn't I. For Christ's sake James, we've had this arranged for days." The look on his face was one of angry exasperation.

James shrugged his shoulders. "Sorry mate, have to think of the old folks sometimes."

"Fuck you then." Greg strode off. Kirsty who had been a curious spectator to this spat, raised her eyebrows, James looked embarrassed.

"Bit over the top wasn't it. You two aren't, well I mean you're not gay are you James?"

Now that was a question James had rather she hadn't asked. He turned his eyes away from the retreating Greg, to concentrate on

Kirsty. Once again he was aware of a strong feeling of attraction towards this girl, tight jeans showing off a neat bottom, beneath her loose jacket and tank top the definite hint of a bulge when she moved in a certain way. There was more to it than that though, gestures, movements, way of speaking, femininity, he supposed it was, which he found charming.

"Of course not, just good mates, he's a bit moody at times that's all." He wondered how she would react if she knew his sexual exploits with Greg over the last few weeks, hardly to be considered as hetro, that's for sure. Perhaps he was genuinely bisexual, because he was only too conscious of the direction in which his libido was pointing him, right now.

"Are you really stuck with dinner at home."

He said "yes" and didn't know why. Perhaps he saw anything else as a betrayal of his mate. He still needed a friend whatever his feelings towards the opposite sex.

"Okay, but I'm going to hold you to your promise on that work." Her smile, for the first time, was less confident. James couldn't remember making any promises but he was glad of the opportunity that provided.

"Could get away after dinner for a bit. Quick drink at the Imperial or something."

James was in for a surprise that evening that had nothing at all to do with homework. They had one drink, then Kirsty suggested they go for a drive. It turned out that she was in fact eighteen, apparently had fluffed her first year and was taking the course over again. She had passed her driving test, had her mother's car for the evening. James may have felt he was being swept along but rather enjoyed the precocity of his new friend. He had always found it difficult to talk to girls in any depth yet it was becoming easier talking to Kirsty as time went on. The prospect of a drive, and all that might presage, was having a profound effect on his libido. As soon as they got in the car, he was possessed by rampant tumescence, not helped by the passionate kiss they exchanged. What had started as a gentle lip contact, quickly became a passionate exchange which left them both out of breath.

Kirsty broke away. "Let's find somewhere a little less public shall we?"

As they drove out of the car park, James, even in the midst of his lust, thought about Greg and the blatant betrayal that this episode, represented. True he had told Greg he didn't think he was really gay, yet his actions had belied his words on many occasions. Kirsty, following a sign post to a small village, the name of which he didn't recognise, turned off the main road. After driving along the narrow lane for a couple of miles, she pulled into a field entrance, and turned off the engine.

The sound of the engine had barely faded away, before they were at it like a couple of ferrets. Kirsty suggested they might be more comfortable in the back seat.

James was amazed that it was all so easy, this sex thing with girls. This particular girl didn't appear to mind where his hands went. It wasn't long before he fumbled the button on her jeans, and pulled down the zip. He encountered no underclothes.

When his exploring fingers touched hair, he paused at the sheer enormity of what was happening, but not for long. As he went further and deeper, Kirsty made small animal-like sounds.

There was aroma of sexual musk in the air, that nearly drove James mad.

She had already uncovered him, and as he moved with unbridled impatience to get on top of her, his whole body shuddered. She heard him say through clenched teeth, "'Fucking hell, fucking bloody hell."

She could feel his hot emission on her belly, but ignoring that, she attempted to soothe the slumped body of her would-be lover. She kissed him with understanding tenderness, brushing the damp hair away from his forehead. "It doesn't matter, James, these things happen, there'll be other times for you." James felt frustrated and embarrassed in equal degree. His very first sexual encounter with a girl, and he had blown it something terrible.

"I'm so sorry Kirsty, what a plonker you've landed yourself with."

"James, my sweet, is that the first time you've been with a girl, or at least tried to?" She couldn't help a soft giggle, before quickly resuming her comforting manner.

Chapter 22.

One lunch time, while having lunch with Rosalind, Naomi was provided with yet another reason for dissatisfaction with her employer in general and with Bill Clarkson in particular. "What do you mean sacked, what on earth have you done to bring that about Ivan?" Ivan had asked if they minded him joining them for their lunchtime visit to the pub. The two women guessed that something might be up, because Ivan usually brought sandwiches, hurrying through them at his desk.

"The recession, falling-off of business, last in first out. Bill was his usual smiling self telling me how good I was, how easily I would find another position. Do you know, he even went on about me starting my own business, all tongue-in-cheek of course. He knows something about my financial position, what it costs to set up in practice, but he made it all sound like he was worried about my future, devastated at having to let me go." Ivan was obviously very upset by the turn of affairs, not far from tears, emotional hurt at what was happening to him.

Naomi and Rosalind made sympathetic noises, but the guy was quite clearly in a state of shock. It was difficult to know what to say from a practical point of view. Not surprisingly, Naomi thought back to her own thoughts in the recent past, although things were different now. It would be marvellous to join with Ivan in starting up their own business, but with a husband out of work for three months, and the capital demands such a move would make, she quickly put the idea to one side.

"Is it absolutely out of the question Ivan, I mean setting up on your own, a bank loan perhaps, interest rates are low." Rosalind had been quiet for a while, but now she intervened with a show of animation, trying to encourage their depressed colleague. She looked at Naomi, and Naomi knew straight away what she was thinking.

"I'm afraid Ivan's right Rosalind, now's not the time. Who's going to want a new solicitor in times like these and as for a loan, the chances of getting one, for what after all would be a gamble, are non-existent, whatever the theoretical interest rates. Any company willing to make either of us a loan in these circumstances would want to charge exorbitant rates. Then there's security, I could guess what Peter would say if I went home and said I wanted to put the house up as collateral."

"I've got some money." Rosalind said. The other two were silent, was there a fluttering of hope in Ivan's mind, a vague stirring of excitement creeping into Naomi's brain. "Quite a lot actually. I wouldn't mind investing it in a promising new business. Mind you I would want to be a business partner, my money, you two providing the expertise, and you'd have on office manager thrown in."

"Rosalind that's very sweet of you, but there's no way I could let you take such a risk," Naomi said, but what she was really thinking was different from what she had just said. Despite the risk, the huge difficulties, was there a chance?.

"Yes Naomi's right, and Rosemary will want me to start looking for a job..." but Ivan too, was feeling the pull of a dream.

"Tell you what," Rosalind suggested, "why don't we all meet up at my place one evening, have a look at some costings: no harm in talking is there?"

They left it at that. All of them walked out of the pub with their minds in various degrees of doubt, and turmoil. They had gone so far as to fix a date to accept Rosalind's invitation, which she turned into one for supper. In the meantime, they would carry out some research, cost of premises, what other expenditure would be involved, cost of insurance, and so on. Another consideration vital to any such scheme was, what clients might come over to them if the impossible did happen.

Naomi returned home, still excited by the lunchtime possibilities, trying to curb her enthusiasm for what was as yet only the germ of a idea. How she would love to tell Bill Clarkson he could stuff his job. She didn't immediately seek out Peter because she wanted to check her contract of employment, which she kept in a filing cabinet in the kitchen. She remembered about the three months' notice, but was bothered that there might be some restrictive clause setting a time limit for her setting up business with another firm.

"You're back then?" Peter came into the kitchen with a drink in his hand, looking bleary-eyed and untidy, as he often did these days. "Good day?" He asked without enthusiasm. Naomi's exuberance collapsed, yet there was an act to be played out between man and wife. For the time being she would play her part.

"OK," she said, with a dredged up smile, "what about you, any luck on the job front?"

Naomi was only too aware that her husband was having a rotten time. Seeing him in his constant depressed state made it difficult for her to see him in the way he was before his redundancy. She tried to make allowances, but couldn't help thinking, from time to time, that the man had given up. My God, she chided herself, my level of tolerance is beginning to run low.

"What do you fucking think, there are no bloody jobs out there are there." For the last three months his days had been bleak with boredom; that in itself was deadening even without the constant disappointments. On top of everything else, he found he resented the normality of Naomi going off to work each day. When she started to grumble about her boss, he sometimes got angry, couldn't help reacting by saying she at least she had a job. During those three months or more since he had been out of work, Peter had applied for jobs both in his area of expertise and outside, and had only had one interview, which turned out to be a dead loss. The court case had come and gone, guilty of careless driving, a fine and costs but he had not seen the lady in black since then, which was one tiny consolation, almost worth the legal hassle.

Days spent in desultory housework, taking George for gloomy walks, watching daytime television, had left him in a wretched state of mind. Even when he went round to Simone's flat he found it difficult to lift his spirits. He worried that she was getting a bit fed up with him. He dragged his thoughts back to the here and now. "What do you want to eat then? I could go and get fish and chips."

She nodded, watched him grab his coat, and slouch out of the door. If anything came of this thing with Ivan and Rosalind, she was in for a time and a half selling the idea to Peter. On the way to collect their dinner, Peter called in at the Red Fox, but none of his drinking pals were there; it was still early. He chatted inconsequentially with Henry for the time it took to drown a pint of Otter, then hurried out to complete his mission. Peter didn't like himself as he was now. It was one thing having come to that conclusion, but it was quite another matter doing something about it. The nights were drawing out he noticed as he trudged back home Even the thought of Spring did nothing to lift his spirits.

The night of the meal at Rosalind's, Naomi told Peter it was a sort of out-of-hours seminar, leaving him to fend for himself. Even though he spent his time with Naomi being pretty bloody and unfair, he still missed her when she wasn't there. The evenings were better than the days, perhaps because he had someone to listen to his moaning. He put a lasagne in the microwave, taking it through to the living room to watch the news after pouring himself a Scotch. For some reason he went over to the window and looked out, before starting his meal; it was still quite light. His heart gave a jump. There she was, not standing and staring as she used to, do but walking past. The other night, the night of the dinner at Robbie's, perhaps the sighting had not been a figment of his imagination after all; the woman was still haunting him.

Without knowing what on earth he was going to do, he pulled on his shoes, grabbed his coat and went out into the road to start walking in the direction Mrs Benson had been heading. She was still in sight, moving quite slowly. Without any plan, not even understanding why the hell he was doing it, he started to follow her. Eventually she arrived at the Blandford estate, a mixed area of council houses and private property that had once all been council owned.

She walked up the path of one of the smaller semi-detached houses with an unkempt garden, before putting her key in the door. She had not looked round once in the time he had been following her. Now here he was outside the house of his nemesis, not knowing why he was here, or what he was going to do, if anything. He walked on for several yards past the woman's house, still undecided about his course of action.

There was anger inside of him, the need to blame someone for his present condition. Although he was rational enough to realise that the woman had little to do with his problems, his irrational self saw her as a symbol of his troubles. Before he had found that sad little girl, everything had been fine. He felt guilty about putting blame on her mother, but he had done all he could for her, now she was persecuting him for no good reason.

He walked back the way he had come, turned into the path to the Benson house. He knocked, there was a pause before she came to the door. The deadpan expression on her face as she saw who it was, didn't change one iota. She stood back a little way, inviting Peter to step into the narrow hallway. She appeared unsurprised by his presence. "Mrs Benson will you please leave me alone. I have troubles of my own right now and you harassing me doesn't improve matters. I've said many times how sorry I am about your daughter, but there is nothing more I can tell you that would help."

"I don't know what you mean Mr Shadbolt." Her blank face looked at him where he stood just inside the door, as though what she saw was of no interest to her whatsoever.

"Come off it, you know exactly what I mean. Only a short while ago you were outside my house, surely you don't deny it." He wanted to kick some reaction out of this miserable woman, get her to admit that what she was doing was wrong, pointless.

"I may have walked past your house, not a restricted area is it?"

Her words were spoken with total lack of expression, as dead pan as her face.

"What about the other night do you deny..." He stopped, feeling powerless in the face of the woman's total lack of response. "I must warn you that if you pester me again, I will go to the police."

"You do as you think fit, Mr Shadbolt. Now please leave me alone or it might be me who goes to the police." She moved towards him leaving him no option but to back out through the door, which she then closed firmly after him, leaving him stranded on the door step, angry and exasperated and no farther forward

Peter walked home disconsolately. It had been a stupid idea anyway. He was deeply depressed. The thought that he might expect to see that woman in black again hanging round his house, did nothing to improve his mood He saw her as a kind of Jonah putting a blight on his life. To talk about a symbol of his downfall sounded dramatic if said out loud, but that's how it seemed to him, that evening.

Naomi wasn't home yet, there was only George to offer him unconditional tail-wagging affection. He found his whisky glass, emptied the contents in one stressful swig, his lasagne was cold. He couldn't be bothered to reheat it, yet despite his dejection, he was hungry. In the kitchen he cut himself a couple of slices of bread, a lump of cheese, adding butter, before returning to the living room, where he refilled his glass. It was dark now.

As he sat munching on his bread and cheese, gazing out into the night, his depression weighed on him like a black cloud. Somewhere among the dark thoughts that milled around in his mind was one that told him he was pathetic, that he should get up and do something, not right at that moment, but with his life in general. For the moment the whisky seemed a better option.

"What on earth are you sitting there in the dark for?" The sudden flood of light startled him, he must have fallen asleep.

"What's this mess, why didn't you eat your dinner?" She picked up the plate with the sad-looking lasagne. Her meeting had been exciting in its possibilities. She wanted to tell someone all about it, but Peter didn't look like he was in the mood for that sort of excitement this evening, so she kept quiet.

The next morning, Naomi had already left for work, Peter was still in his dressing gown as he often was in the mornings lately, when the front doorbell rang. On the doorstep was Inspector Goddard with another plain-clothes man.

"Sorry to disturb you so early Mr Shadbolt but..." Peter ushered the two men inside into the living room and invited them to sit down. There was a deadly seriousness about Goddard's manner this morning, which augured more trouble.

"Mr Shadbolt, I'm sorry to have to tell you that poor Mrs Benson is dead, her neighbour had a door key, went to check that she was alright, found her upstairs lying on her bed. She'd swallowed a large number of sleeping pills."

Peter felt relief, guilt that he felt relief, guilt that he might have done more to help the woman, slight unease at the close proximity of her death to his encounter with her last night. "That is sad news, inspector, but I'm not sure how I can help."

"Well you probably can't, but there is just one slight mystery. The neighbour I spoke of said Mrs Benson had a visitor yesterday evening. She didn't have many visitors, so I understand, so the visit stood out, you might say. Forgive me asking Mr Shadbolt, but have you spoken to Mrs Benson or seen her recently?"

Peter could have explained exactly what had happened yesterday and that would have been that. Instead, inexplicably, he lied. "No I haven't seen the lady since the court case, that in itself has been a bit of a relief as you can imagine."

He looked the inspector in the eye and lied, and he had no idea why, unless he thought his visit had driven her to an extreme action, and he didn't want to get implicated. It wouldn't do the woman any good now, him getting involved. Peter would have liked the interview to have ended then. He smiled in a way that should have indicated *'that's it then is it?'* but the inspector showed no sign of getting out of his chair.

"Sorry to keep you Mr Shadbolt, but there was one other rather odd thing about the lady's death, nothing to do with you of course but, when the neighbour found her, there was a pillow over her face. Strange thing for her to have done don't you think?"

Peter shrugged his shoulders but the inspector appeared to be waiting for a reply. Did the man suspect there may have been someone else involved in the suicide, did he suspect some kind of foul play. "I'm not sure why you're asking me inspector. I mean, do you think there is more to it than simple suicide?"

"No, we're certain about the cause of death, the pills without doubt." He scratched his head, exchanged glances with his sergeant, who had not said a word during the whole time the policemen had been there. "No, but the pillow you see, why the pillow? We wondered if someone else had been there that's all."

Did they know something that they weren't saying, had he been seen at the woman's house, now was the time to come clean, to clear the air. Peter sighed, ran his hands through his uncombed hair. "I'm sorry inspector, I lied, I did see the woman last night, she was hanging about outside my house. I followed her home to ask her to keep away from me."

The sergeant's pen was busy writing in his notebook.

"I see, perhaps you could explain to us why you found it necessary to lie." His tone was a shade or two less polite, than previously.

"Look inspector, that woman has blighted my life for several months, I just didn't want to get involved that's all." He sighed, raising his hands in supplication. He went on to tell his visitors the full facts.

Finally they rose to take their leave. "We could have been off sooner, Mr Shadbolt, if you had told us the truth in the first place. For what's it's worth I have some sympathy with you. Having said that, I don't take kindly to being obstructed in my work. I will need you to come to the station to make a formal statement, but I believe what you have told us now, to be the truth."

The look the inspector gave Peter as they left the house was one that spoke of human frailty, and how that made his life more difficult.

The underlying feeling that possessed Peter, when the

policemen had gone, was one of incredulity that he could have been so stupid. There had been nothing to gain by lying. He couldn't, for the life of him, see why he had done it. Just one more sign that his life was falling apart. His depression was back deeper than ever, there was no light at the end of the tunnel.

There would probably be no repercussions from his stupid lie Nevertheless, he saw it as another failure of judgement. He didn't like the person he was becoming, he was beginning to lose self-respect. Moreover he was angry, angry with Naomi for being so patient, angry with inanimate objects when they wouldn't do what they were told, angry with checkout girls for no reason at all, angry with the stupid contestants on the 'Weakest Link', but most of all angry with himself for not finding a job, for not thinking of something productive to do as an alternative.

He went upstairs to shower and dress. What was he going to do today, besides taking the very grateful dog for his usual long walk. Then to the police station to make his statement, get it over with, suffer the embarrassment of having acted so stupidly and then what? All this time on his hands: he should have used it to write his opus, but he had hardly added a chapter to his so-called novel over the whole time since his redundancy.

It was warm in the late April sunshine as he walked into town, not that Spring meant much to him in his present state of mind. He walked because that used up time, how pathetic was that. He had to take action, do something to take him out of this infernal rut.

At the police station Goddard, whom he had come to think of almost as a friend, wasn't there, but the statement was straightforward enough, although the sergeant who saw him asked him, as he was leaving the station, to let them know if he decided to go away anywhere; that made him feel like a criminal, served himself right though for lying in the first place.

Chapter 23.

After lectures, a couple of days after James's escapade with Kirsty, Greg came over, all smiles. "Dad's away again for the night, how about staying over at mine, get some beers in, watch the footy?"

"Not tonight Greg, I've got too much work on. I need these 'A's if I'm going to get into a decent university."

His friend shrugged, seemed to accept the excuse, then his mood changed to one of anger. He grabbed the front of James's shirt. "You seeing that girl, James?"

"Me and Kirsty did have a drink together the other night, but I wouldn't call it 'seeing', we're just mates like you and I are mates." He smiled, slowly pulling his shirt out of Greg's grip.

"I thought we were a bit more than that James," Greg was still scowling. "What was all that sex about, bit more than mates, if you ask me."

James tried to keep things relaxed, still smiling. "Think perhaps we were getting a bit intense, bit serious, you know Greg, let's cool off for a while shall we?"

"You fucking bastard, little tart wiggled her arse at you, and you dump me just like that. You don't know who you are James or what you are, that's your trouble. Wonder what that bird would say if I told her you've been shagging me, for weeks." The venom in his expression was so fierce that James feared that he might actually follow up his threat to talk to Kirsty, which would mean his embryonic relationship with her would come to a very abrupt end.

"Look Greg I told you all along I wasn't gay. I enjoyed being mates but the other is something else and I..."

"Fuck you James, that sucks. Do you really think we can carry on being mates when what you were really looking for was a bit of cunt. You go and chase your piece of tail, but don't come whining back to me when you find out you're on the wrong track." He turned away, striding angrily across the open space towards the classroom.

James had enjoyed Greg's friendship, quite apart from their times in bed, but somehow now the break had happened, he didn't really mind, time to move on. Kirsty seemed interested, and so was he, certain now where his sexual orientation lay. He still worried though that Greg might do the dirty on him, tell her about the extent of their relationship; and what that would do for his chances. He couldn't imagine she would be thrilled by the thought that her boyfriend had been shagging a bloke before she came along.

That was for the future. Today the sun was shining literally, and metaphorically. It was with a sense of a burden lifted, that he got ready for his next class.

Naomi had done it, made the decision to leave Bradford, Lang and Oldfield and now she was facing the music. "What the fuck is this Naomi?" Bill Clarkson was holding her letter of resignation in his hand. She stood up and came from behind her desk to face his wrath. "It's exactly what it says on the tin Bill, I'm leaving the firm." Clarkson's face was red, steam almost coming out of his ears, as Naomi described it later. "But why the hell, you're doing well, part of the team, great prospects, I just don't get it. I've just had to let Ivan go now you drop me in it, by walking out on me." She kept her calm, no point in a row.

"That's not quite how I saw things, Bill. In my opinion my chances of a partnership were remote. Your approach to management borders on the bullying, sometimes; I just think I'm better off out of it, that's all. You've got three months to look around for someone else; in the present market conditions you should have plenty of choice."

Her boss calmed down, then turned on his usual smile. "Can't we work something out here Naomi, bit more money, some kind of plan for the future. Come on now, let's schedule a meeting to discuss a package that will suit you; you're far too valuable to this firm to let go, always been highly appreciated you know, what do you say?" His charm had often worked before, not particularly with Naomi, but with other people in the practice." He waved her letter in the air, making a mock move to tear it in half.

"Sorry Bill I've made up my mind, there's nothing you can say that will change it I'm afraid." She spread her hands in a 'that's it' gesture. The smile disappeared, the anger returned.

Naomi got the impression that he would have loved to say *'well fuck you then'* but instead, he asked coldly, "Where will you go? No one's taking on staff in the present market. I suppose you must have something in mind or else you wouldn't burn your boats here."

"Ivan and I are going to set up our own practice." If he had been angry before, now he was apoplectic.

"And just where will you get your clients from may I ask. You needn't think you're going to have access to files in this office. In the circumstances, my dear," heavy sarcasm on the 'my dear', "I must ask you to clear your desk. Oh, you'll be paid all that you're entitled to including your three months' notice, but any attempt at poaching has to be nipped in the bud. And that goes for your friend Ivan the terrible as well."

Chapter 24.

Of course he wouldn't have gone if he had known what had taken place between Naomi and Clarkson that morning, but he didn't, so he went. By mid-morning, on a bright day, Peter decided on the spur of the moment to go away; he didn't know where, but in twenty minutes flat, he had crammed some casual clothes in a bag with his shaving gear, grabbed his laptop, told George to get in the car and driven away.

Perhaps he might visit his mother, see how she was coping with that bastard Gerald, or maybe go and see Margaret and Sebastian in Kent. He hadn't made his mind up, although the direction was East, East along the M5. As he drove he felt a certain sense of exhilaration, he was doing something instead of moping around the house. It seemed to him, as he drove along, that that was all that mattered for the time being.

When he reached Bristol, he made another on the spur of the moment decision. Instead of heading on East, he saw the signpost to Wales and followed it onto the M4, over the graceful bridge, through the toll-booth and into another country.

A vision of Snowdonia came into his mind, he had been there before, a wild land where he could seek relief in violent exercise, climbing mountains, tiring George out with long walks. Then as he drove towards Cardiff, he began to see signposts that gave him other ideas. When he stopped to let George out for a run, he consulted his road map, concluded that there were plenty of wild places farther south, which would suit his mood. He saw names he recognised like the Forest of Dean, the Black Mountains, the Brecon Beacons, all of which provided a sense of excited expectation, a desire to explore.

Just before he reached Newport he turned North, heading towards Abergavenny. As he patted George where he sat, quietly patient, in the passenger seat, he was beginning to think of where he would stay for his first night in Wales. His long-term intention was to try and rent a cottage of some sort, deep in the wilds from where he could go out each day, and maybe exorcise some of his ghosts, but for that first night a pub would have to do. As he got close to Abergavenny he saw a place, the Butcher's Arms. There hadn't been many pubs along the road, so he decided this one would have to do. He let George out of the car and the two of them made their way through the front door of the pub. There were men drinking in the dimly-lit bar, only men, and, when Peter entered, the chatter died like a sudden lull in a storm. He was watched, you might almost say stared at, as he moved to the bar. "Looking for a room for the night, wondered if you have accommodation here."

"Dogs," the grim-faced landlord nodded down at George sitting at Peter's feet. "Don't allow dogs sir. We don't do rooms anyway." He didn't seem at all anxious to get any business from this intruder. The noise in the room had gradually returned to the original volume now. Peter had to speak up to make himself heard.

"I was actually looking for a cottage in the long-term, a cottage to rent somewhere in the Brecon Beacons area."

"Sorry sir, suggest you try the Park Rangers, I believe they rent cottages in the Park."

Peter had been in need of something to eat and drink, but didn't fancy staying in that unwelcome atmosphere. There would be other pubs. He turned to go when a man sitting at a table near the bar shouted at the landlord. "Tell him about Max Williams, Dai."

The man behind the bar shrugged. "Right then, there is this farmer over near Govilon, rents a cottage out, early in season so you should be okay." The man who had shouted got up and came over to the bar.

"Not far from Abergavenny, is Govilon. When you get to the

village drive through, and about a mile on the other side you should see a sign 'Manor Farm', not that it's much of a manor mind, but he has that cottage for rent, see."

Peter thanked the man, and made to leave the pub. As he went out through the door, another voice called out, "Look out for Megan, she eats Englishmen for breakfast." The whole bar thought that was funny. Peter left to the sound of loud laughter sounding in his ears. He wondered what was so funny, but at least he had a lead to go on, somewhere to stay.

The directions he had been given were accurate, and despite it getting dark he found the Manor Farm sign. Driving up the rutted track, he arrived in front of the farmhouse, a rather unprepossessing building, crammed between two barns. There was no one around, so he knocked loudly on the front door. No reply, he knocked again, still without answer. He was beginning to think about trying again for a pub to spend the night, when George gave a sharp short bark. He turned to see a man at the entrance to one of the barns.

"You looking for someone?"

In the semi darkness Peter could just make out that the speaker was a big man dressed in rough working clothes. "Yes I was looking for Mr Williams. I was told that you, if you're Mr Williams, had a cottage to let, and I'm interested in renting one."

"Who told you that then?" Before Peter could explain he went on. "Too early in the season, place not ready yet, sorry, they should have warned you about that." He walked over to where Peter stood outside the front door and bent down to pat George. "Nice old dog you've got there."

"Well thanks anyway, can you recommend a local pub that would put me up for the night, one that takes dogs?"

The man blew out his cheeks. "Plenty of places in Abergavenny, I reckon, don't know about the dog though." He patted George again. "Tell you what, if you don't mind it being a bit rough I can open up the cottage, at least a roof over your head for the night, isn't it. Wait on there, I'll get the key."

He disappeared into the farm house, leaving Peter on the

doorstep. He was back quickly, leading the way past the barn, down a path through what appeared to be an orchard, trees around anyway, until they reached a building, the details of which were hard to make out in the darkness. Key in the door, slight grating sound as it swung open. The light switched on revealed an interior rather better than expected. The door opened straight onto the living room, which was furnished comfortably from what Peter could see, if a little chintzy. There was a musty, unlived-in smell but that was only to be expected. "Big for one bloke but can't help that, three bedrooms upstairs. You settle yourself in and I'll go and get some sheets and such." His manner was friendly, almost jovial.

As Peter explored the kitchen, then the upstairs, he began to think he had struck lucky. Williams came back with sheets and a duvet. "Place hasn't been aired, but there's no damp so you should be alright. Bit of pie for you, don't expect you've brought supplies with you, tea, milk and sugar, best I can do, shops in Govilon tomorrow. Television works, or it did the last time I tried. Right then, sleep well, talk about rent in the morning." Off he went like a man who had made a decision, and was pleased about it.

The thought was retrospective, but it suddenly struck Peter that he must be completely bonkers, taking off like that on a whim. Naomi would have been home long before now, she would be wondering where he was. He dialled her on his mobile and got the expected "where the hell are you Peter." It was a difficult telephone conversation because he couldn't really explain what had made him decide to do a runner. His refusal to tell her where he was, infuriated her. She was still shouting at him, when he rang off promising to ring tomorrow.

Naomi had not told him that now there were two of them out of work, deeming it not a sensible thing to do to someone who had apparently gone completely mad. Peter put down a bowl of water for George, tore off a hunk of the pie for him which he wolfed down with greedy relish. It struck him, watching the disappearing act with the pie, that dogs didn't appear to ever suffer from indigestion.

He explored the kitchen, made himself a pot of tea, switched on the television for company, without the contents registering to any degree. Then, for the first time since he had set out on his odyssey, ruminated on what it was all about. What on earth could he gain by secreting himself away in the wilds, what was he going to do with his time, was it fair on his family? He must have been tired because he suddenly jerked awake to find it was nearly midnight. He let George out, made up a bed in the best of the rooms upstairs. After a quick wash he dropped off to sleep far more quickly than had been happening at home, over the last few months.

Not having drawn the curtains the night before, Peter was woken early by sunlight streaming in through the window. He felt remarkably refreshed, and as far as he could remember his sleep had not been disturbed by any stress dreams. He was only half awake but thought he detected the low sound of voices coming from downstairs.

He dragged himself out of bed, rubbed some focus into his bleary eyes and covered his nakedness with a dressing gown. As he made his way down the steep stairs the voice became louder. Its owner appeared to be talking to George. When he entered the kitchen, he discovered a buxom young girl wearing jeans and a tee-shirt with the words 'I love Megan' emblazoned across her ample chest, talking to George.

"Bread, butter and homemade jam," she smiled, "Dad said you arrived quite late, going to need some breakfast, I thought. Like your dog, very friendly, what's his name?" She spread her hands over the food she had brought where it lay on the table, as of making an offering to the needy or like a magician about to demonstrate a trick.

Peter rubbed his eyes, blinked a couple of times. He hadn't expected breakfast to be delivered by a nubile young female, smiling in the morning sunshine and making a fuss of his dog. From her tee-shirt he gathered that this must be Megan. His mind went back to the pub the previous evening and the shout, "Look out for Megan," followed by the noisy laughter. Now he could understand the male prurience behind the laughter. She was certainly a fine specimen of young womanhood, apparently bursting with health and life.

"George, his name's George," Peter bent down to pat the animal, who had come across to him, deigning to desert his new friend for a moments or two. "You must be Megan," he said, nodding in the direction of the girl's chest. His libido was already hard at work in the face of this bright young sex-goddess.

"Got it in one, " she said, looking down her front, pulling the tee-shirt tight, accentuating her curves a degree or so.

"Thanks for the food, didn't expect this kind of service, thought you Welsh were supposed to be a bit unwelcoming."

"Just a one-off, new visitor and all that. What's your name then? Why're you here. Early in the season isn't it, and all on your own-y-o." She made a pot of tea, pushed the toaster across the table and handed him the bread knife.

Peter obediently sliced the loaf. "Name's Peter Shadbolt, just needed a break that's all and this is a beautiful part of the country from what I've heard."

"Not running away from the law are you? That would be exciting." She smiled again. Peter couldn't make out why this sexy young girl was being so friendly. Perhaps they didn't get many visitors on Manor Farm. He had thought of her as a girl but revision became necessary, when there was a scrabbling at the door before it burst open to reveal two small children, one boy and one girl both around the age of four or five.

"Mummy what are you doing in here? We couldn't find you, we want some breakfast." When they saw Peter they stopped in their tracks, staring at him wide eyed, suddenly silenced by the discovery of a stranger in the cottage.

"Hello kids, this is Mr Shadbolt, come to stay with us for a bit, say hello to him." Neither of the children spoke. She put her hand on each of their heads, ruffling their hair. "This is Gwendolen, Gwen most of the time, and this little scruff here is David. Come on kids let's go and get some breakfast shall we?"

The two children scampered out, followed by their mother, who shrugged, offered a smile over her shoulder, and was gone. Peter's first thoughts were that she must have been very young when she had the kids, she didn't look more than eighteen herself.

Anyway George had liked them, all of them, producing a full display of tail wagging and hand licking. Peter had some toast with the very tasty homemade jam, then went up to shave. When he found the water was hot, he took a leisurely life-giving shower, emerging dripping and rejuvenated. The day seemed to him fresh with possibilities. He felt a frisson of excitement, as he looked forward to exploring his new surroundings, both on the farm and in the locality.

All that, despite telling himself that he should be thinking about his motives for this retreat from his normal life, about what he was going to say to Naomi when he rang her tonight. There were things to be done first, shopping, food for himself and the dog, an exploration of where he was, a general settling in, all of which he looked forward to.

Peter remembered from his arrival last night that the nearest village, Govilon was not far from the farm, so he decided to walk in to have a look around. He was entranced by the panoramic views of the countryside, which he took to be part of the Brecon Beacons National Park: hills on the skyline, a river running close to the village which he later discovered was the Usk; there was even a canal with a wharf. He noted the village had a shop, but the day was bright and warm, so shopping would have to wait.

He set off to the delight of George, to walk at first along the canal and then branching off into the countryside. He felt exhilarated, a sense of freedom, sheer enjoyment with the day and his surroundings. Eventually despite his exuberance he began to tire, and meandered back to the village. A pint of beer in the local pub, what better way to finish his first morning in paradise?

"Are dogs alright in here?"

The man looked up from reading his paper behind the bar. There were no other customers. "No problem sir, what can I get you?" He smiled, more welcoming than the landlord Peter had encountered yesterday, then drew a pint of bitter with friendly relish.

"Quiet today," offered Peter, taking a draft of his beer.

"Might be few in later but you know, round here, weekday lunchtime is not a popular time." He pulled a face. "Not that any time these days is particularly popular. A waste opening, half the time, don't know why I bother. It'll pick up once the season starts, I suppose, but then they'll all go back home and I'll be back to this."

"Beautiful spot, at least you have that to be grateful for."

"Can't live on the scenery though can you?" the man sighed, running his hand through his sparse hair. That's what you're here for I expect, what is it walking, fishing, cycling?"

"Just a break, nothing specific, although I am looking forward to exploring the countryside." He took another swig at his ale, pleasantly surprised by the landlord's willingness to chat. "I'm staying at Manor Farm, just up the road, one of Max Williams' cottages. I expect you know him."

"Yes we know old Max. Have you met the rest of the family?" For some reason he seemed amused by his own question.

"Well I've met Megan, and her children, but not their father."

The landlord's smile broadened. "Quite a girl is our Megan. You won't meet the kids' father because he isn't around, always been a mystery that has, who was the daddy. Some say that ...well never mind what some say, I'm not one to gossip."

Peter left it at that, finished his beer, before walking back towards the farm to collect the car, not wanting to carry his supplies all the way back to the cottage. As he entered the vicinity of the farmhouse and the barns, he heard a screech of laughter and turning the corner found Max Williams and his daughter engaged in some form of horseplay among a stack of hay bales. When the pair saw him, they stopped fooling about, looked at each other rather sheepishly before standing up and coming towards him. "You alright Mr Shadbolt? Just larking about that's all."

Peter remembered the landlord stopping half way through his

talk about Megan and it crossed his mind that perhaps he had been going to say something else about the children's father. Could it be that village gossip might suggest that the father could be someone closely connected to the farm?

Chapter 25.

James had been coming home for meals more frequently of late. "Where's Dad then?" He had not deigned to be in for a meal the previous evening, so tonight was the first time he had noticed the absence of his father.

"Your father," Naomi emphasised the words, "has gone away for a while, says he needs a break from his family." She felt bitter. Here she was trying to establish her own enterprise, with all the hassle that that entailed, and her dear husband, whose support, and indeed help, she could have done with, had buggered off, God knows where.

The impending co-operation between herself and Ivan had yet to get off the ground, he was still working out his notice with Bradford, Lang and Oldfield, although he half-expected to be given the same short shift as Bill had doled out to her. Indeed one of her worries was that Rosemary Campion had expressed fear about the plan for independence, which appeared to have weakened Ivan's resolve to some extent. The fact that there were no jobs available with local practices countered, that to some degree. Nevertheless Naomi needed support herself, and now her bloody husband had gone on safari.

"He hasn't left you Mum has he? Where's he gone, anyway?" James had been going through a stage of what felt like a rebirth. He hated that he had let Greg down but felt relief in his heart of hearts, happy confirmation that he wasn't gay. Kirsty appeared to like him, not just because of his expertise with Physics. She had not teased him about their first abortive sexual encounter, and he had another date lined up for Saturday. This thing with his parents, if it was a thing at all, was a nuisance. He didn't want to get involved in family squabbles just now.

"Not as far as I know, James, but for some reason he won't tell me where he is, promised to ring again tonight. You want something to eat do you? Nice of you to drop by this evening." She smiled despite her words, James grinned back. In actual fact, she very much welcomed her son's company, even if it was only for the short time it took him to eat his food, although this evening, for once, he appeared ready to talk, rather than scooting straight upstairs to await the call that dinner was ready.

Naomi starting to get the meal ready, half-turned towards her son to ask "Where's Greg these days?"

"We've split Mum. I'm seeing this girl, Kirsty she's called."

Naomi laughed inside; James wasn't gay after all, despite all Peter's worries and he wasn't here to get the news. The telephone rang.

"You better speak to your son, I'm in the middle of cooking."

"Where are you Dad?" Evasion, monosyllabic exchanges, she grabbed the phone.

"This isn't funny Peter, where the fuck are you?" On the point of telling him that she had left her job and was embarking on her own risky enterprise, she decided against. Fuck him, if she was on her own then so be it, let the sod play his games, she had a life of her own to lead and could manage quite well, thank you, without the support of an errant husband.

"Peter tell you what, you ring me when you're prepared to tell me where you are, and what's going on. Until then don't bother calling me." She rang off, and in the aftermath of her anger, she began to wonder if her suspicions, aroused by that blue letter, were coming to fruition. Perhaps that was why Peter was being so secretive.

"That went well." They both laughed. It struck Naomi that her son had re-joined the human race, that girl must be having a good effect on him.

Peter had had more success with a call he made earlier. This being a Wednesday, he had to let Simone know why he wouldn't be round that afternoon. At first she had been a bit shirty, she could have worked on, if she had known he wasn't coming. Then she began to sound interested, when he explained where he was, quite excited when he invited her down to his country idyll for the weekend. She couldn't get away on Friday, she said, but would leave early Saturday morning. That was why he was standing in the area allotted to car parking in the Manor farm yard. Simone had phoned him to say she expected to be with him in about twenty minutes. Megan was busy round the barns, but took time out to come over to speak to him.

"You look as though you're waiting for something Mr Shadbolt, or someone."

"Yes I am expecting someone, hope that will be alright with your Dad," On the spur of the moment, without knowing why he added. "It's my wife actually, just for the weekend." Perhaps, he thought, that was the easiest way to explain his visitor without stirring up unnecessarily prurient interest.

Simone drove into the yard, just then. Megan stood around, her curiosity obvious, leaving Peter with no option but to introduce her to 'his wife'. Simone raised her eyebrows, but played the game calmly, and with a smile. She patted George as he jumped up at her in excitement. Then as they walked arm in arm through the orchard towards the cottage Simone, not unnaturally, asked. "What's all this about a wife then?"

"Just seemed easier than anything else that's all." Any further conversation was cut short by the need to concentrate on their introductory kiss which was long, wet and pulsating.

She stopped his eager hands, took a deep breath, kissed him again, lightly this time. "Hang on a bit, long drive, plenty of time, want a cup of tea, and for you to tell me what the fuck you're doing in Wales."

They sat at the kitchen table, the kettle had boiled. Peter tried to explain the inexplicable. He didn't know himself why he had taken it into his head to abscond in the way he had, so it was hard to say much about it. "Haven't even told Naomi where I am yet, she's pretty peeved with me." He sighed, gesturing his unsettled feelings. Of course sex came next. Later, lying in post coital lethargy, next to a naked Simone, nothing else seemed very relevant; for the time being Peter was very content.

The weekend passed quickly, more sexual activity including on the Sunday when they took lunch into the countryside for a picnic. Simone, always one for adventure, insisted they take off all their clothes even though where they had stopped at the edge of some woods was rather exposed; she said the risk of being seen added spice to the act. The demands of lust meant that obedience was a must.

Even the idyllic must come to an end. On Sunday afternoon Simone drove away. She had meetings on Monday, she said, and had a living to earn. She had appeared in high spirits when they said goodbye, enjoyed the weekend but then didn't seem sad at all to be going home. Peter felt rather resentful at that, when his own feelings were of loss.

When her watched her car disappear he felt suddenly very lonely, the delights of a cottage in the country seemed less attractive, without Simone. His mood was one of sighing and regret. George appeared to sense his master's sadness, lying quietly at his feet for the rest of the evening.

Mood being what it is, when the next day dawned bright, and softly warm, Peter felt glad again, promised the faithful hound a long trip to explore the countryside, and in particular the hills, the highest point of which he had discovered was Blorenge mountain. He packed some sandwiches and drove in the direction of the hills. After parking the car, he discovered there were three recommended walks up the mountain. He decided on the middle option, two and a half hours, the sign said.

The area obviously had an industrial history, ruined buildings, narrow gauge rail tracks and other debris were scattered around, reminders of the iron works once located on the mountain slopes. There were some splendid views of the Black Mountains and the Brecon Beacons. At one vantage point, they stopped to eat their sandwiches. The day continued bright and balmy but as Peter sat looking at the panorama around him his mood changed, once again. It would have been so much better to have someone with him to share the experience; he was after all a gregarious man by nature Doubts were creeping in about whether this getting away from it all thing, was all that it was cracked up to be.

After the descent from the mountain, Peter fancied a beer. Sipping his drink, his thoughts about what the hell he was doing tucked away in a cottage in Wales, returned. He thought about what Naomi had said about not bothering to ring her again unless he was prepared to say where he was, that seemed fair. To have invited Simone to stay for the weekend, while carrying on his secretive tactics as far as his wife was concerned, was most definitely not right, might be construed as betrayal by any fair-minded person. This evening he would offer an olive branch, perhaps invite her down as well. At the very least he would try to explain why he had absconded in the way that he had.

He was hungry. A fry-up was the easy solution. He had reached the delicate part of making sure the eggs were cooked but not overcooked, when there was a tap on the door. He shouted an invitation to come in while he extracted the eggs from the pan before adding them to the unhealthy mound of bacon and sausages already on the plate.

"Dab hand with the old frying pan I see, Mr Shadbolt." Megan had a different tee-shirt on today, something about Las Vegas, and she was wearing shorts. The picture she presented was one to stir the libido of any red-blooded male, no bra it appeared and shorts so short they left no doubt as to the extent of her thighs. "Dad wanted to know if you needed milk." She put a can on the kitchen table, then sat down next to it, her face wreathed in the smiles of someone who knew what effect their presence was having on the other party. "Your wife was very pretty, what did she think of your little hideaway then, didn't stay long did she?"

It seemed obvious to Peter that the milk had been an excuse to visit, cynical maybe but there can't have been much excitement for a young girl to do in a small village like Govilon. Out of politeness he put his dinner in the oven thinking Megan would take the hint and leave him to his meal. "She enjoyed herself

Megan, but she had to get back to work you know."

"Don't mind me Mr Shadbolt," she nodded in the direction of the oven, " I like to see a man getting stuck in, you carry on and have your dinner, got anything to drink?"

Peter handed her a can of lager from the fridge, extracted his dinner plate from the oven, then started, somewhat self-consciously, to make his way through the pile of food in front of him. "My name's Peter, sounds terribly formal all this Mr Shadbolt stuff."

Megan drank from the can, wiped her mouth on the back of her hand, pulled her tee-shirt down in what, might or might not, have been an unthinking way, appeared happy to settle down comfortably, to watch him eat. "I do like your dog, Peter, he's a real sweetie, aren't you George?" She stroked George, who for the moment was more interested in the possibility of a piece of bacon coming his way. "How long are you thinking of staying in our lovely Wales then, Peter?"

She thumped the obviously empty can down on the table, leaving Peter feeling constrained to ask her if she would like another. "I'm not sure Megan, why have you got bookings for the cottage then?"

She took another swig from the second can, ran her tongue over her lips which combined with an arch smile, sent a message to Peter that this nubile young thing was on a vamping mission. Young mother, sublimely female, probably available, why not, but then you couldn't go round fucking any woman who arrives on the scene and may be willing. Besides he had a wife and a mistress, Such a double infidelity for the sake of short-term prurience, was outside his notion of what was right. He quickly dismissed the temptation, if it had been there at all. Anyway he may have been kidding himself, misreading the signs. After all most young women these days, it seemed to him, set out to make themselves outrageously sexually desirable; it gave them the edge for whatever might follow.

Megan lingered, but the moment, if there had been one, had passed. Eventually she left with a pout and a shake of her hips, when Peter explained he had to catch up with work on his laptop. In fact it wasn't altogether an excuse to get rid of her, he had been doing some writing since he had arrived in Wales, one page at a time, constant need to refer to what he's written earlier, because of his only occasional attention to the story. Slowly, very slowly, something was emerging. He found that last thing at night and when he woke in the morning, while he was still in bed, he would revise what he had written earlier to make it sound more authentic, then to plan what came next. Gradually the novel was gaining a form of integrity, which gave him an unexpected degree of satisfaction.

The night after Megan's milk visit, Peter came to a firm decision, it was only fair; he would ring Naomi, tell her where he was and try and explain why he was here. The second part was going to be difficult, as he still didn't know himself what he hoped to gain from his little holiday. She was, to say the least, cool on the telephone, but Peter felt duty-bound not to react to some of her bitchy comments.

She still didn't tell him about her dramatic departure from Bradford, Lang and Oldfield, that there were two of them now unemployed. In fact things were going rather better with her enterprise, negotiations were underway for office space, Rosalind would be available to help soon and Ivan appeared to have stiffened his backbone, in the face of there being no alternative.

"Why don't you come down for the weekend and we can discuss things at length, perhaps prove to you that I'm not completely mad."

"Too busy. Anyway, do you really expect me to encourage this escapism. I know you were very fed up with being out of work, but ignoring the problem isn't solving it is it? We'll speak some more later," she added in a lighter tone before putting the phone down.

Ten minutes later, to the astonishment of his father, James rang to say that if he wanted visitors, why didn't he bring his girlfriend down for the weekend. Peter was relieved to gather that his son wasn't gay, although he wasn't sure why that should be important. He recognised that the suggested visit was probably a scouting expedition instigated by Naomi, but nevertheless it was a bigger step in father-son relationships, than had happened for years, so he welcomed the idea.

Chapter 26.

He yawned, stretched and farted. Charlie wrinkled up her nose, digging him hard in the ribs with her elbow. She found the farting inconsiderate and distasteful; it was her bed and a small one at that, but then again it wasn't the first time, so what the hell.

"My God, is that the time?" Charlie put the clock down with a bump, rubbing her bleary eyes in an attempt to restore full vision. "That's another lecture I've missed."

"What the fuck, you've missed it now." He pulled her languorously towards him. "You smell so sexy in the morning, bit unwashed and all that."

"Thanks a bunch," she laughed, went along with the lazy invasion of her body, relishing the decadent exercise of having sex at eleven o'clock in the morning, when she should have been working.

Eventually Charlie dragged herself from under the duvet, leaving Phil fast asleep. Great guy, lots of fun, but his idea of sleep patterns was different to what she'd been used to. Her course work was beginning to suffer. While she showered, she determined on a new resolve.

Once dressed, she sat at her desk, attempting to put that resolve into practice. She had only completed two paragraphs of her essay, when a disturbance from the direction of the bed, and the sound of groaning indicated that her companion from the night before, had woken up at last. As he stumbled naked towards the bathroom, he stopped to massage the back of Charlie's neck, leaning over her shoulder to read what she'd written. His contribution was hardly helpful. "Balls, all balls, theory, theory, got nothing to do with what actually happens in the field."

"Oh fuck off Phil, go and have your shower, you smell disgusting." He did just that, after some comment to the effect that she hadn't seemed to mind how he smelt, an hour or so ago.

Despite her failing to make much progress with her essay, Charlie weakly succumbed to the now dressed Phillip's suggestion that they go and have a drink before rehearsals after lunch.

His play, 'Off the Hook', was coming on fine according to Phil, although Charlie wouldn't have known one way or the other. She attended most of the theatre sessions because she liked Phil. Carrying out odd jobs behind the scenes, made her feel part of the action.

The theatre crowd were enthusiastic up to a point, but only too ready to abandon rehearsal to retreat to the bar for yet another night on the beer, before moving to somebody's room to continue talking, more drinking and smoking weed. If she made an excuse not to attend one of the meetings, Phil merely shrugged. It was that off-hand manner that usually made her decide to go anyway. If the bloke had looked as if he cared, she might not have felt the need to be quite so attentive. It was all great fun, very cool and all that, but her work was suffering. The last meeting she had had with her tutor had been painful, to say the least..

Phil was older than most of the students around him, on a post graduate course he never spoke about, and which appeared to take up very little of his time. He had a certain charisma, a presence, which left no doubt as to who was in charge of the Theatre Society. Everyone involved seemed to accept that fact, carrying out his instructions, without question.

Charlie sometimes found his manner to be bossy and inconsiderate. She often felt excluded during the period of the rehearsal, as he barked out instructions at his cast, only paying her any attention when he wanted some odd job to be done. Even when they all went off, after the rehearsal sessions to drink themselves silly, he didn't really treat her like his girlfriend, exclaiming his theories about theatre to anyone who would listen, flirting with any woman who happened to be paying particular attention to him.

It was only when they broke up for the night, that he appeared to remember her presence, at which time he would put his arm round her possessively, walk her away, taking it for granted she was his for the night. No woman likes being taken for granted. Charlie was no exception, but she had fallen for the guy, and there were some aspects of being the head honcho's girl, that she liked, so she put up with the situation.

As well as weed, Phil smoked ordinary cigarettes, and often in the middle of a rehearsal he would stop, saying he needed to have a break before going outside to have a cigarette. Usually by that time, he would be looking frazzled, hair all over the place, sweat running down his face, the very picture of a director under pressure.

They usually left him alone out there to recover his dynamic, but one evening, for some reason, Charlie decided, after a few minutes to follow him out. There was no sign of him outside the door, but when she turned the corner of the building there he was with Amelia, their faces spread across each other's in passionate embrace. Phil's eyes opened, discovered Charlie was there, broke away and grinned like a schoolboy found stealing from his mother's purse.

Charlie was broad minded, putting up with Phil's constant flirting, giving it little weight, but what she had just witnessed was beyond that. She went back inside, collected her sweater, brushed past the apologising director, heading for her room. As she expected, the knock came on her door not long after the incident. Phil's voice came through the woodwork assuring her that Amelia meant nothing to him, a quick snog was all it was, she shouldn't be so sensitive, and so on. When Charlie failed to respond he eventually went away, leaving her to ruminate on what had happened.

In fact the kiss had probably just been a one-off. Should she get upset about such a minor peccadillo. It probably meant nothing as the man said, and despite her fury, she began to realise that she didn't want her fling with Phil to end in this way. One thing was certain if it was to continue, he had some grovelling to do. Anyway she would get an undisturbed night's sleep, which was something, then in the morning work on her essay before going to that day's lecture.

Her sleep was fitful that night, her dreams confused, but certain scenes came back to her when she woke in the morning, scenes where she was in a group, people were getting at her, accusing her of ruining something, but she didn't know what; whatever it was they were angry with her. The attacks went on and on for as long as the dream lasted. It left her feeling frazzled.

It had been a dream, that was all, soon to go the way of all dreams, out of mind, so she made an effort, getting up, taking a long soothing shower before she had her muesli and orange juice. After that she made a determined effort to concentrate on her essay. Her thoughts kept straying back to the previous evening, wondering whether Phil would try again to make it up with her.

Despite her resolve to work all morning, she couldn't keep it up, finally collecting some notes she might need for her lecture, she made her way to the door. When she pulled it open, there was a single yellow rose lying on the floor, just outside the door to her room. Phillip was a dynamic guy, full of enthusiasm, kind when he thought about it but romantic, never, and if it was him, and it couldn't be anyone else, why yellow, trust the bastard to be different. She picked up the flower, went back inside her room to put it in a glass of water. Did he really think one rose would be enough to make up for what he had been up to with that Amelia?

Chapter 27.

James look pleased to be in Wales, a different James, different from the angry boy of recent memory. He grinned at his father. After a moment's hesitation from both of them, they hugged. Kirsty stood by, watching father and son greet each other with a smile on her face, while she made a fuss of the dog. Peter kissed the cheek of the girl, who had apparently wrought this amazing change in his son, before leading them down the orchard path to the cottage. They put their bags down in the hall.

"I've got the room first on the right at the top of the stairs. You can take your pick with the other two." Times being what they are, James now seventeen and Kirsty must be eighteen at least, they were not likely to be using more than one of the rooms, he surmised. This girlfriend who had so magically appeared from nowhere seemed a sensible girl; it was she who had driven them down in her mother's car. "Hope you guys had a good journey. Look why don't we have some lunch, then perhaps take a walk. Don't want to sound as if I'm organising you but I have some tickets for the theatre this evening, in Abergavenny. Now just say if you'd rather go off and do your own thing, but that's what's on offer." He sounded, to himself, like some uncertain tour guide trying to enthuse his visitors, uncertain because he wasn't sure yet just how to treat this changed son of his.

James had his arm round Kirsty's waist. "Sounds great to us, okay Kirsty?" She nodded. That decided upon, they all sat down at the kitchen table, while Peter produced the makings of a ploughman's lunch. They were well into the cheese and pickles before James looked straight into Peter's face and asked. "What the hell are you doing here Dad? None of my business but Mum is hopping mad. She's hurt, doesn't understand what you're trying to prove." He stopped eating, waiting for an answer. Kirsty looked a trifle uneasy, this was family stuff, absolutely none of her business.

"It's not a matter of trying to prove anything James. I was bored out of my mind, just needed to get away, try to view my life from a different prospective." It must have been the first time in his life that he had been in a position of having to explain himself to his son; it was difficult.

"Why keep where you were a secret, that was unkind."

Peter sighed. "You may be right, can't explain really, but she knows where I am now, she could have come down." James took a bite out of his hunk of bread apparently ready to let the subject drop.

They drove over to Abergavenny early, to explore, found there was a market in full swing, which they wandered round for a time before walking through some beautiful gardens and up to the castle most of which was in ruins, finally arriving at the Melville Theatre in time to get something to eat, and have a quick drink. The play was called the 'Ministry of Fear', adapted from a Graham Greene novel, something of an experiment, the programme informed them.

The afternoon and evening passed enjoyably, Peter still trying to get used to this new son, who had at last joined the human race While the two kids were absorbed with each, they still made the occasional effort to involve him. Once back at the cottage after the short drive home, Kirsty asked Peter what he thought of the play. His view was that he didn't think the novel suitable for adaption as a play, and that the director seemed unsure whether to make the thing funny or serious, left it hanging somewhere in between.

After some more general chat about the play, Peter opened a bottle of wine, and the three of them sat round the kitchen table drinking and talking until one o'clock in the morning. Kirsty had asked at one stage if they could visit Hay on Wye while they were nearby; she had always wanted to explore the bookshops for which it was famous.

When the two youngsters eventually went up to bed it was obvious that they would only be using one bedroom as they made their way arm in arm up the stairs. Peter stayed at the table finishing off the wine, pleased with the visit, but now left alone, becoming introspective or at least retrospective, as often happened recently. His escape to the wilds of Wales no longer seemed a solution, a gesture that impressed nobody, especially Naomi. Anyway it wasn't fair on her, whatever it might have done for him, if anything..

James and Kirsty came down late for breakfast looking slightly sheepish as they said good morning. It wasn't far to Hay, but Kirsty said she didn't want to be late starting back, her mother would be worried, so they set off mid-morning, wandered round the book shops, had a snack lunch at the Swan at Hay, sampled the real ale, or at least James and his father did, getting back to the cottage by mid-afternoon. Peter saw them off with regret, a sense of homesickness pervading his feeling, further confirmation in his mind that this idyll had run its course.

When Monday came round, he had almost decided to pay Max Williams what he owed him and, tail between his legs, return home to who knows what. That evening his plans were again changed, or at least delayed, by a phone call from Naomi. She had something important to tell him, something that couldn't wait until he had finished 'fucking about' as she put it. She had made up her mind to come down at the weekend to pay him a visit. Peter's first reaction was to tell her not to bother, he was coming home anyway, but then thought perhaps a weekend in the country might be good for both of them, give him a chance to try and explain his feelings, her the chance to have a go at him in peaceful surroundings, so he let things lie.

The next day dawned deliciously bright and sunny so Peter decided to take some sandwiches and go for another of the long walks, he had been taking since coming to Wales. That morning he set off with his mind clearer than of late, Naomi's impending visit perhaps, his decision to return home, whatever it was, he felt the need to exert himself, to push himself to some extreme. His mood was cheerful. All the striding through the undergrowth, seeking new horizons, discovering new hills, following pretty streams gave him a satisfying sense of wellbeing. George was enjoying himself too, dashing off every so often chasing some creature that probably wasn't there, then coming back to make sure the boss hadn't deserted him. He must have walked for three hours or so before he began to slow down, and think about finding a nice spot to eat his sandwiches.

Sitting beside a small lake, rested and ready to go on, Peter felt the first drops of rain. A look at the darkening sky told him that this might be more than a shower.

It had been a bright day when he set out, rain was the last thing he expected. He was most definitely not dressed for it. As the rain began in earnest, he ran for a group of trees, reaching shelter just as the clouds opened, and the real deluge arrived. At first it was rather exciting, the sound of the rain crashing through the trees, the smell of the earth newly saturated. After a while the novelty wore off, the rain clouds showed no signs of passing over.

It wasn't cold, but he was bored standing under the trees, so he decided that getting wet wouldn't do him any harm, and set off to retrace his steps from this morning. At first he had no difficulty recognising land marks he had noted on the way out. Soon he reached a point at the start of another wooded tract that didn't seem familiar. In fact everything looked rather different in the gloom and the pouring rain.

He cast about for a while until he finally recognised a stile, he thought he had climbed that morning. This went on until he saw from his watch that it was already five o'clock, and he still hadn't reached the farm. George was looking despondent, staying close to Peter's heels, while Peter himself was now quite literally soaked to the skin. He was almost despairing when he saw some farm building emerge from the murk. To his great relief found he had stumbled his way back to Manor Farm, more by luck than judgement.

He squelched through the orchard to let himself into the cottage, exhausted and relieved. He found a towel, gave the dog a vigorous rub down , restoring warmth and some dryness to the poor animal. Then duty done, he went upstairs to strip off his clothes before standing under a very hot shower for twenty minutes or so. He dried off and put on his dressing gown. Down in the kitchen, he didn't have time to put the kettle on before there was a knock on the door. There, on the door step, was his landlord's daughter, dressed in a heavy old rain coat, and carrying a bottle.

She was through the door before he could invite her in or otherwise, plonking what turned out to be half a bottle of whisky on the kitchen table. "Saw you going through the orchard. Like a drowned rat you looked, and poor old George. Thought you might need something to warm you up, half-inched this from my old man I did. Get the glasses out then, let's have a shot."

It wasn't a bad idea, the whisky, so the glasses came out. Megan under that heavy coat was dressed in her usual trade mark jeans and tee-shirt, the logo said something about real equality for women. Before sitting down at the kitchen table, Peter poured a measure of Scotch into two glasses. Megan chucked the raincoat on the floor, then plonked herself down next to Peter, pulling down her shirt as usual, to show off her bosom, licking her lips in between sips of whisky. "Where'd you go then, get lost did you, nasty storm that one, isn't it."

"Don't really know, it was a nice day so I just followed my nose, no idea where I was, then the bloody rain started, didn't let up, so I tried to find my way back. Actually I did get lost a couple of times but got here in the end."

Megan gave off heat like a human radiator. Every so often he could feel her thigh touch his through his dressing gown. He despaired at his own lack of control; his tumescence was rampant, and he prayed there would be no occasion for him to stand up, away from the protective table. The girl reached for her glass, and in so doing her hand brushed against his. Here we are again, he thought, young woman offering herself, thin cloth separating their flesh, virile man with two women already. They drank some more whisky, she nudging ever closer. Peter decided that, with Naomi coming at the weekend, he could never look her in the face again if he gave in to temptation. Anyway he could be wrong; maybe the girl was just after some company.

"Megan you really are a sweetie, thanks so much for the whisky, but I really must try and do some work."

She looked at him, eyebrows raised in mock surprise, but showed no sign of leaving. "Come on now, Peter, you've got to relax after the soaking you've had." Her thigh most definitely pressed against his this time; any doubts about the young woman's intentions were banished.

If she'd put her hand on his thigh just then, his resolve might have failed. As it was he kept faith with his better side, edged his chair away from hers, knocked back the last of his whisky in one gulp, smiled at her as though he had no idea what she had been up to. Then screwing the top back on the whisky bottle, he moved it in her direction. " Better let you Dad have what's left."

"Fuck you then, you're a bastard did you know that, don't know what you've missed, getting old before your fucking time, that's you." Megan was one angry girl; she grabbed the nearly empty bottle, picked up her raincoat, gave him a look that would have frightened a scorpion, and stamped out of the back door leaving it wide open behind her.

Peter's feelings, as usual, when it came to his relations with women, were mixed. Curiously the regret he felt was nothing much to do with missing the chance of having sex with a nubile young woman, more to do with having hurt Megan's feelings by refusing her advances. After all she had been pretty kind to him since he's arrived at the cottage. He had scorned what she had on offer, and hell hath no fury like a woman scorned, so he shouldn't expect much kindness from Megan from now on.

Putting thoughts about Megan, what might have been, to one side, he turned instead to Naomi's visit, and how they would react with each other. He couldn't leave Simone out of his thoughts either. All of which left him no nearer knowing what he wanted to do about his marriage. As it got darker, he stayed sitting there; objects around him became less distinct; the darkness could be felt warm and velvet as the light faded. George's wet nose touched his naked thigh to remind him of his presence, receiving the expected pat in return.

He woke un-refreshed the next morning, having suffered a return of the stress dreams in which all sorts of problems arose including, he vaguely remembered, having his car stolen. He ate breakfast, before walking up to the farm to tell Max that he would be leaving in a week or so. As he came round the corner of the barn he noticed a man, who he had never seen before moving hay bales. The man turned to look at him, but didn't speak. Max put in an appearance just then, breaking the momentary silent impasse between the two men.

"Mr Shadbolt, this is Kurt, he's helping out for a few days." The man relaxed his stare, nodded, then carried on humping bales. "You wanted to see me?" Max walked a short distance away from the man with the bales.

"Guy's a walker he says, run out of money", nodding in the direction of the man he had referred to as Kurt, "I felt sorry for him,. let him sleep in the attic for a few days while he helped out on the farm. Hasn't got much to say for himself, beginning to wish he wasn't here now, there's something a bit sinister about him."

Peter nodded, not very interested in Max's lost sheep, if that's what he was. He explained about Naomi's impending visit, then the fact that after that he would be picking up sticks, going back to Devon. As he left the yard, Kurt looked up from his task, watching until he was out of sight. Max was right, he thought, an unpleasant man but it was none of his business who Max wanted to employ. It did rather mischievously cross his mind to wonder what Megan would make of this Kurt.

Peter found himself once again pondering on the impending visit of his wife. What was she going to say about his selfish fleeing of the family home, what was this important thing she had to tell him about. The thought that she might want a divorce, crossed his mind. The peace he had felt when he first arrived at the cottage, was now replaced by the same restless feeling that had possessed him before he had left Devon. He found it hard to concentrate on anything for long, picking up a book, reading for a while, watching some inane programme on the box, taking George for short walks, eating too much snack food, drinking too much beer. He was back again to not liking the man he was becoming.

The Friday before Naomi's visit he had drunk himself into tiredness, before going to bed fairly early. Terror struck sometime in the night. He woke to a sensation of weight holding him down, an arm round his neck. As he struggled to consciousness, his first thought was that it might have been Megan fooling about, but almost immediately the force of the attack, the weight on top of him dispelled that idea. As he fought for breath, he came to the shocked conclusion that someone was trying to murder him.

Peter always slept naked and on his front, so his assailant had little trouble at first, holding him down. He flailed with his arms, reaching out behind him, but there was no force in the blows. Then to his absolute disgust he realised that his attacker was also naked. He could feel the man's rampant cock thrusting wildly between his buttocks in an apparent attempt to rape him. Peter was assailed by a mixture of fear and disgust. The man on top of him was strong. Struggle as he might, the guy kept his tight grip round his neck. The thought of being raped by a man was so traumatically repulsive that Peter fought like a wildcat to get free. He was a big man himself and gradually his attacker was finding it harder to hold him down.

They fought on, Peter scratching and tearing at the man on top of him, causing the grip round his neck to slacken slightly. The wild panic of his waking moments, had now been replaced by more rational thoughts of how he could escape. With the slightly greater freedom he now had from the loosening of the arm round his neck, Peter managed to stretch out his arm. Grabbing the bedside lamp, he lashed out as hard as he could, connecting with the man's head. The blow lacked any real force reaching backwards as he was, but it had some effect. It was enough for the man to shift his body trying to avoid further strikes, As he did so, Peter managed to partly role out from under him, and with a surge of adrenalin fuelled effort, pushed him off the edge of the bed, both of then landing on the floor with a crash. As he scrambled to his feet; the man made a grab for his legs; Peter kicked him as hard as he could in the face. The pain in his foot was exquisite, but for the moment anyway, he was free.

He half-ran, half-limped down the stairs through the already open front door and down the path through the orchard as fast as his legs would carry him When he reached the farm house he banged madly on the front door, still shaking in fear, screaming to be let in. He was vaguely aware of George's wild barking, only later noticed that the dog had followed him in his wild run through the trees.

Max came to the door, rubbing his eyes. Peter brushed past him slamming the door shut, locking it behind him. Only then did he feel some relief from his fear. He was shaking like a leaf, obvious to the farmer that something pretty awful had happened to his tenant. Max handed him a coat from the hook in the hall but not before Megan had appeared on the stairs, grinning at his nudity, before realising the state he was in..

"Police, ring the police, man attacked me in the cottage." In his agitation Peter was finding it difficult to be coherent. Despite that, it was clear to Max that some sort of attack had taken place, serious enough to scare this guy half to death. He dialled 999 to give a rough and ready account of what he thought might have happened In the slightly calmer atmosphere that followed, Max ushered, a still shaking Peter, into the sitting room, made him sit down, poured a glass of brandy, watching while the victim gulped it down.

"Why on earth should anyone want to attack you, Peter? You feeling a bit better now are you, better have some more brandy." Max looked at Megan. They were both thinking the same thing. With all the commotion that had been going on for the last few minutes, why hadn't their lodger emerged from his room to find out what the commotion was about. Max went upstairs, came back grim faced. "He's not there, looks as though that Kurt chap might have been your attacker Peter."

"The filthy bastard was trying to rape me, Max; he was lying on top of me, when I woke, fucking naked, the bastard trying to rape me." The second glass of brandy went down Peter's throat, began to take effect. His shaking was subsiding, he could think more clearly. "Sorry, Max, if I sound rather frantic, but the idea of being raped by a guy, repulses me in a way I just can't describe."

"I don't suppose female rape is much fun either." The stare Max gave his daughter at this point put a stop to further invidious comparisons. Perhaps the sweet young thing was still suffering from the brush off the other night.

After about half an hour they heard a car pull in the yard. Max let the two policemen into the house, took them into the sitting room, where Peter was slumped in the chair, still in something of a daze, not helped by the brandy he had drunk on top of the beer he had consumed earlier in the evening.

"I take it you're the man who was attacked sir?" Peter nodded. "You will no doubt be relieved to know that your assailant is already in our custody, just had a message on the radio, handed himself in at the Abergavenny station not five minutes ago."

"How the hell could he have got to Abergavenny, he was busy attacking me less than an hour ago. How do you know it's the same guy anyway?"

"Came clean straight away, said he assaulted someone here on the farm. Bicycle sir, must have stolen it I suppose, you lost a bike, have you Mr Williams?"

Max went out to check if his machine was missing. The policeman's phone crackled. He moved into the hall to take the call. When he came back he shook his head and sighed. "Seems your attacker is a Kurt Rowlinson, already on the sex offenders' register as a paedophile, so the attack on you is a bit out of character, as it were." He sounded apologetic, as though such an assault was against the rules.

"I'm very sorry for what happened sir, but we will need you to come in and make a full statement some time tomorrow, you understand. The good thing is if he's admitted the offence you won't have to give evidence in court."

Max came back to confirm his bike had gone, the policemen left. It seemed to Peter an anti-climax after his state of utter terror, almost routine as far as the police were concerned, but leaving him with a hollowed out feeling, very unnerving, uncertainty about what he should do next. There was relief in there somewhere, relief that it could have been worse.

Megan went back to bed. Max walked with Peter back to the cottage and after chatting reassuringly for a few minutes, he too went back to the house. Peter locked the door behind him. Despite the fact that it was still the middle of the night, Peter couldn't face going back to the bedroom where that sick bastard had tried to bugger him. A subdued George had fallen asleep in his basket, while his master sat at the kitchen table drinking mug after mug of strong sweet tea, feeling slightly fuzzy after the large therapeutic brandies Max had pressed on him.

The horror of the trauma was still very much with him, his revulsion over the attack was strong, the memory of being held down by force was frightening in the extreme, particularly the sense of helplessness it had invoked. Thinking over the circumstances of the attack, he now wished he had had the courage to stay, to strike out at the man, beat his face to pulp. A case of fear of violence reverting to the violence of revenge, sort of self-preservation, you might say, but it was all in the mind anyway because he hadn't done that. He had run away as fast as he damn well could. Did he blame himself, maybe a little, but then when he thought about it, he reckoned most men would have done the same in the circumstances. It wasn't the same as an upright fight, someone coming at you by surprise, in the dark, not that he would have been much use even in a straight forward confrontation. He hadn't fought anyone since his school days, but at least the horror of the sneak attack wouldn't have been there.

Eventually, Peter decided sleep was not on the agenda, so he moved into the living room, opened up his laptop, trying to record some of the horror of his experience, his feelings of fear and revulsion. He had a file for ideas, thoughts and suggestions he might use in the future. Working on ideas proved to be therapeutic but after typing away for some time he tired, until finally, without switching off his machine, he slumped back in the chair to fall into a troubled sleep, full of wild images, images of fear and violence, but without specific form, a vague amalgam of threat and terror.

The undrawn curtains let the bright sunshine in through the living room windows, waking Peter early. Waking was hardly the word, because what he actually did was fight his way to consciousness through a confusion of memories and dreams, finding it hard to get his mind working on an even keel. Eventually he managed to damp down his emotions, told himself that he had to face the here and now. Even then, he felt quite awful, tired and frazzled, a black feeling of depression oppressed his consciousness. He realised that he was still naked under the coat that Max had handed to him the night before, decided that a shower, shave and getting dressed might equip him better for the day ahead, As he moved to the stairs a subdued George came out of the kitchen to look for a sympathetic pat.

Chapter 28.

Some needs remain, whatever traumas might assail us. When Peter came downstairs again he felt hungry, very hungry. He cooked a large plate of bacon and eggs, supplemented with fried bread. Now clean and fed he was beginning to feel almost human. The two things on his mind were the statement he had to make to the police in Abergavenny and the impending visit of Naomi with all the baggage that might entail.

As some of the cobwebs blew away, he began to think tentatively about the events of the previous night. How desperate Kurt must have been to sexually attack a grown man, how perverted, yes, but how unlikely to succeed. Then why cycle straight over to hand himself into the police. He must have known Max had a bike parked at the back of the house; perhaps he had intended to surrender to the police whatever the outcome of his assault.

When he got to the police station in Abergavenny, he was told that the officer assigned to take his statement, had been called out. Would he mind coming back in an hour. Peter rang his wife to tell her he might be delayed, but she had her phone switched off.

Naomi had no difficulty in finding Manor Farm, although when she drove into the yard there was no one about. She had started out early; perhaps Peter hadn't expected her to arrive so soon, gone shopping or something. She was walking towards the farm house, when the door opened and Megan appeared. In fact, although Max knew about Naomi's visit, he had omitted to mention it to his daughter, so she was surprised to see a stranger in the yard.

"Hello, looking for someone?"

"Yes, Peter Shadbolt, I believe he's staying in one of your cottages."

"Oh yes, Peter. Actually we've only got the one – cottage, I mean. We had a spot of trouble here last night; he's gone into Abergavenny to speak to the cops."

"Oh my goodness, is he alright? what was it all about?"

"Sorry, but can I ask who you are?"

"I'm his wife, Naomi, didn't he tell you I was coming down?"

Megan's eyebrows shot up in surprise. Whether by accident or not, her next words changed the Shadbolt family for ever. "His wife, but I thought that, I thought, well never mind." She stopped, giving the impression of being confused about something.

"What did you think, why should you be surprised, what's been going on here?"

"Nothing, I was getting mixed up that's all. Peter will be back soon I expect, I'll show you the cottage. I'm Megan by the way."

As they walked through the orchard Naomi's thoughts revolved around why the girl should have been surprised when she had said she was Peter's wife. "Look Megan, tell me, has there been someone else down to stay with Peter?"

"His son and girlfriend were down recently." She appeared nervous.

"And?"

"That's about all, as far as I can remember." When Megan opened the cottage door, George gave Naomi an ecstatic greeting. In the midst of the commotion Megan walked towards the door. "Sorry I've got work to do, must go."

She started back down the path, glanced back over her shoulder, then hurried away as though she had a train to catch, leaving Naomi with the most emphatic impression that she had not answered her question about visitors, with complete honesty. Perhaps there had been more to Peter's escape to the country than merely a wish to take a break from his problems at home. Her thoughts slipped back to that hateful, blue letter received months ago now, shoved to the back of her mind as being irrelevant in the scheme of things, until now..

There were questions to be asked, and she was going to ask them. While waiting for her husband, she looked round the cottage, before making herself a cup of tea. A short while later as she sat at the kitchen table drinking her tea, it came to her that her exploration of the cottage might have been a cloak for looking for evidence of occupation by another party.

When Peter got back to the cottage husband and wife greeted each other with a kiss and a hug. "Sorry I wasn't here when you arrived love, but there was an attack here last night. I had to make a statement to the police in Abergavenny."

"That young girl told me there had been some sort of trouble but an attack, an attack on who Peter?"

"On me, actually." He went through the whole story, getting some relief from the telling. Naomi couldn't have been more sympathetic, her hand reaching out to touch his cheek, as he tried to explain the fear and loathing of the attempted rape.

Eventually he ran out of words. The two of them ate lunch, bread and cheese, then strolled out with the dog to enjoy the afternoon sunshine. "Peter has anyone else been here to stay with you in the cottage?" It was a question out of the blue, taking him completely by surprise.

"James and Kirsty came to stay, as you already know."

"I wasn't thinking of them; has anyone else been to stay here?"

It's an old rule that if you're going to lie, never hesitate. Peter hesitated, and he was lost. His face confirming, to Naomi, that the suspicions she had been harbouring, were justified, and explaining the confusion shown by young Megan, when she had arrived.

He didn't say a word.. "How long has it being going on Peter, who is this other woman you've been fucking. At least I assume that's why she was here, not just to pick primroses." They had stopped walking, she was right in his face. "Say something, you cheating bastard." Her face was twisted in anger, yet she stayed calm, waiting to hear from her faithless husband, curious, despite her anger, to know how he would respond.

He sighed, spread his hands in a gesture of surrendered apology. "I'm sorry Naomi, no excuses, I did have someone down here for the weekend, of course a woman, I'm guilty as charged."

Naomi still kept her temper, still went on with why she had come to Wales in the first place. "I came down here, to tell you that I've left Bradford Lang and Oldfield, to set up a practice with Ivan Campion and Rosalind. Now I find my husband has been betraying me behind my back. All that wasted sympathy and understanding about your redundancy, and all the while you've been getting all the sympathy you needed from other sources. No wonder you didn't want to tell me where you were." There were tears hovering about the edge of her eyes, sorry for a lost cause perhaps, sorry at something the pair of them once had.

"OK I've been unfaithful, but that wasn't why I had to get away. The woman only came down for one weekend that's all, she hasn't been living here or anything like that." Even to his own ears the words sounded pointless, one weekend or a millennium's worth of weekends, it remained a betrayal..

"I see so you think occasional philandering is acceptable do you." She shook her head slowly from side to side, sighing a deep sigh of utter exasperation. "So just what do you intend to do now, Peter?" That indeed was the question, He only wished he could begin to answer it, as much for himself, as for Naomi.

Strangely enough Naomi didn't continue to berate her husband during their walk back to the cottage, maybe the distance between them had already been there, the revelation a mere confirmation. She hardly said another word until they got back inside the cottage. Then spoke quietly, with cold politeness. "I'm not driving back today, so if you could find a spare room for me for the night, I'd be grateful."

The gulf between husband and wife, created over the space of a few minutes, was so wide, that they might have only just met as strangers, rather than having had a marriage of twenty years. They remained polite to each other, Peter tentatively asking about the progress of her enterprise: she offering incredulity and sympathy over the ordeal he had been through the night before. They talked about James and Charlie in a civilised way, but it was as though they were tidying things up before going their separate ways. Neither of them mentioned the future, and while Naomi would drive back home tomorrow, Peter wasn't sure what he would do.

Any further discussion about infidelity was put to one side, although that didn't prevent it hanging over them like a Sword of Damocles, even while they talked, ate a meal together, even watched television.

Naomi went upstairs early. Peter waited until he heard her come out of the bathroom, before going to bed himself, worn out by last night's events, and today's emotions. Little sleep the previous night, he was dog-tired, could have done with the comfort of a woman's arms. Despite his deprivation, he eventually fell into a fitful sleep punctuated again with vague images of fear and anxiety. It was quite late when he woke and when did finally stagger wearily down stairs, there was no sign of Naomi. He called her name a few times but there was no answer. When he checked the other bedroom her things had gone and so, obviously, had she.

Packing and taking George for a short walk, didn't take long. He said goodbye to Max, saw Megan looking out of the window. She didn't wave. Then he was off, on the way back to heaven knows what. He took it easy on the drive home, so it was mid-afternoon before he arrived, to find Naomi in the kitchen, drinking coffee and reading the Sunday paper. She looked older somehow, face strained and grey looking. "You're back then. I've moved most of your stuff into the spare room, until we decide how we're going to play this thing, you alright with that?"

Peter nodded. He found the calm way his wife was dealing with the situation made it more difficult for him than it would have been had she ranted at him. It left him feeling rather helpless. Naomi was in control, and he had to wait to see what she would do, which might be to petition for divorce without further ado, or maybe they could live together in armed neutrality, hoping things would eventually get back to normal. Alternatively she might try to chuck him out.

The obvious hardly occurred to Peter, that what happened next was largely down to him. After all he was the one having the affair, he was the one who had breached the marriage trust. The tension between husband and wife was relieved slightly by the appearance of the new James, who seemed pleased to see him home. He didn't know whether Naomi had told their son that things were not as they should be between his parents.

An interlude had gone by. Peter was now back where he was, Wales had been just a dream tailing off into a nightmare. He still had no job, the future reached out ahead of him like a bleak everlasting plain. And then there was Simone, what was he going to do about Simone? Not surprisingly the atmosphere in the house remained fraught. Even with efforts to avoid each other, husband and wife could not help crossing paths every so often. James went off to meet Kirsty, Naomi made herself an omelette. It would have been easier if his wife had shouted at him, but the silence between the couple was devastating.

When he lay in bed that night, his thoughts turned for the thousandth time to the practicalities of his situation. What would happen if Naomi petitioned for divorce, the house was in joint names so he had a right to be here. Presumably she was getting income from her new set-up. He still had money from his redundancy package, also knew that he would soon be eligible for job seekers allowance, such as it was. He slept in fits and starts, his mind producing the usual disturbed dreams. In the morning he felt like death warmed up.

Naomi went off to work without a word. Jamie went for one of his last days of the college term. Peter was back where he was weeks ago. He tried to make himself useful round the house, but it appeared to need little attention. Reading the trade press produced no job adverts that matched his CV, George continued to benefit from his availability. Eventually he got an application form from the local supermarket, who were advertising for van drivers; anything was better than this hanging about all day doing nothing. He filled it in, before delivering it back to the store by hand, two hours later.

When Naomi got in that evening, she said she wanted to talk, so they went into the sitting room. She accepted the offer of a drink, then turned to face her husband with a direct look, almost a stare. "I know something about divorce Peter, know how to go about it, and that's what I want. The immediate thing to realise is that until the children reach the age of nineteen, assuming they're in full-time education, this house is their home, so whatever we decide between us, it can't be sold as part of any settlement. What's more we can handle the divorce process ourselves without wasting money on solicitors. There are time constraints, the law works slowly, but I intend to start the ball rolling by petitioning for a decree nisi." She paused, eyebrows raised, expecting a response.

"Well, you certainly sound like a solicitor, I'll give you that Naomi." He was taken aback by her matter-of-fact handling of the situation, not that he should have been. After all she was a solicitor herself. He should have remembered very well what Naomi was like, in control, but it still struck him as grotesquely cold and unemotional.

"What the fuck do you expect Peter. Bloody writing classes. I bet you can write some fucking good porn now based on your course work." Her composure had cracked slightly. "You really are a bastard you know, garnering sympathy and all the time you're at it with some fucking bird."

"I'm sorry Naomi, didn't want to hurt you, but we seemed to be drifting apart, then I met this woman really by accident and well ..." He paused, making one of his little hand gestures of apology. "I didn't set out to be unfaithful, but you didn't really want me most of the time and I ..."

"Here we go, you really are the limit Peter. Just because I wasn't ready to have sex every time you felt like a quick fuck. There's more to relationships than ten minutes between the sheets, twice a week. I suppose this other woman is on heat every time you go round to her place, that's what mistresses do, I believe. Tell me one thing Peter what are you going to do now?" Her bitterness was justified, Peter didn't defend himself.

That was a good, oft-repeated question in his own mind, and one to which Peter had no answer. He shrugged. "Carry on looking for a job I suppose."

"Yes I know that but where are you going to live?"

A flutter of apprehension made itself felt in Peter's mind. He hadn't conceived that Naomi would actually try to throw him out of the house, yet that's what her question seemed to imply. "Well for the time being I intended to stay where I am; this house is still half mine. As you bloody well know I don't have the money to be renting accommodation elsewhere." Angry words, he knew, but it was difficult just sitting there taking it, deserved or not.

"I don't want things to get any more acrimonious, Peter, so let's say I agree to your staying. There would have to be ground rules in the new circumstances. I have no intention of cooking for you, cleaning or doing your washing for start. Then I think it would be a good idea if we avoided contact as much as possible. James will be around for a couple of months, and Charlie is coming back from Durham, so that might ease any tensions to a degree."

Christ, the woman was so damn organised, it made him sick, yet he nodded acquiescence to her plans. If she'd had any papers this would have been the stage when she collected them together, before sweeping out of the room. As it was, she walked into the kitchen. He could hear her banging about getting her own and James's supper ready. He poured himself another drink as he speculated morosely what life would be like living this separated existence.

Chapter 29.

Of course Simone knew nothing about Naomi's discovery of their liaison. When they were lying side by side in bed, after Peter had gone round to her flat on Wednesday, he had to persuade her to curb her passions as he had something serious to tell her.

Her response was of a casual nature, no-big-deal sort of reaction. "OK, so what, you were pretty fed up with your marriage weren't you, so why don't you move in here for a bit?" She offered herself for a kiss, which Peter lovingly bestowed, though his mood, for the time being, was subdued, so the kiss was a one-off. Simone, sensing his worries, went out to make the ubiquitous cup of tea. When she came back Peter told her about the attack back in Wales, before going on to explain Naomi's terms for him staying at home.

"There you are then, all the more reason to move in here."

"You're a sweet girl, Simone. I'm really grateful for the offer, but I still have to think of the kids. James is going to be around, and Charlie will come home soon for the summer holidays. It would feel like some form of desertion if I moved out now." He sighed; decisions about loyalty and responsibility were hard, particularly when lined up against a life where frequent, and very willing sex was on offer.

"You must do as you think best." She sounded a bit put-out. Then when she thought of her own two boys, and the extent to which she would go to protect them, she softened. A cup of tea was all very well but in the changed circumstances there was no reason for Peter to hurry home, no secrets to be kept. Yet habits die hard and by late afternoon Peter found himself almost impelled to go back to the house. He had no idea why he should feel that way, knowing the cold reception that awaited him there. Despite Simone's persuasive hands, he hauled himself out of bed, and went to shower.

When he came back into the bedroom, towel round his waist, Simone was spread eagled on top of the duvet in very blatant temptation. Peter's original thoughts about going home were very easily put to one side by the musk of her sex, and the sight of that lovely flesh displayed for his attention. As the towel slipped to the floor, he wrapped himself round that delicious body, appetite renewed, and for the next half-hour nothing more important than indulging his libido, entered Peter's consciousness. Sex has a power all its own to beguile the mind.

When he finally woke from a post-coital doze, he found Simone sitting on the bed at his side holding out a gin and tonic. "Sure you don't fancy moving in, lover?"

Peter arrived home to find Naomi had beaten him to it. In the kitchen, when their glances met, he thought he detected hurt in her eyes, hurt that she knew where he'd been that afternoon, but there was defiance there too. Neither of them spoke. Peter decided to leave the territory to her, get himself something to eat later. He switched on the early evening news, poured himself a whisky. Hidden away amongst all his other problems, it struck him that drinking as much as he did was hardly going to help him resolve his problems.

The telephone rang. He heard Naomi pick up the receiver and then she called out. "It's for you, someone called Gerald."

Peter didn't know any Gerald as far as he could remember. He went into the hall to take the call. "It's Gerald here, Peter." There was a pause. "Gerald Portland, we met last year at your mother's, you remember, went out for a meal."

Peter had begun to remember even before the caller confirmed that this was the man he had disliked intensely, when they met, the guy that had moved in with his mother. "Yes I know who you are, why are you calling, is my mother alright, has there been an accident?"

"No accident Peter, but I have some very bad news for you. Elizabeth is in hospital, it's cancer I'm afraid."

"My God, how serious is it? Why haven't you rung before this? Where have they taken her?" Was his verbal attack something to do with his own guilt? He hadn't visited his mother since calling in on the way back from taking Charlie to Durham last year, had only spoken to her over the telephone on a handful of times since then. Yes he was guilty of neglecting his own mother, now she was ill; no wonder he felt angry, angry at himself, angry at this usurper who had insinuated himself into the family.

"Look here Peter, your mother asked me not to worry you, she's only went into hospital yesterday, it's all happened very quickly. She wouldn't go to the doctor at first then, after tests, all hell broke loose. They rushed her in yesterday, as I said. I'm very sorry Peter, but you're not the only one who's upset, I'm very fond of Elizabeth as you know, it's come as a shock to me as well."

The man sounded genuine enough. Peter modified his tone. "That's alright Gerald but I asked how serious it is. Which hospital is she in?"

"She's in the Royal General in Northwich. Look, Peter, this is hard to say, but I'm sorry to have to tell you that the doctors are diagnosing her illness as terminal. I realise you will want to come up as soon as possible. Please feel free to stay at the house when you come up, you'd be very welcome."

Fucking cheek, inviting him to stay at his own home, not that in reality it had ever been his home, but that's what it felt like. Anyway he kept his cool, telling Gerald he would be there tomorrow. When he told Naomi, she at once put aside her enmity to offer genuine sympathy. She had liked his Mum, asked if she come up to Cheshire with him, a request, to which he readily agreed.

Chapter 30.

Charlie had eventually forgiven Phil for the thing with Amelia while he, for his part, had done his level best to be nice to her. That was of course when he wasn't hung up with directing the play. Things in that respect were coming to a climax now as the first night of 'Off the Hook' loomed. The summer break was nearly on them. Charlie wondered if Phil would have any suggestions for the holidays that might involve the two of them, but then she remembered him saying something about needing to work.

She made excuses for him as the big night approached, excuses for the fact that the only attention he paid to her now was when they were in bed, and then it was a quick fuck before he fell into untidy sleep.

As the day of the first performance loomed, Charlie had been asked to do what she could to advertise the play, and to sell as many tickets as possible to undergraduates and staff alike. On the night itself, Charlie felt rather left out as the cast, and the backroom guys rushed around like blue-arsed flies. There was little she could do except sell programmes. The theatre was only about half full by the time the curtain went up, which was disappointing. When, shortly before the off, she went behind the scenes to wish them all luck, a scowling Phil was glaring at the audience through a crack in the curtains. He barely acknowledged her best wishes, shrugging away from her attempt at a kiss. "Fucking plebeian shits, wouldn't recognise art if it came up and bit them on the arse."

Charlie was only too aware that this thing that absorbed Phil's every waking moment was lightweight by any reasonable measuring, but this, or any other time for that matter, was not the time to express such an opinion. She took her seat, applauding loudly at all the right moments. Even with the sparse audience, the play seemed to go down well. Afterwards they all went to a party in the college bar.

Later a few of the stalwarts squeezed into Phil's room to carry on drinking. Phil had appeared angry at first but, as the evening wore on, he mellowed, began flirting with the female members of the cast along the lines of congratulating them for their performances. The attention he paid to Charlie was limited to an occasional hug in passing, one quick kiss at the start of the celebrations. As the numbers dwindled, and drunken students stumbled back to their own rooms Charlie found herself left with just Phil and Amelia for company.

Amelia said she was off. As she went out of the door she exchanged a surreptitious look with Phil, which Charlie intercepted by chance and was immediately suspicious remembering the previous occasion when she had found the two of then snogging. Anyway Amelia went but, almost at once, Phil took Charlie by the shoulders, looked into her eyes and sighed, "Look love I'm absolutely shagged out, do you mind if we call time for tonight?"

The bastard didn't want her. Charlie thought she knew why. She accepted his apologetic kiss and brief hug before going on her way, angry and upset. She started to walk back to college, then, on a whim, and with suspicion lurking in her mind she changed course, returning instead to Phil's room where she hammered loudly on his door.

She heard his voice from inside, asking who was there, but didn't answer, merely carrying on with her pounding at the door. Finally it opened to reveal a dishevelled Phil in boxer shorts. She pushed past him. There in his bed was the lovely Amelia, who had the cheek to grin at the angry intruder. Charlie turned to face Phil, who smiled sheepishly, shrugged as if to say, 'Okay you've caught me bang to rights, I'll come quietly'. Charlie did the nearest thing to snarling, then slapped him as hard as she could, before walking out leaving the door open behind her.

All that was last night, now the telephone call telling her that her gran was dying. That finally decided her, studies would have to wait, the semester was over for her, back to Exeter by way of Cheshire was the plan. That would take some organising. Charlie was fed up with her lack of success with boyfriends, but she had another two years at uni, she would get over that bastard Phil quickly enough in the holidays.

Chapter 31.

The drive up to Cheshire was subdued to say the least, James playing computer games on his portable console, Naomi and Peter exchanging polite, very light conversation. The question of how they were all going to fit into his mother's house for the night was one question mildly taxing Peter's brain. The fact that he and Naomi were not sharing a bedroom at present would raise eyebrows and questions. Was Naomi going to tell the kids that she was petitioning for divorce? How would they take it? He needn't have worried about accommodation, because the ever-efficient Gerald had arranged with the next door neighbour, who was a widow living alone, to make a couple of rooms available if needed. Margaret and Sebastian were staying in nearby Nantwich with Sebastian's mother and father.

When they arrived, Peter's first thought was to go straight away and see his mother in hospital. That was before Gerald stepped in to suggest that it would be better to wait until the morning. Elizabeth, he said, got very dozy in the evenings; she wanted to be at her best when the family visited. Naomi had been ready to cook something for them to eat, but there was Gerald again on the ball, indicating a casserole simmering in the oven and vegetables already prepared in saucepans.

Christ, how that bloody man irritated Peter, even more so when Naomi mentioned that she quite liked him, bit fussy maybe, she said, but his heart was in the right place. They had just finished eating, when Peter's mobile rang to tell him that Charlie was at Northwich station, would he pick her up please. She had apparently got a bus to Manchester, caught the train from there.

That was good, give him the chance to explain something of the situation between himself and Naomi, then she could tell her brother. When father and daughter met they embraced warmly enough, although both of them were feeling the strain of recent events. Charlie still affected by Phil's lousy behaviour, Peter finding it difficult getting round to telling her that he had been playing away. Then there was the shadow of the dying woman, which was why they were all here anyway.

Peter's explanation of his affair with Simone sounded very lame to him. Even when Charlie leaned across to give him a little hug, he still felt like a sod, a sod who was breaking up a family. In the circumstances Charlie did not tell her Dad about her own disastrous love-life. That could wait for another day. It was decided that the kids would stay in their grandmother's house, while he and Naomi would sleep next door. The widow, whose name was Mrs Rampton, didn't turn a hair when they said they preferred separate bedrooms. Families were families. It was absolutely none of her business how they organised their sleeping arrangements.

In the morning Gerald was at it again, insisting on cooking bacon and eggs, before they went to the hospital. When they arrived Margaret and Sebastian were already in with Elizabeth. The nurse said that too many people at one time would be tiring for the patient; they should wait until the first lot of visitors came out. When it was their turn, they found Elizabeth in a room with one other old lady, who was asleep. It was a shock for Peter to see his mother, quite a large woman, looking so diminished in size. She smiled at them, squeezing every one's hands in turn but, when she spoke, her voice was barely a whisper. As the visitors worked on their forced cheerfulness, the old lady's attention began to drift, her eyes closing now and then, while Gerald hovered over her, his concern obvious.

Peter wondered how on earth she had deteriorated to this degree in such a short space of time; that was before the guilt came back. If you don't see your mother for months on end, it shouldn't be a surprise if she looks totally different when you do.

The nurse came in to tell them the visit was at an end. They each said their goodbyes, wondering if it would be for the last time. Peter was the last to lean over the bed, and as he did so, his mother grasped his arm with surprising strength. "Peter there's something I want you do for me."

"Now Mrs Portland, you'll tire yourself."

Peter was just about to tell the nurse that his mother's name was Mrs Shadbolt when she spoke again. "Don't fuss nurse, there is something important I have to say to my son." She spoke quietly, but there was strength of purpose in her voice which brooked no intervention..

The others filed out. "Yes Peter, I'm Mrs Portland. I kept it quiet, not sure you lot would approve. Gerald has made me very happy ever since I've known him. I'm only sorry I won't be around much longer to be with him." She paused, the effort was tiring her. "Peter, I have altered my will to leave the house to Gerald. I want you to promise that you won't fight against my wishes. There's still a bit for you and Margaret, and a small legacy for your children." Her head fell back on the pillow, her hand reached out to find Peter's. Her eyes closed now, but her grip still firm. She whispered. "Promise me Peter, without the house, Gerald will be in a mess and I couldn't bear that."

Her eyes opened again briefly, the pleading clear to see. "Peter hated the idea of that horrible little twit ending up with his mother's property, but there was no denying the old lady's entreaty. "Alright Mum, I promise to let the will stand as you wish."

The grip on his hand relaxed, she appeared to have fallen asleep. He kissed her forehead, then quietly left the room.

The next day Mrs Portland was moved into a hospice. That, as if they didn't already know, confirmed that she had little time left to live. It became a matter of whether the two families would wait here in Cheshire until the end or go away and return when the doctors pronounced that the end was very close. Naomi said, with tears running down her cheeks, that she had better get back to her new business. She made Peter promise to ring her when there was news that the old lady's death was imminent. The children went back with Naomi, and Sebastian left as well. It was down to brother and sister to do the visiting, with Gerald always a constant presence.

Margaret's take on Gerald was completely different from Peter's. When he told her about the promise their mother had made him make in the hospital she didn't seem to mind. "Sad that she didn't think she could tell us she was getting married again. Probably down to my brother, I should think, if you made the feelings you expressed, to me, obvious to Mum." She reached out to touch his arm affectionately, showing she wasn't handing out blame.

"Yes, well, the man did come out of the blue didn't he? What's his background, professional widow-seeker perhaps. "Peter regretted his bitter words as soon as he said them, but then, they could have been true, such things did happen.

"You're wrong Peter. Whatever the man's background, he is genuinely fond of Mum, and she's no fool. I'm sure she would know if she was being conned."

They were sitting in a pub after telling Gerald they had some family business to discuss, which was partly true, although in Peter's case it was mainly because he needed a break from, what he saw as, the pompous little shit. They moved on to talk of their respective families. Peter confessed to his extra marital shenanigans and talked about his depression at being unemployed. Margaret knew about the job situation but was shocked to hear about the threatened divorce.

"My God, Peter, you're in a bit of a mess aren't you. Do you intend to live with this other woman, Simone or whatever her name is?"

"Good question, Margaret. Our house is in our joint names and there's no violence involved so I could stay where I am, but it's a grim existence. On the other hand," he looked rather sheepishly at his sister, "my thing with Simone was really just sexual. Neither of us had any long-term intention of settling down together, she didn't want me to leave Naomi, was just happy with our weekly meetings."

"That's maybe what you think, Peter. In my opinion you're being naive. I'm sure she said all that to you, but it must be a lonely life for her, lover once a week, kids at the weekend, think about it."

The next few days were tedious. In between visits to Elizabeth there was little for Peter and Margaret to do. Each time they went into the hospice their mother appeared to be losing ground in her fight against death, seemed to be shrinking before their eyes. Then the last time they went they were too late, she had slipped quietly away an hour earlier. The nurses hadn't telephoned because of the regularity of the visits and the fact that they needed time to prepare the old lady before they arrived. Even Peter had to accept the genuineness of Gerald's grief and, if he couldn't pluck up the humanity to put an arm round the man's shoulder, he felt for him. Margaret was less restrained and fell into a long embrace of mutual sadness with her stepfather.

That was it then until the funeral, the details of which Gerald said he would organise without any help from the family. He would let them know the details as soon as arrangements had been made. "Elizabeth wanted to be buried in the churchyard of Hartford church, she told me that." That was the last thing Gerald said before Peter and Margaret left him to grieve on his own.

As Peter drove home, he was wishing that he could have offered Gerald more genuine sympathy but, if the truth were known, although he couldn't bring himself to like the man, he suspected that Margaret was right about his genuine affection for their mother.

Chapter 32.

Back home, Naomi was kind to him, even cooked a meal for the four of them. It was a sad meal not only because of Elizabeth's death, but because the children now knew about the split between their parents.

After dinner Charlie mentioned, almost apologetically, that she was going out for a drink with Justin Bankworth, the boy who had once been the boy next door. Naomi commented, "I thought you said when you went off to Durham that the lad was a complete bore. What's happened to change your mind. What happened to that Rupert chap you brought home for Christmas?"

"Things move on Mum, Rupert's history." What she was really thinking was that, at least, she could rely on Justin, which was more than could be said for the wankers she had met at Durham in her first year. There was no way she was about to explain all that to her parents.

James was going out too. Since Charlie had come home, the old rivalry between the siblings had almost ceased. She asked him about Kirsty without the mockery that might have been the case a few months earlier.

So there they were, Peter and Naomi left to watch television with very little to say to one another. Peter wasn't concentrating on the programme on the screen, he was dwelling on his neglect of his mother in recent years. No wonder she had welcomed Gerald into her life when her own children paid her so little attention.

Uninterested in watching the box, and having talked with Naomi about his mother, which was about the only subject they could discuss without fear of dissention, Peter fell back on his usual recourse, that of taking George out for a walk. It was a glorious evening, soft as velvet, smells of earth and growth in the air following the rain shower early on. His mood was one of melancholy, rather than depression, sadness for things lost, sadness that he didn't seem able to make a decision these days. On that walk, on that evening, he didn't much care for the man that he was.

Not really a day for a funeral. High summer, hot, too hot for comfort, everyone overdressed for the weather. Peter delivered his encomium with controlled emotion, whereas when Margaret spoke, she was beset with tears. The sermon had been alright; at least the vicar had known Elizabeth, which provided a personal note to his words. Now watching the priest going through the ancient burial rights, the mourners were sad, but not distraught, apart from Gerald, who was openly weeping, and Margaret who still looked upset. As the priest's words droned on, Peter found his regrets, at what he hadn't done for his mother when she was alive, were being overtaken by thoughts of his own predicament. Should he give up Simone and try to re-establish a relationship with Naomi, what should he do about getting a job. His ridiculous indecision depressed him.

Ashes to ashes, pinches of soil onto the coffin, then it was all over. The grandchildren talking with some relief after being released from formality, renewing interrupted acquaintance, the adults quieter, but all strolling away from the grave, except for Gerald, who still stood, apparently making his last goodbyes. Peter couldn't help thinking that he was over doing it; after all he had only known Elizabeth for a few months, as far as he knew; could you really be that grief-stricken for someone you had known for such a brief time?

"I'm sorry Peter, she was a nice lady." Naomi put her arms round Peter, but then she had done the same thing to Margaret, and to Gerald, when he finally joined them, so it meant no more than sympathy for someone's loss of a close relative.

"You alright Dad?" Charlie's affectionate hug seemed to be

about more than his loss, seemed to express sympathy for the hurt he must be feeling about the split from Naomi, about his loss of a career. As far as she was concerned, whatever he had done or not done, he was still her dad, and she loved the old bugger. For Peter it was a spark amongst the gloom of his thoughts, one for which he was grateful. His stomach clenched with the extent of his love for his warm and wilful daughter. "I'm fine love, just feeling a bit guilty, now the old dear's gone, that I didn't give her enough of my time."

Gerald began to organise family and friends into various cars, to take them back to what Peter thought of as his mother's house, although it was now, to all intents and purposes, Gerald's house. He had arranged for caterers to come in to provide the food and tea and coffee, had himself laid in alcoholic drinks for those needing a stimulant.

Naomi's feelings were ones of genuine sadness and sympathy for Margaret and Peter, but she couldn't help worrying about how Ivan and Rosalind were getting on without her. The business was her baby, and while she needed the input of the other two, she was the driving force. Without her, nothing much would happen; she had to be there to guide the ship. It was only two days she would be away but she worried nevertheless.

She sighed to herself as she watched Peter being consoled by Charlie, a little touch of jealousy in there somewhere. What about this divorce, she wondered. Peter had accepted her ultimatum without protest, so she had taken the first steps in the process. Still she hated the idea of her life being ripped apart and then, once the children were out of the picture, the division of the spoils. Even now it seemed to Naomi that closure could be avoided, if only Peter made some gesture of reconciliation towards her; a more genuine apology, confirmation that this other bitch was consigned to the past, but no, he just moped about the place, seemingly without ambition to try something different; van driver for Tesco, is that the best he could come up with?

The Shadbolt family stayed the night making use of the neighbour's hospitality again. Nobody wanted a formal meal in the evening after the wake, but James and Charlie opted for some chips. Gerald told them about a chippie within walking distance, so they set out to buy a takeaway. "What about this girlfriend then James, what's she like?" There was no teasing now, and James took her question on its face value.

"Nothing serious, she's taking the same course as me at college."

"I bet there's more to it than that, James. You know when you and that Greg were so close, I was beginning to wonder if you two were..." She stopped and giggled. "Well you know, 'at it' together."

James wished the earth would open up and swallow him whole. He felt the flush irresistibly colouring his neck and face. "We were just close mates that's all, still see him at college." How he regretted that relationship now, particularly the memory of having sex with a bloke. What the hell would Kirsty say if she ever found out.

"It wouldn't have mattered if you were; there's nothing wrong with being gay." Charlie was being reassuring, or so she thought, but the only thing James wanted was to get off the subject. As if to answer his prayers the next question swung the subject wildly, if embarrassingly in another direction. "Have you had her knickers off yet, young James?"

He was used to Charlie being outrageous, and on this occasion, her question came as a relief taking them, as it did, well away from his association with Greg. "None of your damn business Charlie," but he grinned. This evening was the first time that he could remember that his big sister had treated him as an equal, not some grubby and annoying little schoolboy. It felt good to have someone close, who understood the contemporary scene, might even become a confidante in the future. They got their chips and strolled back to the house eating then out of the paper, telling each other what had been going on in their lives over the last few months, or at least some of it.

The family set off, back home, early the next day, having first gone through Elizabeth's will. Peter and Gerald were named as executors. The details would have to be sorted through probate, as there were investments and a house involved. The children were delighted to hear they would come into a £1000 each as soon as the formalities were concluded. Charlie already had an idea of what she would do with her share even before they reached home.

Chapter 33.

Back home, Peter went next door to collect an ecstatic George from Mrs Stackhorn. It had always seemed strange that the miserable old bugger, always complaining about invasions of her garden and other trivial matters, should be happy to look after their dog whenever it was needed. The kids went off to find their respective friends, Naomi rushed into town to see what had happened to her infant enterprise. Peter immediately reverted to depression. The supermarket had turned down his application; they didn't say why, but he could guess that with his CV they thought he would be over-qualified for the job.

That evening was similar to many recent evenings, with Peter taking a loving George for a walk, then returning to restless indecision. The house was empty: Naomi obviously involved with her new business and the kids still out. He found a couple of chops in the freezer and occupied himself with preparing some dinner, which he took into the living room to eat on his lap while watching some junk on television, his whisky on the table at his side. He must have fallen asleep because the next thing he knew was Naomi shouting at him from the doorway.

"Peter, this is never going to work. If you think I'm going to get home after working myself silly, to start clearing your mess, you've got another think coming. The kitchen looks as though a hurricane has struck; it's not on Peter, I'm telling you." Lately she had looked tired, probably due to the stress of setting up the new business, but her anger was not constrained. He recognised, with real bitterness, that she was right.

"I'm sorry I was going to clear up but I fell asleep."

"Drank yourself to sleep more like. I really don't know what's happened to you Peter. You seem to have lost any drive you might once have had. Surely there must be something you can find to do instead of moping round the house all day mucking the place up, voluntary work or something." Naomi gave a weary shake of her head, ran her hand through her hair. Any regrets about the divorce were rapidly being chased away by her husband's inconsideration, his failure to take any positive action.

"I've tried, as you damn well know." It sounded pathetic even to Peter's ears.

"You've got a good brain, good experience, you could be useful to some organisation. As far as I can see you haven't tried hard enough."

Sleeping in front of the television always left him feeling dull and lethargic. He could do without this tirade, justified though it may have been. "Suppose you just tell me what I'm supposed to do, you're so full of bright ideas."

"For God's sake Peter, look at yourself, you're pathetic, fucking pathetic." She left the room closing the door behind her with a bang.

There was one decision he could make, that was to move in with Simone, accept her offer. It was a big decision and would of course cement the divorce action, but he and Naomi were done, finished, so what did it matter, anything was better than being treated like a useless layabout, even if that's what he was. He would ring Simone tonight to ask her if she had been serious about her invitation. That was action of a sort. With it came a determination that he would do something about a job, maybe re-train for something. Naomi's words had goaded him; he would show the bitch. As he went outside to make the call to Simone, he could hear Naomi angrily clattering about in the kitchen. Oh well it was too late to do anything about that.

Simone couldn't have been nicer about it, even sounded excited at the prospect. When he came in from the garden his entry coincided with Naomi coming out of the kitchen; she glared at him.

"You'll no doubt be pleased to know I'm taking some action tomorrow. I'm moving out, so you won't have to worry about your precious kitchen getting messed up."

Naomi was on the back foot for a moment, regret, perhaps, that she had driven her husband out of the house, but she soon recovered her equilibrium. "Going to stay with your other woman are you Peter; she's fucking well welcome to you. I just wonder whether she will still want you when you're moping about her place all day long instead of popping in for a quick fuck now and then."

"Oh go to hell, Naomi, will you, just get off my back." Peter went to bed angry but vaguely relieved that he had made the decision, tentatively looking forward to the next day.

Moving in with Simone was difficult. She had told him where to find the key. He drove over in mid-morning, with the few things he was bringing with him. The flat had Simone's personality stamped all over it. Peter was left with the sensation that he was making a short term visit, finding it difficult to accept that this could be a long term arrangement. Even finding somewhere to put his clothes was going to prove a problem, so he left his cases still packed in the hallway, to await Simone's return in the evening. As he wandered round what was to be his new home, for the near future at least, he was seeing the flat really for the first time, taking in the details he had barely noticed on his many visits previously. In the past he had usually just been passing through on his way to the bedroom.

The strangeness of his surroundings was unsettling. He had strong pangs of regret about leaving behind all those things he had lived with for years, the familiar furniture, the pictures on the wall, his books, although he had managed to bring a few of those with him. He was panicking. Would this work and, if it didn't, what would he do? There was no way he would go crawling back to Naomi with his tail between his legs. After leaving his cases in the hallway, Peter went into the town to get something to eat for lunch. It seemed a violation, at this early stage, to start cooking in Simone's 'state of the art' kitchen. As he sat in the pub drinking a pint of beer with his sandwich, he remained in a state of uncertainty, found that he was already missing George. He had felt it would be unfair to add a dog to his own presence in Simone's home, but leaving him behind was deeply hurtful.

Peter spent most of the afternoon walking round the shops, until finally he decided to return to the flat, risk making a cup of tea, before switching on the television. It was a relief when he heard the sound of Simone's key in the lock. She was back early, probably because she understood how difficult moving in would be for Peter, and wanting to help. .

"You got here then?" Usually when Peter came to visit they would be locked in tight embrace as soon as he put foot over the threshold, but today there was some hesitation before Peter kissed Simone quietly on the lips, and she hugged him close to her chest.

This was a new situation and they both realised it; no rushing into the bedroom this evening; they must feel their way into this new arrangement with mutual care. Simone, who had called in at the super market on the way home, began to prepare their evening meal, while Peter fussed about trying to help, but mainly getting in the way. The most useful thing he did was to pour Simone a generous gin and tonic which she accepted with a little kiss of gratitude. The evening passed pleasantly enough, Peter eager to load the dish washer, Simone finding some space for him to put his clothes.

Despite all the mutual consideration there remained little periods of awkwardness brought about by each being over-polite to the other. It wasn't until they were both in bed, that they found an ease of contact that they recognised as familiar and unrestrained. That brought about a more relaxed state of mind in both of them. Their new living arrangement might just work.

"What did she say when you said you were leaving then Peter?" They had made satisfactory love, but Simone wasn't yet ready for sleep. She lay with her head on Peter's chest, squinting up at him with a soft smile playing around her lips.

"Not much," he kissed the top of her head, "something about going to my other woman."

"Well she knows now, probably make her accelerate the divorce petition I suppose." She snuggled down, kissing a nipple, smiling contentedly. "Tomorrow, lover, we've got some talking to do. I'm not daft, I know how strange it must be for you moving in here, all my things scattered around the place, nothing of you, but I want to do something about that. You could bring over the odd picture, favourite objects, something to add your personality to the place."

"Thanks sweetie that's great, but I also want to discuss finance; not after a free ride am I?"

"You've just had a free ride." She laughed. "Okay Peter whatever you want, I'm sure we'll work everything out." To put a stop to discussion for the night she reached down his body, easily persuading him to concentrate on sexual intimacy rather than practical matters. This time they fell asleep after a quiet but satisfying culmination.

Peter had been in Simone's bed many times before, but had never woken up in it, in the morning. He felt strange, slightly disorientated as he took in his surroundings in more detail than he ever had before. Simone came out of the bathroom wearing a dressing gown, glowing after her shower. She sat down on the edge of the bed and leaned over to give her lodger a kiss. "Morning lover, did you sleep well?" He stretched luxuriously relishing the rapid tumescence that soon prevailed.

"Like a baby." The presence of this gorgeous, deliciously-smelling woman, made him randy as hell; his hands were searching urgently under the folds of her dressing gown.

Simone laughed as she got up from the bed. "Haven't got time Peter, I've an urgent meeting this morning." She kissed him again then teased him by reaching under the duvet to give his cock a quick squeeze, before darting out of his reach to start getting dressed. She laughed again his groan of frustration. "You'll have to get used to the idea, Peter, that this is a working household, not a house of pleasure; or at least not all the time. I really must be off, help yourself to whatever you want for breakfast."

He watched her finish dressing, watched her gulp down a cup

of coffee, heard her run downstairs and the front door bang shut, then he was alone, wondering, as he had done for many days in the recent past, how he was going to get through the day. He was in a new location but having too much time on his hands was not going to be solved by that.

Anyway, for a start he decided to ring what used to be his home number, have a word with the children, if they were up. He waited until he thought Naomi would have gone to work, then dialled the number. A yawning voice answered the phone recognisable as Charlie's, despite the sleep content. The kids, he thought, were all set to live their own lives, and what he and Naomi did was probably not of any great concern. That aside they were his kids. The feeling that he needed to keep in contact, to let them know that he still loved them, was not walking away from them, was strong within him..

Charlie managed to stifle her yawns, seemed glad to hear from her Dad. In a short space of time she told him that James was still in bed, that she and Justin Bankworth were going over to France for a couple of weeks, that she loved him, was sad about him and her mother splitting like that. "Life's a pig at times Dad, but you can hardly blame Mum after she found out about your bit on the side, can you?"

"I'm not blaming her for anything, Charlie, but, you know, these things happen."

"Not unless the two people concerned want them to happen." That was an unusually serious comment for Charlie. "Anyway Dad, you going to stay living with this other woman on a permanent basis, or what?"

There wasn't much more to say, so they agreed to meet up for coffee in town the next day, which was the day before she went off to France with the boy she had called a bore less than twelve months ago. Peter asked her to persuade James to come along as well. The phone replaced, he was left feeling pangs of regret over what he had done to break up his family.

Chapter 34.

While Peter was settling in with his mistress, Naomi was working her socks off as usual, three appointments this morning alone. It was going well. Ivan and Rosalind were growing in confidence and enthusiasm every day. When she took a short break at lunchtime to eat her sandwich and drink a cup of coffee, her thoughts turned to her errant husband. Her pride had decreed that she start divorce proceedings but in reality she hated the idea. If Peter had agreed to drop this other woman, she felt certain that they could rebuild their life together again. There were vestiges of love in that consideration, but also the fact that she hated the turmoil that would result from divorce and, she had to admit, she hated the idea of being without a partner, even if they weren't exactly soul mates. Now the blighter had moved out to live with his other woman that put an altogether different slant on the situation.

Peter, in his new surroundings, felt a new drive to get his life together. He bought local and national newspapers, trade magazines, registered with employment agencies on the street, and the internet, but despite all his efforts found nothing that appeared to suit his qualifications. Even turning his attention towards manual work produced no job opportunities he thought he could manage.

Towards the end of the day, feeling downhearted, he sat outside a café in the new precinct to drink a cup of coffee, watching a couple of pigeons cadging for crumbs. The euphoria of last night's sex with Simone had dissipated. Even the thought of many more to come failed to make up for the day's failures. It was glaringly obvious that Simone, kind and considerate as she was, would eventually tire of having a live-in lover, who did little except mope about the place all day, which come to think of it was exactly what Naomi had said the night before he left home.

When the weekend arrived Simone went off to pick up Phillip and Michael as it was her weekend to have them with her. On Saturday they took the kids out for the day to Paignton zoo. It wasn't a great success with both the boys reacting badly to Peter's presence.

Then, on Saturday night, after a strained day, during which the children continued to show their resentment of Peter's being around, Simone shocked him by asking if he minded sleeping on the sofa that night. She said she didn't want to upset the children further by letting them see her sharing her bed with a man who, to them, was a stranger. Peter couldn't for the life of him see that it mattered. She and Roger had been apart for years, surely the kids had accepted by now that their parents were leading independent lives, so what the hell. Whatever he thought didn't matter, it was Simone's flat, they were her children, he was after all a guest, so of course he agreed to a night of discomfort.

He woke in the morning to find Phillip, the older of the two lads, standing by the sofa, frowning down at him. He must have been about nine, quite old enough to recognise that having a strange man to stay in his mother's home meant something even if he didn't know what. "Why are you living her with my Mum?"

What do you say to a nine-year-old child who sees you as an unwanted intrusion into his life. His parents may be living in separate houses, but they were still his parents, outsiders were not welcome. A routine had been established since his Mum and Dad had split; Phillip wished they would get together again, but failing that, at least he had got used to that routine. Now it was being disrupted by a total stranger, and he resented it. To be fair, he would have thought the same way if his Dad had invited a woman into their home.

"Your Mum and I are friends, that's all Phillip."

The boy sniffed, pursed his lips as though thinking, then came out with words that put Peter well and truly in his place. "My Mum and Dad are going to live together again soon, so we'll all be in my Dad's house." He didn't actually say *'and so there'* but that's what it felt like. Peter, still half asleep, sat up, rubbed his eyes, wondered how the hell they were going to get through the rest of the day.

"That will be nice for you all." Sounded feeble but in the face of the child's antagonism, it was all he could think of.

The blanket had slipped off Peter's shoulders. "You haven't got any pyjamas on." He envisioned the boy going back to his father to report that naked men were sleeping on his ex-wife's sofa.

"No, I find it more comfortable to sleep without them." He was saved by the arrival of the child's mother.

"You're up early Phillip, want some cocoapops for breakfast?" She ruffled his hair, grinned at Peter, "Coffee?" He nodded, and when mother and son left the room he hastily pulled on his trousers before following them into the kitchen. Phillip was saying something about Peter sleeping without pyjamas, while Simone was trying to explain that was quite normal for some people, suggesting that he get on with his breakfast cereal. She passed a mug of coffee over to Peter, grimacing over the child's head.

"Where's that sleepy head of a brother of yours?" The boy looked up from his cereal, his face serious.

"Dad says he would sleep until tomorrow if he let him, says he even took a long time being born. Is that true Mum, did he take a long time?" Simone laughed, kissed the top of the boy's head. "Can't say I kept note of the time sweetie, but it was worth it however long it took, and that applies to you as well my darling." Peter couldn't help noticing the moisture in her eyes as she spoke to her son. It was only too obvious how living apart from her children was desperately painful for her, how having to say goodbye to them after each visit was a small trauma in itself.

When Michael eventually came downstairs, he still looked half asleep, had to be persuaded to have some breakfast. He only began to show some animation when Simone suggested they go to the park and play football. "Haven't brought my Manchester United shirt, Mum."

"That doesn't matter, we all know who you support."

In the park the children rushed about kicking the ball with Peter and Simone joining in. The morning went better than yesterday although walking back after the session Phillip, hand in hand with his mother, looked over at Peter and said, "You're not much good uncle Peter, not a patch on my Dad, he can tackle really hard, and run fast as well."

Peter laughed, nodding his agreement, recognising only too clearly what the comment had pointed out, that there was a missing figure from the morning's play, that he was only there on sufferance. Simone gave him a sympathetic look. The moment soon passed with the two boys arguing about whether Manchester United or Arsenal were going to win the league next season After lunch she took the boys home to their father in Bristol.

When she got back to the flat she was miserable. While Peter started cooking a bolognaise for dinner, he sat her down with a large gin and tonic, but her spirits remained low. They said little to each other, watched television for a couple of hours, until Simone said she was tired so they went upstairs early. In bed she snuggled up to him, head on his chest and cried a little bit. It was the first time he had ever been to bed with Simone when they hadn't made love. He didn't have to be particularly perceptive to realise that tonight was not the night for sex.

Monday morning Simone was out of bed early, full of her usual energy and showing no signs of yesterday's melancholy. Peter offered to get her coffee, but she told him to stay where he was, kissed him long and hard, evaded his clutching hands, and was out of the flat by eight-thirty. Peter stayed in bed thinking of what he was going to do to start off another week of tedium. He must have dropped off, because he was jolted awake by a loud bang that appeared to come from the area of the kitchen. He lay still, listening for further sounds. There was nothing. Perhaps he had imagined the sound, but then just as he was relaxing again, there was the unmistakable sound of the kitchen door creaking. It was only slight, but Simone had mentioned the previous day that the door needed a drop of oil, so he recognised it straight away.

There was no doubt about it, there was someone in the flat. Peter was no 'do it yourself hero' but he couldn't just cringe in the bedroom, hoping the intruder would go away. His guts churned with fear, he shivered, yet it wasn't cold. He had to do something. Sliding out of bed, then putting on his dressing gown, he went softly over to the bedroom door, and listened. There was another sound, although he couldn't make out exactly where it was coming from.

No doubt now, there was someone in the flat. Weapons, what could he use as a weapon. He looked round the bedroom but there was nothing obvious. Then he thought of his squash racket in the wardrobe. Not much of a weapon, but at least something to hold on to, strike out with, if a confrontation came.

He listened again at the bedroom door, before easing it open, and peering through the crack. There was nothing to be seen but from the sitting room came the unmistakable sound of someone moving around. He slipped out of the bedroom, moved quietly towards the open sitting room door. Tense as piano wire, he put his head round the corner. A youth was picking up objects, apparently looking for things worth stealing.

"What the fuck do you think you're doing?" Peter raised the squash racket threateningly in the air. The boy, that's all he was, small and furtive, turned towards Peter, a look of utter shock on his face.

"Fucking hell." He backed against the wall, eyes darting about in his face. As Peter moved forward the boy covered his head with his arms. "Don't hit me, I'm sorry, thought the place was empty." He slid down the wall to sit crumpled in a protective heap. There was suddenly a foul smell in the air, the lad had shit himself with fear.

Peter looked at the miserable pile of humanity in front of him. Despite himself, his angry fear was at once tempered with sympathy. This boy was obviously no threat, but what was he to do with him now? His first thought was to ring the police straight away, and that's what he should have done, but curiosity and human interest came to the fore. "I'm not going to hit you, but what the hell do you think you're doing in this flat?"

For the first time the boy's eyes met Peter's directly; he was calmer now, aware perhaps, that he wasn't going to be attacked. "What do you fucking think," he snivelled, adding with restored confidence, "need to live don't I, thought the bird lived here had gone to work, didn't know there was anyone else in the place." His arms were away from his head now, the hatred was apparent in his staring eyes.

"How old are you, how did a young lad like you get involved in burglary?" No answer; the police would have to be called. Peter thought of the ignominy of being carted off to the police station with messed up pants He decided to give the child, which was how he saw him now, a break. "Alright, son, let's see what we can do to clean you up while I think about what to do with you. Come with me and don't try and run for it."

The boy scrambled to his feet, slouched after Peter into the bathroom. "Right take off those stinking things and wash yourself down in the bath; I'll get you some things of mine to wear."

"I'm not fucking taking my trousers off with you in here. You some kind of pervert or what?"

"Please yourself; if you'd rather the cops take you off stinking of shit that's up to you. And I'm not giving you the chance of bunking off through the window so you'll just have to put up with me in the room."

The boy scowled furiously, but then slowly turned his back on Peter, and let his trousers fall to the floor. Still with his pants on he stepped under the shower, running the water before taking them off as well. He soaped himself thoroughly and when it looked as though he had finished, Peter handed him a towel. The trousers joined the pants in the bath to be disposed of later. He took the boy into the bedroom, handed him some underpants from the drawer, and then an old pair of trousers. The boy turned his back, moving as far away from Peter as he could, before letting the towel slip to the floor, and putting on the clothes. "You want a cup of coffee then?"

He looked suspiciously at Peter. "What's the game then, why haven't you called the pigs." His frown was distorted with continuing suspicion, giving the impression of a cornered rodent.

"Do you want coffee, or not."

"Got anything to eat have you?" Even in cleaner clothes the boy looked a picture of abject misery, hair long and dirty, face somehow crimped and grey. Peter got bread from the bin, butter and cheese, put them on the kitchen table. The boy cut a thick slice, took a couple of bites, before adding a wodge of butter and hunk of cheese, which he wolfed down with greedy haste. He gulped some coffee, his eyes flitting from side to side, as though half expecting the food to be whisked away or something unpleasant to happen.

Neither said anything for minutes as the food was being dealt with, then the youth looked up and, mouth still full of bread, said. "What's the game then, why you acting decent, what's the catch?" Confidence was returning now, fear dissipating, but it was still a mystery what this bloke wanted. He had been caught bang to rights, why was he messing about like this, why no call to the pigs.

"I'm not up to anything. If you want to know I'm curious to learn how a young lad gets into burglary. How old are you?" By now Peter was beginning to wonder himself if he had gone quite mad. For reasons he wouldn't have been able to explain, he wanted to find out a few facts about the young intruder.

"Fucking old enough aren't I, need to steal to live don't I. No hand-outs from the state for kids my age, less you want to live in one of them homes or with them bastard foster parents." The rest of the loaf was fast disappearing; the boy had been very hungry indeed.

"Don't the social workers catch up with you?"

"Course they fucking do, but it's easy to go on the run again." He scowled into his coffee. The fear may have gone, but he was still one very miserable child.

"What's your name?"

"Why you want to know? Jimmy's my fucking name for what that's worth." Peter thought of James and the privileged life he had lived compared to this snivelling example of youth, then decided, on a whim, not ring the police.

Further questioning, further reluctant answers followed. It transpired that the boy had recently run away from a foster home where, from what Peter could understand, he had been physically and sexually abused. Finally the boy left with Peter's trousers and all the money he had on him. As he edged cautiously through the front door, he turned to look at Peter, shook his head before running off without any another word, not even a straightforward thank you.

Peter stood in the doorway, watching him run down the street, thinking about what was going to happen to him over the next several years. The boy reached the corner, stopped running, turned round to look back towards the flat, raised a hand in the air, before vanishing round the corner. What a way to start the week, but the episode had given Peter food for thought. He was bored out of his mind so why didn't he do some volunteer social work, if there was such a thing. He remembered now that Wendy had talked about voluntary work at that dinner which now seemed so long ago. Naomi had suggested something along those lines in one of her tirades. Having a direction to move towards, however vague, raised his spirits on that Monday morning. Perhaps the events of that day has been his Damascus moment. The thought amused him.

Chapter 35.

Peter hadn't played squash for weeks, so it was something of a surprise for Robbie Barkworth when he rang to suggest a game. It was a very one-sided encounter with Robbie running out an easy winner, and an exhausted, out of practice Peter wondering if he's ever been able to play the game. In the bar with pints in front of them, Peter asked after Wendy, before responding to counter questions about his own recent life. Robbie knew about Simone, but was shocked to find out that Naomi was divorcing him.

The incident with the young burglar had remained firmly at the forefront of Peter's mind. When he related what had happened to Robbie, it was, perhaps, because he wanted an opinion about his idea of getting involved in social work, perhaps it was also because he was genuinely concerned about the fate of lads like Jimmy.

Robbie grinned over his beer. "Can't really see you in that role Peter, you've been too long in the rat race to change your spots."

That annoyed Peter; he frowned. "Alright, you cynical bastard, but it could just have been my Damascus moment you know." He was still attracted by the thought that an incident could come along and change the whole direction of a person's life. "You don't think I'm really serious do you?" The more he tried to convince Robbie about that fact, the more he began to realise that he was serious.

When he got back to the flat he found Simone in a thoughtful mood. He thought at first she was still worrying about the intrusion into her flat by that young burglar, but then it seemed to be something else altogether. There was a distracted air about her, less ebullient than normal. She had kissed him when he got back, although there appeared less enthusiasm about her embrace than might have been expected. He thought no more about it until they were in bed later that night. She abruptly raised herself on one elbow, looked at him with a very serious expression on her face. "Peter I'm sorry but I've got to go up to Bristol this weekend, so you'll be on your own. I hope that's OK."

"No problem, but it's not your weekend for the kids is it?"

She lay back in the bed and looked up at the ceiling. "No it's not, but something has cropped up and I have to talk to Roger. There's some details about the arrangements for the children. It's better done face to face rather than over the telephone. Will you miss me sweetie?"

As she snuggled up to him, he sensed that she was not in her usual randy mood. Well he was knackered after his game of squash, so an early resort to sleep was all right with him. In fact he mused as he slipped into unconsciousness this would be another of the few occasions he had been to bed with Simone without them having sex. He was left wondering, as a last thought, what the trip to Bristol was really about.

Saturday on his own. Out with the laptop, surfing the net for information on social work. It was great having a goal in mind, something to aim for, however unlikely or impossible it might be. It took him only a few minutes to discover that his First in Economics would qualify him to take a two year MA in social work, which was better than the three-year standard course, and there were several universities offering the course.

He was getting more and more excited as his initial vague ideas began to morph into practical opportunities. Already he was asking himself whether he was too late to apply for the Autumn start. His mind was racing, impatient now to take positive action. Finance for mature students would have to be looked into but there were bursaries available to social-work students administered by the NHS Business Services Authority, which might pay for tuition fees with an allowance for practice placement costs. One thing was certain; the money from his redundancy and the relatively small amount left him by his mother would not last for two years.

His frantic research was interrupted by a call from Charlie on his mobile. She was back from holiday with Justin, was suggesting they get together in town for a coffee together with James, who had asked to come along. Peter was uplifted by this contact from his kids, agreed to meet later that morning.

He arrived at the café first and got to his feet when he saw them coming towards the table. Charlie was as beautiful as ever, but James was sporting a black eye and bruising on his face. He hugged them both before ordering coffee, then asked Charlie about her visit to France, how it was going with Justin. He was asking the questions, but all the while he was dying to tell them about his plans, the total change of direction he hoped his life was going to take.

"France was fine Dad but me and Justin, well no, that's all over, I'm afraid. I should have followed my gut instinct, realised he was not right for me, but after those blokes at uni, I thought perhaps the boy next door might be a refreshing change. He's a nice lad, kind and considerate but, hell, he bores the pants off me. My fault, I admit, but I need someone with a spark of adventure in them. Justin is old before his time, ready to marry, settle down with a safe job, and a nest of kids; I want to live while I can and find some excitement." Her eyes shone. That wasn't due to sadness over Justin, it was excitement about the possibilities that life offered.

Charlie had always displayed an impatient restlessness, so this latest development was no surprise. His heart gave a little jump when he thought about what might happen to his wilful daughter as she progressed through life, and how much he cared. Of course he cared about his son too, although the relationship here was subtly different from that with his daughter. He smiled at James and raised an eyebrow. "James, what about you, taken up prize fighting or something?"

James shrugged. "It's nothing Dad." He touched his damaged face. "Some idiot was after my mobile. I wanted to hang on to it, so there was a bust-up. I came off worse." He shrugged again. Peter thought for a fleeting moment about the possible social implications of such an attack, another Jimmy perhaps, but quickly reverted to a tribal response. "My God, James, that's terrible, have you been to the police?"

"No point Dad, they'd never catch him and I don't want all that hassle." The truth was very different, in fact. He and Kirsty had been walking back from the student bar two nights ago, when some bloke wearing a balaclava had jumped on him, punched him a couple of times, then ran off into the bushes. The only words his attacker had uttered was "You bastard," repeated a couple of times. It was enough for James to recognise Greg's voice.

He told Kirsty that he had no idea why he had been assaulted, and wasn't about to tell his father anything different. The whole thing with Greg was embarrassing in retrospect, all he wanted to do was to put that episode in his life behind him.

In fact when he thought about the incident, he didn't even blame Greg; he could understand how his friend had felt betrayed when he had decided to opt for Kirsty. It was really nothing to do with the sex in itself, it was the betrayal that must have hurt.

As far as James was concerned though, the sexual element of their friendship was something he wanted to forget. In fact he would be mortified if anyone found out. It crossed his mind that Greg might seek for revenge by dropping a few words in the ears of fellow students. He wondered, not for the first time, how Kirsty would react if she knew what had happened between the two boys.

Peter had listened to his children with fatherly patience but now, no longer able to contain his excitement, he told them about his plans to go back to university. They took the news with incredulous looks at their dad, maybe wondering if he had gone just a little bit potty, but said little. Perhaps they needed time to absorb this strange change of direction their father had decided upon..

Simone came home on Sunday afternoon. Peter was very glad to see her after a lonely couple of days. He noticed a difference in her as soon as she came through the door; gone were her usual exuberance, and her playfully provocative way of greeting and, instead, her kiss was brief, almost asexual. She looked worried, appeared to have something to tell him. The first thing she did was ask Peter to pour her a large gin and tonic. That was strange in itself, she was no great drinker, normally would have waited until evening before even thinking about having a drink. He had been impatient to tell her about his own dramatic career change but this was not the time.

Peter carried out her instructions, helping himself to a whisky while he was at it. "Alright love, spill the beans. What's happened in Bristol to upset you?" She took a deep swig of her gin, looked very directly at him, sighed, licked her lips, all the while slowly shaking her head in what seemed to Peter to be a sad way. He feared the worst. "Something to do with the kids is it, Simone? Come on love let's have the bad news. Whatever's happened, I'm sure we can fight the blighter, if that ex-husband of yours is up to some new trick to stop you seeing them."

"Not quite like that Peter." She came over and sat on his lap nestling up close to him, openly weeping now. "Something's happened that's changed everything, or at least will change everything, if I agree to do what Roger is proposing."

"For God's sake love, tell me. Whatever it is I'll stand by you." He kissed the top of her head, holding her tightly in his arms.

That started off another torrent of tears. "I know you would Peter, I know you would, but it's you or the kids. I'm sorry but the kids have to come first."

"You're telling me that Roger doesn't like me here, is that it? Threatening to stop you seeing them, unless you chuck me out, the fucking bastard." Peter felt anger rising in him, knew he was bound to lose out in a battle between him and Simone's children, but it was all so petty, the sod didn't want her, but he didn't want anyone else to have her, was what it was all about.

Simone raised her head so she could look directly into his face. "As I said Peter, it's not quite like that. Roger has offered me a sort of deal. I go to live with him and the kids in Bristol while we try again to make a go of it."

"But what the hell, I thought you hated the guy, how can you suddenly change your attitude overnight, and why now, out of the blue like this?" He was very angry, but also baffled by this turn of events.

"Well sweetheart, it's not as strange as it may seem. First of all Roger's investments are not producing enough for him to live on in the present market conditions. He's been offered his old job back if he wants it and that involves some overseas travel, so then there's the problem of the kids, and who would look after them while he was away. So you see it's a logical plan, and I get my kids back full time." She kissed him through the tears that ran freely down her cheeks.

"So that's us finished then?" He sounded bitter; he was bitter. All Saturday's euphoria vanished in the blink of an eye. Of course he knew how much she cared for Phillip and Michael. Who could blame her for making such a decision, but he hated the idea, divorced from his wife, or soon to be, deserted by his lover. He sighed. "Are you going to remarry Roger then?"

"No, in fact the deal is that we live separate lives, there's room in the house. I would do my job part time, that's not a problem, and I would be there for the kids. It's not ideal but I did once love the man, perhaps I can do it again." She sniffled as she went on, "but Peter I'll always love you. This thing between us meant more to me than the sex, glorious though it was. I've never talked about it before, because I thought you just saw me as a bit on the side. Actually you mean a lot more to me than that."

They went to bed early, spent a long night talking and making love, but it was quiet love making. Simone expressed her sadness in the tender way she pleasured her lover, seeking to give him whatever he needed with selfless consideration. That damped down Peter's own passion but didn't stop the two of them appreciating the joy of each other's bodies over and over again, until they finally fell asleep tightly entwined in each other's arms.

At one point, before the night was over, Peter stopped his caresses to look down at Simon's naked body illuminated by moonlight through the uncurtained window, wondering how he could possibly live without her. His guts cramped at the thought of the barren life that lay ahead of him. Becoming a social worker had, over a few hours, faded into a distant unimportant dream when set alongside the loss of Simone.

Chapter 36.

Charlie was, for once, helping her mother prepare the evening meal. "So how is your dad getting on then, found himself a job yet?" Naomi's every waking minute in recent months had been consumed with getting her business off the ground. Ivan was a good guy, but the drive required to establish a portfolio of new clients, and to preserve those that had followed them from Bradford, Lang and Oldfield, had to come from her. Rosalind was playing her part, had already had to take on a secretary to help with the mounting office work. Soon they would need more help. All good, but all time-consuming in a way she had never experienced before.

"You'll never believe this, Mum, but he's talking about retraining as a social worker." Naomi looked with some astonishment at her grinning daughter.

"A social worker, what on earth brought this about? Doesn't really sound like Peter to me." What she didn't say was that a lot of things about her 'soon to be' ex-husband, had taken her by surprise, not the least of which was his flight into the arms of another woman. He had seemed so set in his ways, career mapped out, family man, and all the time he had been screwing another woman. For some reason, unknown even to her, she had not yet applied for her decree absolute.

Was it the finality of the thing that stopped her going ahead, did she think that he might come back, she really didn't know. What she did know, what she wouldn't admit to anyone, not even her children, was that she missed having a husband around. More than that, she missed having Peter, in particular, around. He was a bastard, of course, but he was a familiar bastard. There lingered still, an affection that couldn't easily be thrust aside by a piece of paper.

"Seems he had a run in with a young burglar at the flat where he's staying. That convinced him that social work was what he wanted to do. Two years taking a Masters I think he said."

"Good job he's getting free board and lodging then." She cut short the conversation to go back to her cooking, but had to admit to herself that she had been interested in Charlie's news.

The flat sold quickly. Peter and Simone moved gradually apart, the coming separation an inevitable sadness. The lingering time before Peter moved into his grotty bedsit, and Simone moved to Bristol, was horrible. They still slept in the same bed, made half-hearted love occasionally, but the light had gone out of their relationship.

The marking time was not good for either of them.

Peter had one bit of good news. Despite the lateness of his application UCAS had fixed him up with his masters course at Exeter university.

It appeared that they were so desperately short of social workers, they were prepared to cut corners to rush students through the system.

He did have to attend what they called a mature students' interview that went down reasonably well, despite some sceptical questions from the panel about why someone of his age should want to suddenly go into social work. At the end of it all he was given a place.

Lectures would start in October.

When he watched the van disappear round the corner Peter felt bereft. Simone had fussed around all morning, while the movers loaded up the van revealing an agitation, that even at this very late stage, spoke to Peter of uncertainty.

"Of course I'm fucking worried about how it will turn out, my split with Roger was pretty nasty, but as I've explained I'm not going back to his bed, only to his house."

Peter must have looked sceptical because she continued. "Yes I know what you think, Peter, but I've done it now, must make the most of it, and with the kids there, we'll just have to make it work."

When they said goodbye she stayed in his arms for what seemed like forever, hugging him tightly to her, until the van driver coughed, asked if she was ready for the off. She told him to go. She would be along in a minute, but then was unable to tear herself away from Peter's enclosing arms. When finally she did wrench herself away, the tears poured down her cheeks. As she clambered into her car and accelerated away, he heard her shout through the open window. "I'm sorry Peter, I'll always love you," and then she was gone, leaving Peter on the point of tears himself, regret hanging like a great weight round his neck.

He walked back to his bedsit, made himself a cup of coffee, tried to read one of his recommended course books, but couldn't concentrate. He felt loneliness so absolute that it seemed to crush the very life out of him. He knew he shouldn't be blaming Simone for taking the decision she had, but he did, and that made him feel even worse. His surroundings were depressing, cheap furniture, quite awful décor and, worst of all, very few of his own things around him. He remembered with startling contrast the house he had left behind to live with a lover who had now deserted him. For a fleeting moment or two he considered swallowing his pride and moving back home, but the thought of the cold, strained life with Naomi that would ensue made that impossible.

The day passed slowly. Towards evening, Peter decided to walk, to escape from the claustrophobic surroundings of his flat. He walked through streets he had never passed through before, pretty grim for the most part, until finally he decided he needed a drink. The next pub he came to, he went inside, without even looking at the name, and asked for a pint of bitter. He stood disconsolately at the bar wondering what people saw in going to pubs on their own.

It wasn't busy that night, and he might have left after another pint or so, had it not been for the arrival of two women, who came to the bar, chatting and laughing. One was a tall, dark-haired woman, her friend was shorter with blonde, rather unruly hair. The smaller woman had a neat, elfin face under all that hair. She glanced at him and smiled, to which he responded with a surprised, weak smile. They took their drinks over to a table in the corner, leaving Peter to continue with his pint in morose isolation.

He was about to leave the bar after downing a second beer, when the woman who had smiled at him came over to order more drinks. "All on your own this evening then?" It crossed his mind, just for a moment, that they might be on the game, but dismissed the idea straight away. The woman seemed to have a naturally friendly personality. He came out with a short little laugh that sounded odd even to him. "Yes, just a quiet pint or two."

"That sounds as though you want to be left in peace to drink your beer."

"Sorry, that came out wrong, I wasn't trying to be stand-offish, bit fed up this evening."

"Why don't you come over and join us, tell us your woes if you like."

"That's very kind of you, but I'm not good company tonight, I'm off when I've finished this." He smiled properly this time to show he was grateful for the invitation. Yet the blonde woman's friendly personality appealed to him. He had been tempted, but then thought better of it.

"Suit yourself but it might be good to have a chat with a couple of scatty women." She turned away to order the drinks. Then as she started to carry them back to her table she turned to him again. "Come on, be brave." Her smile was attractive, the invitation enticing. He would only spend the rest of the evening moping if he went home now.

"Why not." He followed the woman across the room. "Better introduce myself, I'm Peter." He held out a hand towards the second woman who took it without apparent surprise; perhaps the two of them had discussed inviting him over before the blonde had gone to the bar for a second round.

"Nice to meet you Peter, I'm Samantha and this flirt here, is Annie." Peter gathered from that brief comment that the idea to invite him to join them had been Annie's rather than her friend's.

Both women must have been in their middle thirties, both attractive in their different ways. It turned out that they were mature students, studying psychology, back early for the new term.

"That's a coincidence, I'm lined up to start a masters in October, studying social work, might see you girls around campus then."

"My God Peter that's courageous. Have you worked in that area before?" Her surprise might or might not have had something to do with Peter's age.

"No, it's a new start for me. I lost my job and, well it seemed like a good idea at the time I applied, so there we are."

Annie smiled at him. "That's great Peter, although I suspect that's not why you're in here drinking on your own."

"Annie you really are the limit. Tell her to mind her own damn business Peter, I would."

"It's a long story Annie, let's just say I have split with my partner and leave it at that."

They did leave it at that. The rest of the evening passed lightly, and amusingly, with the women describing some of the exercises in psychology they had undertaken last term. It turned out that Annie was divorced, while Samantha had never been married, but was rather friendly, as she put it, with one of her married lecturers.

They stayed till closing time. Peter got up to shake their hands, was thanking them for a pleasant evening, when Annie, after a glance at her friend, asked him if he would like to come back to their flat for a coffee. They strolled companionably the short distance to where the women were living, Peter with thoughts about female company and where such an invitation as this, might lead. He had said goodbye to Simone only a few hours ago, but he needed to talk and a soft shoulder to cry on. Friendly Annie might be the girl to provide that opportunity.

Once inside the flat Samantha grinned at her friend. "I'm whacked, Annie, I'm off to bed. Good night Peter, nice to have met you." Her departure was rather obvious, leaving Peter with thoughts about being set up, pleasantly set up, but set up nevertheless Annie made them coffee. They settled down in opposite, rather clapped-out, armchairs to drink it.

Annie was nothing if not direct. She leaned forward in her chair with a look of earnest concern on her face "I was married once, Peter, so I might have some idea of what you're going through. I know I'm being nosey but it sometimes helps to talk about these things."

She was attractive, as much by virtue of her personality as her looks. Peter was grateful for her interest, yet he could see little point in reciting his woes. Three pints of beer was a lot for him. He felt tired, whereas Annie appeared eager to act as counsellor for as long as it took. "You're obviously a kind person, Annie, but my story is really very mundane, of no interest to anyone but myself."

She leaned across the space between them to put her hand on Peter's knee, nothing sexual, just comforting. "That's fine Peter we'll talk about something else shall we, more coffee?"

He sighed, licked his lips and blurted out. "My wife is in the process of divorcing me, my girlfriend has gone back to her husband, I'm without a job, going back to university, no idea how I'm going to get through the next two years financially, or in every other way. There, I told you it was bloody mundane, didn't I?" There was a faint realisation that he was playing on her sympathy, he wanted her to feel sorry for him, pathetic though that was.

Annie went over to sit on the arm of Peter's chair. She touched his cheek softly with her lips and then his mouth; actions were speaking louder than words. Both of them had been aware, when the invitation to come back for coffee was made, that this was probably how the evening would end. Even as they slid to the floor Peter felt he was betraying Simone, but the need for solace was irresistible. He made one last effort at respect. "Are you sure this is what you want Annie?"

"Fucking shut up Peter, get on with it."

There was little romance in their coupling, only the necessary clothes removed, the act nasty, brutish and short. Annie had wanted the romance, the chance to bare herself body and soul in the search for affection, but the man she had chosen was full of bile, bitter over what he had lost and she, sadly for her, was no substitute for that loss. When he sank back beside her, lust satiated, she kissed his wet brow, sorrowing for his nostalgia, guts wrenching with her own unsatisfied need.

"Sorry about the floor Peter. Sam and I share a bedroom and I doubt she would appreciate us rutting in the bed next to hers." It was an attempt at humour, to lighten the moment.

Of course Peter felt wretched. He was only too aware that the way he had acted was utterly selfish, that fact only making him feel even more unhappy. He made an effort, turning to pull her towards him, kissing her with what she knew was sympathy." I'm sorry Annie, that wasn't very good was it?"

"My fault for going for someone on the rebound." She sniffed, and Peter wondered if she was having a little weep. "Look Peter it doesn't matter, it was only a little old fuck after all, you weren't making any promises were you?"

He kissed her again. "No, but I am a bastard, you should be kicking me up the arse, not being nice to me."

She laughed. "I seem to meet a lot of men who are bastards." Peter thought he recognised the sadness of experience breaking through in that laugh, which didn't help his feeling of self-loathing. "You want another coffee then?"

He watched her walk across the room still without her jeans or pants rekindling desire in him once more. When she came back with two mugs of coffee, he quietly asked her to leave them on the table, lie down next to him again. This time he was gentle, carefully considerate and slow. He was pleased when he sensed her reaching climax this time, a small consolation in the scheme of things.

Peter had no idea of the time, but when he woke he was alone.

He realised retreat was the only course open to him, so he quietly let himself out of the flat, still full of regret that he hadn't told Annie what a lovely girl she was, what a great mate she would make for the right man. He wouldn't ever go back to that pub again, wouldn't walk down the street where the women had their flat, although he knew that in months to come he might well be sorry he hadn't given Annie a chance. Simone had gone. He had to get used to the idea, but there was no way he could start a new relationship with another woman in the foreseeable future, given his wounded feelings..

He felt the night air cold on his face as he walked home to the flat, tired and depressed; Autumn was coming. With a jolt it suddenly occurred to him, as he dragged his weary body along, that this part of town was where Mrs Benson had lived and, he remembered, had died. His thoughts waxed maudlin, travelling back in time as he remembered that little child lying in the woods, for whose death nobody had been found responsible, as far as he knew. He thought about George and the dog's simple affection and zest for life. He thought about his comfortable home and his children and finally he thought of Naomi. It's true their marriage had come apart at the seams. Had he tried to make it work or just relied on having Simone as a safety valve. He had just spent a night with an attractive woman, yet now he had never felt so lonely in his life.

He slept late the next day, woke befuddled, reluctant to get out of bed, until the demands of his bladder made it imperative. The only thing he could look forward to, with any pleasure, was the start of his masters course in a couple of weeks' time. Even there he was full of doubt as to whether he was cut out for a career in social work. It wasn't the academic aspect of the degree, it was the placement that he would be required to undertake, and what that would tell him about his emotional strength that worried him. If he failed on that, there was no hope for him actually becoming an effective social worker.

Charlie rang later in the morning to remind him that she was off to Durham the next day. He invited her for a coffee but she said she had far too much to do, a refusal which he saw as out of the ordinary; she was usually only too happy to have a chat with her Dad. On another day, at another time, the small refusal would have meant absolutely nothing, the casualness of youth, but today it hurt. One more thing to add to his depressed state of mind making him wonder if he was losing contact with his children. He determined that he would take James out for a beer in the near future, take more interest in his college work, try and forget his own troubles.

A few days earlier Peter had contacted the CAB to see whether he could do voluntary work alongside his degree work, but the commitment they required, the length and intensity of training put him off. He remembered that, later in the day, he had agreed to attend an interview with the local organiser of SAAFA to see whether he could be useful to them so he made an effort to smarten himself up. He liked interviews and, in the normal course of events, he liked meeting people. Anyway it was something to do. His spirits lifted somewhat at the prospect.

As he sat drinking his coffee, trying to read the Telegraph, he couldn't help thinking about Simone, and what might have been. He metaphorically shook himself, realising, only too clearly that she had gone for good. He must get used to the idea of living without her. What did surprise him was how strongly he felt her loss. After all they had both agreed that their relationship was nothing more than a mutual arrangement for the purpose of sex, yet he had been totally shattered by her departure.

Today he still felt bruised and unhappy, but the sharpness of the pain of losing her was beginning to lose its edge. New beginnings, perhaps not on the relationship front but at least, he had a new life ahead of him. He found he was genuinely beginning to look forward to the new challenge represented by his degree course.

With time to fill in the days before his course started, Peter had taken to wandering round the shops during the day. "Hello Peter, how are you?"

He looked round the crowded bookshop, for a moment failing to pick out Naomi from among the other shoppers. "Naomi, I'm fine thank you." His smile was weak, the meeting totally unexpected; his reaction was wary to say the least. "What about you? From what I hear from Charlie the business is going great guns." She looked confident to Peter, in rude health, and pretty pleased with herself, a marked comparison to the worn look he remembered the last time he had seen her.

Naomi, for her part, would have found it difficult to describe her feelings, questing perhaps, even a slight sense of pleasure, although why that should be, she didn't know.

"What's all this I hear about you taking up social work then, wouldn't have thought it was really your cup of tea." People were jostling them on both sides. It would have been easy to say "see you around then" and walk away, neither of them did.

Peter was feeling awkward in Naomi's presence, guilt at his disloyalty still lingered, also a strange sense of being a loser now Simone had left the scene, a fact that he had no intention of telling Naomi about. Yet he needed to talk to someone, and who knew him better than this woman with whom he had shared a good portion of his life.

Naomi was aware that Peter was uncomfortable, yet she too felt the urge to talk. Was it triumphalism or what, she didn't know but whatever it was, one thing was certain, she was proud of what she and Ivan and Rosalind had achieved, loved talking about it. "Peter, are you busy? Time for coffee, have you?"

He shrugged, nodded. "Yes of course." Adding, "'Plenty of time on my hands right now." That must have sounded unenthusiastic to Naomi, although he recognised in himself, an eagerness to continue talking.

"Do you mind if we go back to the house. I always nip out about this time to let George out for a quick run."

Mention of the dog sent a frisson of emotion running through him.

"Fine."

It was strange, yet all too familiar, being back in what had been his home for many years.

Once George had been persuaded to stop running round in

circles, and Peter was sitting at the kitchen table with Naomi on the other side, it began to percolate through to his inner psyche how much he had missed the familiarity of a home created over years, represented by objects acquired at different times during their married life.

Only objects perhaps, but many of them came with their own particular memory of how they were acquired.

He had only been living away for a few months but, God, how he had missed this very ordinary house with all its associations.

Mug of coffee in front of him, Peter was feeling the prickle of emotion behind his eyelids. He must have looked a bit odd, because Naomi asked with a note of concern in her voice. "Are you alright Peter, you look as though you've seen a ghost?"

In a way he had.

Roy Grantham

Roy was born in Derby in 1934 and now lives in Devon. After a hectic career in commerce and industry, he retired a few years ago to indulge an equal fascination with writing and the intricacies of human relationships.

Recently, he got round to the question of publishing some of the twelve or so novels he has written, together with short stories and very bad poetry. 'The Boy in the Red Sweater' was published in America a short time ago, 'Deeds and Misdeeds' is his second book to hit the shelves. There are several more novels in the pipeline awaiting publication.

When not toiling over a hot computer, or playing very bad golf with his friends, he worked for the CAB for eight or nine years (three as bureau manager), then subsequently worked for other organisations in the Third Sector. Divorced, he has three sons, and is blessed with four beautiful grandchildren.

He believes writing is a joy seldom equalled in other human activities, although on the downside, it is hard work achieving the standards set by most writers for themselves. For all that he is determined to keep trying…

Lightning Source UK Ltd.
Milton Keynes UK
UKOW05f2106031013

218459UK00015B/688/P